Praise for **THE TALENTED RIBKINS**

An Indie Next Pick
Winner of the Faulkner-Wisdom Prize
Winner of the 2016 Rona Jaffee Foundation Writers' Award

"For sheer reading pleasure Ladee Hubbard's original and wildly inventive novel is in a class by itself."
—Toni Morrison

"*The Talented Ribkins* is a charming and delightful debut novel with a profound heart, and Ladee Hubbard's voice is a welcome original."
—Mary Gaitskill, author of *Bad Behavior* and *Veronica*

"What a pleasure it was to take a road trip with *The Talented Ribkins*, a simultaneously gifted and flawed family, sharp-witted but prone to making utterly human errors. Ladee Hubbard has given us a fresh and original debut novel."
—Jami Attenberg, author of *All Grown Up*

"*The Talented Ribkins* is a quest, a treasure hunt, an unearthing of the hopeful and terrible past in service of the future. Wry, with a deft sense of metaphor, Ladee Hubbard delivers a familiar yet uncharted America in which her characters need their superpowers just to survive."
—Stewart O'Nan, author of *West of Sunset*

"[A] sly, pleasurable first novel."
—*Newsday*

"[A] rip-roaring adventure."
—*Entertainment Weekly*

"If you love the works of Paul Beatty and Colson Whitehead, you'll enjoy Ladee Hubbard's wholly unique view of family and legacy with her dazzling first novel."
—*Essence*

"Ladee Hubbard delivers a fascinating twist on DuBois' notion of the Talented Tenth in her debut novel . . . *The Talented Ribkins* recalls Colson Whitehead's first novel, *The Intuitionist*."
—*Paste*

"A marvel . . . exceptionally funny, tender and heartbreaking . . . *The Talented Ribkins* marks Hubbard as a writer to watch. This tale of self-revelation and recognizing one's tribe is quite an arrival, filled with both a sense of discovery and hard-won wisdom."
—*The Advocate*

"*The Talented Ribkins* wears its magical realist elements lightly, weaving them into a realistic family story with a wider cultural context. The novel calls out to a range of other books, such as Toni Morrison's *Song of Solomon* . . . [with] a hint of Thomas Pynchon . . . Hubbard is a graceful and intelligent writer in whose hands the Ribkinses' superpowers are both real and symbolic of the dreams and invincibility we have when we're young, and that are inevitably reshaped by age and experience."
—Colette Bancroft,
The Tampa Bay Times

"Ladee Hubbard has written a celebration of family, as well as of the individual."
—*New York Journal of Books*

"Debut novelist Ladee Hubbard takes you on a magical-realist road trip . . . the book is inventive and fast paced, perfect for those who read Colson Whitehead, Michael Chabon, and / or Toni Morrison."
—*Brooklyn Magazine*

"Both a romp through Florida and a meditation on race, class and politics . . . [It's] Marvel comics meets W. E. B. Dubois' talented tenth."
—*Eugene Weekly*

"A quirky, bittersweet comedy, Hubbard's novel offers an original perspective on the legacy of the civil rights movement . . . Hubbard crafts an irresistible idea of activists with de facto superpowers challenging the racist power structure of mid-20th century America."
—*Atlanta Journal-Constitution*

"Original and entertaining . . . *The Talented Ribkins* is Clark Kent disguised as Superman. It is a story of redemption and the power of family under the thin cover of a mask, cape and tights. And with Hubbard's power of imagination, the novel is nothing short of super."
—*Lincoln Journal Star*

"Crafty and wistful . . . Hubbard weaves this narrative with prodigious skill and compelling warmth. You anticipate a movie while wondering if any movie could do this fascinating family . . . well, justice. To describe this novel, as someone inevitably will, as *Song of Solomon* reimagined as a Marvel Comics franchise is to shortchange its cleverness and audacity."
—Starred review, *Kirkus Reviews*

"*The Talented Ribkins* is a joy. It navigates complex and intertwined issues without ever weighing itself down, and manages to do excellent narrative work while also driving a compelling, propulsive plot . . . Part buddy road trip, part family drama, part social commentary and part magical realism, *The Talented*

Ribkins is in sure hands with Ladee Hubbard, who weaves these parts into a very enjoyable whole. It's a fun world in which to be, freckled with moments of clarity and wisdom that make you ache."

—bookreporter.com

"Hubbard's first novel is an aching ballad to cross-generational companionship and the evolution of identity with age. Readers will fall in love with Johnny, Eloise, and the unforgettable folks who pepper their journey. Hubbard's ear for dialogue and creative character construction make the Ribkins family's story fly."

—*Booklist*

"First-time novelist Ladee Hubbard has created a collection of misfits like no other in *The Talented Ribkins*... fascinating... Hubbard's tale ultimately transcends race, class and time itself."

—*Bookpage*

"Author Ladee Hubbard has done an amazing thing with her debut novel. She's given us a story about history, racism, personal identity, human potential, complicated family relationships, and superheroes. Imagine if W. E. B. Du Bois created Luke Cage, Hero for Hire. Just think how great that would have been."

—superheronovels.com

"With *The Talented Ribkins*, Ladee Hubbard proves herself to be a rare talent who pops onto the scene fully formed as a writer of power and purpose. This is a heart-wrenching quest into the absurdity that is family. Like the best literary fantasies, *The Talented Ribkins* succeeds because the heart that beats at its center couldn't be realer."

—Mat Johnson, author of
Loving Day and *Pym*

"Ladee Hubbard's *The Talented Ribkins* is a first novel of extraordinary confidence and panache. Brisk, funny, tender, scathing, the book is a road story with teeth, a secret history of those black Americans whom W. E. B. Dubois called 'the talented tenth'—underground, in plain sight, sometimes both at the same time—superheroes of reality."

—Zachary Lazar,
author of *Sway*

"*The Talented Ribkins* is tender, inventive, sharp, funny, and smart, like going home for a family reunion and remembering mid-argument that your cousins have superpowers. The Ribkins' various talents and the trouble those talents get them into and out of make this book a riveting read. Its attention to connection, forgiveness, and the problem of figuring out again and again what superpowers it might take to survive being a black family in America make it an important and wildly original debut." —Danielle Evans, author of *Before You Suffocate Your Own Fool Self*

THE
TALENTED
RIBKINS

A NOVEL

LADEE HUBBARD

MELVILLE HOUSE
BROOKLYN • LONDON

THE TALENTED RIBKINS

First Melville House Hardcover: August 2017
First Melville House Paperback: August 2018

Melville House Publishing   14/16 Woodford Road
46 John Street   and   Suite 2000
Brooklyn, NY 11201   London E7 0HA

mhpbooks.com   @melvillehouse

The Library of Congress has cataloged the hardcover as follows:

Names: Hubbard, Ladee, author.
Title: The talented Ribkins / Ladee Hubbard.
Description: Brooklyn : Melville House, [2017]
Identifiers: LCCN 2017018187 (print) | LCCN 2017029786 (ebook) | ISBN
   9781612196374 | ISBN 9781612196367 (hardcover)
Subjects: LCSH: African American families--Fiction. |
   Parapsychology--Fiction. | Paranormal fiction. | Domestic fiction. |
   BISAC: FICTION / African American / General. | FICTION / Fantasy /
   Contemporary. | FICTION / Family Life. | GSAFD: Fantasy fiction.
Classification: LCC PS3608.U23245 (ebook) | LCC PS3608.U23245 T35 2017
   (print) | DDC 813/.6--dc23
LC record available at https://lccn.loc.gov/2017018187

ISBN: 978-1-61219-728-9
ISBN: 978-1-61219-637-4 (eBook)
ISBN: 978-1-61219-636-7 (hardcover)

Printed in the United States of America

2 4 6 8 10 9 7 5 3 1

Design by Bryden Spevak

Now the training of men is a difficult and intricate task. Its technique is a matter for educational experts, but its object is for the vision of seers.

—W. E .B. DuBois

THE
TALENTED
RIBKINS

MONDAY

THE LAST WOMAN

He only came back because Melvin said he would kill him if he didn't pay off his debt by the end of the week. It was why he left St. Augustine, why he had no choice but to drive down to Lehigh Acres and dig up the box of money he'd buried in his brother's yard fourteen years before. The only complication was his brother's last woman, who was still living in the house, because of course he didn't want her knowing what he was after. So he made something up.

"A toolbox," Johnny Ribkins said, standing on the splintered porch of a wood frame two-story, while hard slats of Florida sunshine bore down on his back and the woman squinted from behind the screen door.

"A toolbox?" she said, gray grates masking her face like a veil. "Why you got a toolbox buried in the yard?"

"Oh, it's always been there. Ever since we tore down the shed to build the basketball court." He nodded toward a weed-covered rectangle of cracked cement at the far corner of the yard. "Just seemed like the safest place to put it at the time."

A truck came barreling down the interstate on the other side of the fence, roar of exhaust merging with the mechanical drone of laughter coming from a TV playing inside the house. Johnny removed his hat, swatted at the moisture pooling across his brow, and stared at a rose tattoo that wound around the woman's neck. He hadn't seen her since his brother's funeral but he had to admit she looked less crazy than he remembered. The lace top, miniskirt, and thigh-high boots were gone, replaced by a T-shirt, sweatpants, and white flip-flops. Her once-gaunt cheekbones were now fleshy and jowly, and her hair, deprived of the bright red wig she'd worn to the wake, was gray and cut short. He figured she must have been in her forties, about the same age his brother Franklin had been when he died.

Johnny smiled. "They old tools, see? Like for turning screws so old they don't even make them anymore. Truth is I all but forgot about them until a couple weeks ago, when I got a delivery of antique watches at the shop."

He pulled a handkerchief from the pocket of his shirt and scratched at a line of sweat tickling his left ear. It was hot out there and he could hear how lazy and exhausted his lies sounded. Luckily the woman was none too bright.

"They valuable?"

"Only if you a broken watch."

A hearty "amen" and the sound of applause came from the TV inside the house.

"Tools aren't valuable. The watches are, but only if they're fixed. And really it's more a matter of the fact that they don't make them anymore. Now I've looked everywhere, even tried contacting the original manufacturer to see if I could get ahold of the designs to have copies made. And—"

Where was this going? Why was he wasting time trying to explain himself to some raggedy piece of interloping woman who didn't even have sense enough to invite him inside and out of the heat, which would have been simple courtesy? He didn't have time for this. He needed to find that money, get back to St. Augustine. And—

"So what, Johnny, you some kind of junkman now?"

"Ain't no fucking junkman." It just popped out.

But when he looked up she was smiling. Her lip curled back to reveal the gold filling etched against her left incisor.

"I just thought because of the watches . . . You said they were old."

"They're antiques."

He reached for his wallet. His hands were shaking as he pulled back the screen door and handed her his business card: JONATHAN RIBKINS, ACQUISITIONS AND REPAIRS. RIBKINS ANTIQUES.

"Family business. Two generations . . . Didn't Franklin ever mention it? He worked with me for almost twelve years."

"No, we never discussed such things."

She looked down at the card and then back at him. For a moment he thought he saw something crafty in her eyes, a form of coherency that hadn't been there when he met her all those years ago, else he would have remembered it.

Then the TV let out another "amen" and he decided she must have found Jesus and gotten off the crack.

She handed him back the card. "You sure that's all you want?"

"That's all."

She sighed. "All you Ribkins are so peculiar," she said, then stopped because there wasn't much more to say.

She shuffled down the dark hall. He waited until she was in the living room, then positioned himself at the center of the bottom step and started walking straight ahead, toward the interstate. And as he walked he couldn't help but think about how sad it was to be digging through his brother's yard again after all this time. His half brother, some twenty years his junior, whose existence he hadn't even known about until he was a grown man, when their father got drunk at a party one night and confessed there was another son, someone named Franklin, living with his mama "out in the sticks," and Johnny had been the one to go find him. He thought about all he'd been through since Franklin died, how hard he'd tried to put this place behind him only to find himself, at the age of seventy-two, right back where he'd started. This was especially troubling because Johnny made maps. That was his talent—not just what he did, but who he was, same way his brother had scaled walls. Johnny made maps and Franklin scaled walls, and for twelve years they'd made their living by selling the things they found on the other side of those walls, right there in the antique shop Johnny inherited from their father.

When he'd gone twenty paces he cocked his head to the left and started moving diagonally toward a large oak tree at the far corner of the yard. All of that was supposed to have ended the day his brother died. He'd made a promise to stop stealing, start living right, start doing right—to try to remember what it meant to be a decent man. And everything seemed to be going according to plan until one day he looked up and realized that somehow in his grief he'd wound up working for a man who was under the mistaken impression that he owned Johnny. So here he was, fourteen years later, crouched in the dirt trying to dig up enough money to appease a criminal.

He walked another ten paces, then stopped and stared down at a small patch of dirt and clover.

"You gonna fill it back up?" the woman called from the living room window. "I mean when you finished."

"Of course." Johnny smiled. He was still smiling as she disappeared back into the shadows of a house built for someone else.

He hoisted his shovel. He needed the money. That was all there was to it and there really wasn't any point worrying about the how and why of it now. But it was also true that he'd buried that box for a reason and was breaking a vow he'd made to himself by digging it up. And that, in some ways, was just as troubling as Melvin's threats. Because if all he'd tried to do since his brother left him hadn't been leading anyplace but right back here, then what was the point? And if he couldn't answer that question, couldn't make sense of his own path or justify his existence even to himself, then what was he doing crouched in the dirt, humiliating himself just to hold on?

He put down his shovel and stared at an empty hole, aware that something didn't feel right. He had a near photographic memory, but he had also stood on every inch of that yard, watched it from every conceivable angle, making it difficult to recall with any precision where exactly he'd stood when he first dug the hole he was looking for now. "Why you digging up that tree, old man?"

A heavy-set, big-eyed girl in a red T-shirt and blue jean leggings was watching him from the other side of the fence.

"What do you want?"

"I don't want nothing."

He reached into his pocket, grabbed a handful of coins, fished out the shiniest, and tossed it over the fence. The girl caught it with her left hand.

"Now go on home."

"I am home," the girl said.

She pushed through the gate, walked up the front steps, and passed through the screen door. Johnny shook his head and wondered yet again why his brother's last woman had to be such a trifling mess.

....

"Of course she's your brother's child. Doesn't she look just like him?"

He was in the house now, standing in the dark hall while the woman stood in front of him with her arms folded in front of her chest. The girl sat in the living room watching TV.

"Why didn't you say something?"

"Say what?" the woman said. "This is the first time I've seen you in fourteen years. How was I supposed to even find you? And anyhow, why? I don't need anything from you, Johnny Ribkins."

Johnny looked at the girl slumped on the couch with her feet up on a rickety coffee table, surrounded by huge piles of junk. The whole house was jammed with drab furniture dragged in from who knows where. But worse than the things he didn't recognize were the things he did: the couch pushed against the far wall, his drafting table shoved in a corner underneath the TV set, the lamp with the crooked shade sitting on the floor near the window. Tokens of a distant past he'd all but forgotten yet somehow knew were out of order.

"You're still living in my brother's house."

"This rattrap? In the middle of nowhere? I can't even sell it."

He felt something tense in his chest and glanced toward the yard. "Listen here, woman. You've got no right to be selling anything."

"The name is Meredith, old man, and I already told you I can't. But speaking of rights"—she turned to her daughter—"Honey? Why don't you go on upstairs for a minute and start packing."

"But I'm not going anywhere."

"Get upstairs anyhow. Let me talk to your uncle."

The girl sucked her teeth and stomped out of the room.

"You heading somewhere?"

"Why?"

"I'm just asking."

"Yeah?" She narrowed her eyes. "Look, man. You might as well go ahead and tell me what your intentions are. Because this is a common-law state. You know what that means?"

He did. He stared at the crooked lampshade.

"It means I got the same legal rights as a proper wife. Understand? Now I don't want any trouble from you but I've been living out here for going on fourteen years now so I'll tell you just like I told the bank. Whatever claim to this place you might think you have, you can just forget about. This is *my* house and—"

It was the heat, the heat of her presence, worse than the heat outside. He could feel his breathing catch in his throat and his blood pressure rise, even as he told himself to keep cool and remember why he was there. Melvin had given him just one week to come up with the $100,000 he needed to pay off his debt. And a part of him knew that the only reason he'd been given even that much time was because Melvin didn't believe Johnny could do it, was just waiting for him to fail. But that was because Melvin didn't know about the hole Johnny had dug. Which was to say, how selfish he'd been before his brother died.

"I just want my tools," Johnny cried, then stopped because he could feel himself about to give away how badly he wanted them. He reached for the handkerchief in his pants pocket, put his head down, and patted his brow, trying to channel the appearance of a harmless old man who was confused or anyhow peculiar enough to have come all that way to fetch some worthless junk. And all at once it occurred to him that maybe he *was* just a harmless, peculiar old man—hunched over, blinking back confusion and grief as he stood in the dark hall of a house he'd helped his brother build, yet had given up any claim to long ago.

"Johnny Ribkins, you may not stay here indefinitely, digging up holes in *my* yard."

"Yes, I understand. I just . . . need a little more time. I got distracted by the girl and it's hot out there."

Meredith opened the door and made a sweeping gesture with her hand.

"Her name is Eloise, by the way. In case you were curious."

She shut the door.

Johnny put his hat back on. He stood on the porch for a moment, trying to absorb the quiet of the world outside. Then he took a deep breath, eased himself onto the top step, and stared at his empty hole.

Strange and pitiful, that was what his life had become. His current circumstance was undignified but, if he was honest with himself, no more so than the circumstance that had preceded it: selling his maps to Melvin Marks. That was the part that should have never got started. But decent man or no, he still had to make a living; after Franklin left he couldn't bring himself to go back to working alone, so he'd started working for someone else. Sitting in a small room, drawing up blueprints, waiting for his share. Of course he was getting ripped off. But when he tried to get out of it, Melvin wouldn't just let him leave.

You're not going anywhere, Johnny Ribkins, so you might as well sit your ass back down. You signed a contract when you came to work for me and I can tell you exactly how much it would cost to buy yourself out, because, you see, I got it all written down.

So after a while Johnny started giving himself little wage adjustments. Whenever an unexpected expense came up, it wasn't hard to find ways to simply take what he needed; this he did not consider stealing because in truth it was always far less than what he was owed. It was just a fact that Melvin was getting rich off Johnny's maps, so rich that for a long time he didn't even notice how much Johnny was skimming off the top. It seemed to keep everybody satisfied and for a while everybody was happy—right up until the day Johnny got caught.

The door swung open and Eloise shouted, "It's like one hundred degrees out there. I'm thirteen and I don't like shrimp," then sprinted past him down the steps. She ran over to the other side of the yard and started playing by herself, throwing rocks into the air, then spinning around and catching them in alternating hands, all the while weaving in and out of the sunlight flashing through the branches of the oak tree.

Pull yourself together, Johnny thought. There was nothing to be done about his current situation except be a man about it. He needed to focus, remember where he'd buried that money, and then get back to St. Augustine and deal with Melvin as quickly as possible. That was the way the Ribkins brothers worked: in and out, no flinching, no fucking around. Johnny drew up blueprints not just for the walls he could see but also for the walls behind those walls, and his brother hiked his pants and scaled them. Later on, Franklin would tell Johnny how he'd been exactly right, how he'd turned a corner or pushed through a door and the passageways in Johnny's pictures seemed to magically appear.

"How do you do that?" Franklin sometimes said. Just like sometimes Johnny asked Franklin how he managed to get up there, get up and over that wall or fence or window ledge and then come back to show Johnny whatever it was he'd found on the other side. The truth was Johnny had been drawing up blueprints of buildings he had no access to since before he could read, and Franklin had scaled walls the way other boys masturbated, for years never managing to accomplish much with this miraculous skill beyond a series of trespassing and petty theft charges. No reason for it, just something they'd always been able to do that never made much sense and only rarely seemed useful. Until one day they found each other, and for a while, everything seemed to click.

"Are you really my daddy's brother?"

The girl was watching him from the shade of the oak tree.

"So I'm told."

"Can you prove it?"

"Who else would I be?"

"That's what I'm trying to figure out. You got some kind of identification? Let me see your driver's license."

He reached into his wallet and handed her a business card.

"Satisfied?"

"Mama said you wouldn't have come around unless you wanted something. She said Ribkins are real good at looking after their own but they don't care a thing about anyone else. That's why she doesn't want you in the house. She's worried you might get confused, start thinking you might as well stay."

"Yes, I caught that."

"Is it true?"

"No. Where are you all heading off to?"

"Oh, I'm not going anywhere. She got a job working on a riverboat for the shrimp festival out in Clearwater. She does it every year but I already told her I'm not going this time. I'm staying right here. I'm thirteen now—I can take care of myself."

"Okay," Johnny said.

He heard a whistling sound and turned his head. A group of children had gathered by the gate and were calling Eloise toward them.

"You know, you don't look a thing like my daddy's picture. Plus you're old. If you two were brothers, how come you're so old?"

"That's something you'd have to take up with another party, now, isn't it? Seeing as how I didn't have much to do with it." He smiled. "We were brothers all right. Half brothers. On the Ribkins side. Trust me, we had enough in common, in the ways that count."

She handed the card back.

"Naw, you keep it."

She slipped it in her pocket, then turned around and ran across the yard.

Johnny knew the girl was just telling the truth: he was old. Old and tired. For all he knew, it was a sign of this very infirmity that he seemed to keep forgetting how old and tired he actually was.

He looked back at his hole.

He stood up, positioned himself on the bottom step, and started walking again, this time channeling the cocky stride of his much younger self. He narrowed his eyes, pursed his lips, and tilted his shoulders so that his left side rolled back below his right. He dropped his hips and let his legs slide out in front of him, then sidled across the yard in this manner for a full twenty paces. When he stopped, he realized he was almost twice the distance farther than his careful, plodding steps had taken him earlier. He cocked his head to the left and took ten more winding steps toward the oak tree. He hoisted his shovel and started digging.

Yes, sir, he thought. How you think you got this old? Been around for years, and trust, this ain't nothing. If there's one thing you do know it's how to survive this world. Johnny Ribkins always lands on his feet.

He lowered his shovel and felt the sudden crack of metal against metal. He got down on his knees and pulled out a rusted box.

"Thank you," he said out loud. He glanced over his shoulder.

Eloise was standing on the other side of the fence, leaning against a telephone pole that rose up at the edge of the highway while a boy crouched down in front of her, reached inside a book bag, and pulled out two large cans of cut corn. She shut her eyes and made an "okay" signal with two fingers of her left hand. The boy stood up, leaned back, and hurled the cans as hard as he could straight toward Eloise's head.

"No!" Johnny gasped. By the time he understood what was happening Eloise was holding the first can in front of her face. Her eyes popped open as her left hand floated up just in time to catch the second.

"It's all right, Mister. She caught it, see? She always catches it." The boy smiled. "We just playing."

Johnny turned back toward the house.

....

"They just playing," Meredith said. They were in the living room, Johnny standing next to the TV while the girl sat slumped on the couch and Meredith glared at him with her hands on her hips.

"They were throwing *cans*—"

"You think I like it? You think I haven't tried? I can't get her to stop."

"That's your job, isn't it? You're her mother. You're supposed to make them stop."

"You're not listening. It's not my fault and it's not them. It's *her*. You know how many times I've told her to quit showing off? 'Can catch anything you throw at her, can block any punch.' They all say it and from what I've seen maybe it's true. That doesn't mean I like it and it sure doesn't make it right. But that's the truth of it. The only reason those children keep trying to hit her is because they think they can't."

She straightened her back.

"Now you and I both know damn well it's just some fucked up Ribkins thing she inherited from her daddy."

Johnny nodded. Yes, indeed: a Ribkins thing.

"Tell the truth. All you Ribkins got something peculiar about you. Franklin told me all about it. You think it's easy? Trying to deal with something like that? I keep telling her, all you got to do is let one of them hit you, just one time. Then it will stop of its own accord because folks will know it's not true . . . But see, she doesn't want it to stop. She's showing off. She thinks it makes her look cool."

"Stop it, Mama!" the girl shouted. "I can hear you, you know. Stop talking about me!"

"Also I see you found your damn toolbox," Meredith said.

He looked down at the battered steel box in his hands.

"That mean you're finished? Because I'm trying to be nice. But the truth is I got things to do and you been here all day."

He looked at Eloise. What could he do? She was Franklin's child all right, and a Ribkins. Maybe if he were a younger man with less debt that would have meant something more. But the way he lived, the people he hung out with, some of whom at that moment would have thought nothing of doing him great bodily harm . . .

No. She was better off here. Both of them safer with him pushing on.

"Probably should hit the road before it gets dark."

"That sounds about right."

He frowned. "I'll be back though. You hear me? I'm coming back to check up on my niece."

"It's not really your concern."

"It is though. You're going to have to try a little bit harder to be responsible." He nodded to the two large duffel bags sitting by the door. "You can't leave that child here while you're off gallivanting on some riverboat. Not when you know the kind of foolishness she's liable to get herself into."

"Gallivanting? It's called work. It's a job and I need the money."

"All I know is that's no way for a little girl to play. She could get hurt. It's not funny."

"No, it's not," Meredith said. "You want to know what is funny? Me winding up alone and stuck in the middle of nowhere for the past fourteen years. Me working my ass off six days a week trying to take care of that girl and keep food on the table, only to have some bank tell me I got to come up with twenty thousand dollars or they'll repossess the house. But what's really funny is you showing up after all this time trying to talk to me about being responsible." She shook her head. "Where you been, Johnny Ribkins? What makes you think you've got the right to tell anyone how to raise a child?"

He looked down at the box. "How much you owe on the house?"

"None of your damn business."

Johnny nodded. "I guess I probably should be going."

"That's what I've been trying to tell you," Meredith said.

....

Johnny took his box and drove to Fort Myers. He got himself checked in at a motel, had a nice dinner, and then went to his room and counted his money. When he was certain he had what he needed to satisfy Melvin he climbed into bed and clicked on the TV. He sat through two episodes of *Law and Order* and then switched to twenty-four-hour news coverage of the upcoming election cycle. They were interviewing candidates running for Senate and he happened to catch a few minutes of a man named Dawson droning on about his prospects.

"I know there are some who were surprised when I threw my hat back into the ring, given the fallout from my last campaign. But do you know I receive letters every day from people who need help, who need someone to stand up for them. So that's why I came back. Because I was called . . ."

When he'd had enough of that, he turned off the TV and lay down on his bed, but he could not sleep. He tossed around for what seemed like hours and every time he shut his eyes he heard Meredith's voice:

Just let them hit you in the head one time . . .

Now, what kind of thinking was that? Yet he couldn't it get out of his mind.

He looked up at the ceiling. It was hearing his people called "peculiar" that had him rattled. As if there were something wrong with them. If what Meredith said was true, then Eloise was gifted, unique. And Meredith was right: that was something a lot of folks in the family shared. Little sparks of something special that didn't seem to make much sense and had generally caused more confusion than anything else. Because not knowing what to do with these gifts, many of them spent years trying to understand them, trying to figure out where they belonged and who they were.

They were *Ribkins*.

Johnny sat up. His father had been blessed and burdened with the ability to see in the dark. He had a cousin who spit firecrackers and whose daughter could talk to fish; another cousin had a son whose one true joy was picking locks. And, of course, his grandfather had that sense of smell—the source of his great wealth and eventual undoing. It's where their name came from: the girl's great-grandfather was the original Rib King, said to have invented the best barbecue sauce recipe in the entire southeast. As a result of all his sniffing around after the theft of the recipe, he'd eventually felt compelled to hide. But he couldn't really let go. No one, Johnny imagined, had ever had a better excuse to take an alias than his grandfather—but he'd wanted that trace of memory to remain. When they told stories, when they said it out loud, when they got to remembering who they were. And so they were the Ribkins: born of the rib, still of the rib, and this here, your flesh and bone.

He stood up, walked to the dresser, and riffled through the motel stationery looking for an envelope. When he found one he opened the toolbox, pulled out a few bills, and stuffed them inside.

He put his hat back on.

A Ribkins. He owed a debt was all. And that may have changed his circumstances but it couldn't change who he was.

....

Meredith Sue Clark sat alone in the living room thinking about what Johnny had said about letting folks throw cans at her girl. Even if Eloise never flinched, even if the blows never connected, Meredith could feel them. And she wanted it to stop.

The doorbell rang. She peeked through the blinds and saw a seventy-two-year-old man with stooped shoulders standing on her front porch, hat in hand. She walked across the hall and opened the door.

Johnny reached into his pocket.

"I've been thinking about Eloise—"

"Take her," Meredith said.

TUESDAY

2

A TRUE LIKENESS

It was decided that while Meredith was working on the riverboat Eloise would spend some time with Uncle Johnny, get to know her father's people. This was something Meredith claimed the girl had wanted to do for a long time. Or thought she did.

"Your uncle and me got it all worked out. You're going to stay with him while I'm up in Clearwater, let him show you around. Then you're coming back."

"What do you mean?"

"It's about time you got to know some of your father's people is all. Find out where you come from."

"But I thought you said—"

"Never mind what I said. I might not be a Ribkins but you are. Same as your uncle here."

Eloise nodded. "Well, I can't."

"What do you mean, 'can't'?"

"I mean I can't right now. I got responsibilities, things going on. How do you expect me to just up and leave with somebody I don't even know?"

Johnny shifted his weight on the couch, trying to angle his body over a broken coil that kept poking him in the thigh. He didn't say anything but the truth was he thought the girl had a point. Everything was happening so fast and none of it was what he'd expected when he knocked on their door the night before. All he'd meant to do was give Meredith enough money to tide them over until he'd dealt with Melvin; he didn't want to risk the girl winding up on the street before he could make his way back. Somehow the look on Meredith's face when she opened the door caught him off guard. The slack jaw, the quivering lip, the fixity of her gaze staring back at him even as the muscles around her left eye twitched. Before he knew what was happening, she'd dragged him back inside the house and started confessing all manner of things about their lives he either already knew or didn't really want to hear. And this was his brother's child, last bough on his particular branch of the Ribkins' family tree. Meredith was tired and she was asking for help. What kind of man would he be if he refused?

"Girl, what are you talking about? What things?"

"Responsibilities. I told Donna I would babysit for her on Thursday."

"Babysit? How you figure you're going to do that? You didn't really think I was going to leave you here by yourself, did you? No—either you are coming with me or you are going with your uncle."

He turned away from them, his gaze sliding toward the drafting table where the envelope sat atop a stack of newspapers next to the TV. He'd wound up giving her the $20,000 she needed to pay the mortgage, which, considering he'd just taken five times that amount from the yard, seemed like the least he could do. Except now he had only five days to make up the difference. And Melvin wasn't fucking around. The man may have owed his current prosperity to the accuracy of Johnny's maps, but if he said he would kill Johnny for taking some of it for himself, Johnny knew enough to believe it. However little sense that made, it was still real. As real as these two arguing in front of him now.

"But what am I supposed to do out there? I don't even know anybody."

"That's just it, Eloise. What I'm trying to fix. You think I want to send you away from here? I don't know what else to do. One day it's rocks, next day it's cans. Then what? You tell me, Eloise. What comes next?"

"Nothing comes next. It's not like that."

"No? So what's it like? How long do you expect me to stand around watching you let people try to hurt you just so you can prove to yourself they can't?"

Then Meredith did the thing Johnny had been waiting for and dreading, the thing that should have snapped him awake but instead had the effect of pushing him further down into the couch and the murk of his own mood: she walked to the drafting table, opened the envelope, and removed two hundred-dollar bills from his ancient stash.

"Take this," Meredith said. "That should be enough to get you there. You need more, just let me know. But you are going with your uncle. I want you to spend some time with other Ribkins, talk to people who might understand what you're going through. Because I'll be honest, I haven't got a clue."

Suddenly it was hard for Johnny to breathe. He leaned forward, and before he realized what he was doing, a simple effort to adjust his weight turned into a desperate need to get back on his feet. But he kept getting sucked into the broken coils of the couch.

"You all right?" Meredith asked.

He gripped the cushion and rocked back and forth until he gathered the momentum to propel himself upright. "You two work it out. I'm going to go wait outside."

"Okay, Johnny. We won't be long." Meredith smiled. She was still in her pajamas, hair uncombed, face blank and unwashed. It occurred to him that he had no idea what she'd told the child, how his absence from her life had been excused or his brother's passing explained. Johnny had his own version of things, but given how unflattering that was, Meredith's was no doubt different.

"Take your time."

He pushed through the front door. He stood on the porch for a moment and looked out at the basketball court, the twinkling shade falling across the front walk, the blank expanse of the interstate marked off by a wooden gate half-hidden by shrubs and weeds. His mind finally slipped into the far corner of the yard, where it sat for a moment, dumb and restless, as he stared at the loose dirt covering up his hole.

In truth it was not the only hole he'd ever dug, just the last. It had been preceded by numerous other holes scattered throughout the state of Florida, holes representing not the renunciation of what he now considered a shameful past but rather the many occasions in his life when he simply hadn't felt like sharing. Things he'd let drop and told himself he would come back to deal with later. Because of that, most of what those holes contained was just as small and petty as the mood he'd been in when he dug them. But taken together, they added up to more than enough to make up for what he'd given Meredith. He could still get the money to Melvin in time. It just meant a lot more digging than he'd hoped to do.

He could still hear them arguing on the other side of the door.

"Why you got to be like that, Eloise? Can't you see you hurt the man's feelings? And here he is trying to do something nice—"

He stumbled off the porch and got back into his car. He opened the door, eased onto the driver's seat, stuck his key in the ignition, and then sat there, listened to the beeps the vehicle made when the door was ajar.

When he looked back at the house, Meredith and Eloise were already walking toward the car.

"All set," Meredith said.

The girl flung her backpack into the back seat, tumbled in after it, and slammed the door.

"All this because of yesterday? On account of those cans? So now you all are mad at me? It's not fair."

Johnny winced at the shrill sound of her voice. His hands shook a bit as he reached up to adjust the rearview mirror and tried to imagine the sound of that voice stretched out for miles.

"You're a nice young lady," he said. "Shouldn't be letting people disrespect you like that."

"Might be disrespect if they actually hit me. But they can't. You know that, right? I'm too fast."

"If they respected you, you'd only have to show them once. That's what respect means, not having to repeat yourself. Your mama here tells me they do that to you all the time."

"You hear that?" Meredith nodded. "Your uncle's right."

Johnny sighed. "Nobody wants to see their daughter standing in the dirt, letting a bunch of ignorant children chuck cans at her head."

He watched Eloise's upper lip curl back, as if in slow motion.

"Why you got to call them 'ignorant children'? You don't know them. They're my friends."

"Okay," he said.

Meredith leaned forward and whispered through the driver's window.

"Don't let her upset you with all that nonsense. She doesn't mean it, you know how girls are. She'll calm down once she realizes she's got no choice but to."

Johnny reared his head in involuntary reaction to what he still regarded as the senseless clatter of a troubled mind. But then she reached for his hand.

"Just take care of my girl, Johnny. She needs somebody to help teach her how to walk this world. Somebody that understands."

There it was again, the look he couldn't hide from, the one that had snagged him the night before. He saw a woman who'd been alone and struggling for fourteen years to take care of his brother's child. A woman still trying to smile despite something else they both knew: wasn't anybody else coming around. Whatever help Johnny had to offer was as good as it was going to get.

He started the car.

"Call me when you get there," Meredith said.

He turned the wheel and started driving west.

....

The car rolled down a dry, flat stretch of Interstate 80. Johnny kept his hands on the wheel, eyes trailing the yellow line in front of him while in his mind he was working on a new map. Drawing upon memories of people and places he hadn't thought about in years. Trying to recall exactly what he'd left where. Figuring out just how many holes he'd have to dig to come up with another $20,000 in five days' time. He had a hole out in Fort Myers Beach and another one at a service station in East Dunbar. After that he was going to have to suck it up and pay a visit to his cousin Simone. The woman lived less than three hours away in Sarasota and had had close to $10,000 sitting in her yard for almost thirty years, from when his father first told him he had a brother. Johnny left it there when he'd stopped on his way to meet Franklin for the first time and hadn't been back since, due in large part to an aversion to Simone's third husband, the Judge, so called because he was one. The Judge had never cared for Johnny and over the course of that visit made his low opinions perfectly clear. The last thing Johnny wanted was to confirm them by showing up at their house thirty years later, needing money. Somehow this was especially true now that the man was gone.

"How long is this going to take?"

He glanced at the rearview. Eloise still had her backpack on her lap and clutched it to her chest as if worried someone might try to snatch it from her.

"Not long."

"And then what? What are we going to do when we get there? You got a TV at least? Where you stay?"

Johnny didn't answer. He made a left turn and climbed onto Interstate 75.

"Mama said you make maps. She said all Ribkins got some kind of talent, that that's how come I can catch like I do."

"Maybe."

"How come you're not rich then?"

"Excuse me?"

"If you got so much talent. That's something I'd like to know. Seems to me if you had real talent you'd figure out a way to make some money off it. And then you'd be rich."

"How you know I'm not?"

"Your car is too junky. Rich people don't ride around in junky cars."

"My car is not junky." He looked around at the interior of the Thunderbird, surprised by his own hurt feelings. "There's not a thing junky about my car."

"It's old."

"It's an antique."

"What's that?"

"An antique?" He had to struggle for a moment, remind himself he was talking to a thirteen-year-old child. "Something that gets more valuable with time."

"I never heard of such a thing."

"Well, so what if you never heard of it? What does that prove? It's true. It's how I make my living, girl. I sell antiques. Your daddy did too. Got my own shop. I'm going to show it to you as soon as we get to St. Augustine. Just got to make a few stops first, run a couple of errands." He shook his head. "Anyhow, is that all you think talent is good for? Making money? You don't know anything about me."

"I didn't say I knew anything about you. I just said you weren't rich."

Johnny looked back at the road. He reached for his wallet, set it on the top of the steering wheel. He pulled out an old photograph and handed it to Eloise. "Here."

"What's that?"

"Something besides money. A group I used to belong to. That's me, my cousins Simone and Bertrand, and two friends of ours, Flash and the Hammer. We called ourselves the Justice Committee."

"What kind of group?"

"You learn about the civil rights movement in school? Well, when I was your age instead of worrying about getting rich some people were out there forming groups, fighting for change. Used to be that if you were given a talent, not everybody thought it was just so you could go out and try to make money off it. Used to be people who thought there were more important things going on in this world, believe it or not, than chasing after bling. Other ways to put your talents to use. Next time you got something to say about someone being rich, I'd like you to think about that."

She looked at the picture.

"So y'all were in the freedom movement?"

"We were with the freedom movement. We were freedom movement adjacent. We were the freedom-of-movement movement."

"The what?"

"Never mind. Yes."

"And was my daddy in the group?"

"Naw, he . . . should have been. It was a little before his time."

He put out his hand. "Just give it back."

They reached Fort Myers and rolled down a wide boulevard full of superstores and car dealerships, pink condominiums and high palm trees. He made a left turn on MacGregor and turned down Gladiolus Avenue.

"Where are we going?"

"Shortcut."

They passed a store selling seashells, a kayak rental, and a small hotel. Every now and then a flashing view of the Gulf appeared on the other side of the commercial strip.

"Are we going to the beach? Looks like they're selling snow cones over there."

"No, we're not going to the beach. That beach is no good anyhow. Better one is up the road. Don't your mama ever take you out here?"

"Not really."

"What's that mean?"

"It means no. You ever go to the beach with my daddy? When you were my age?"

"Your daddy wasn't even born when I was your age. He was twenty years younger than me. Remember? I didn't even know I had a brother until I was forty-five years old."

"Why?"

"Your grandpa didn't tell me. Guess he felt bad. You know, messing around on my mama. But of course Franklin didn't have anything to do with that. As soon as I knew he was there I went back down to Lehigh to find him."

They rolled past a stretch of white sand decorated with umbrellas and deck chairs.

"I thought you were from St. Augustine."

"That's right."

"Your daddy came all this way just to mess around on your mama? Why? What was he doing down here?"

"Wasn't doing nothing. I was down here. My first job out of college was teaching math at the school in Lehigh. He came down to check up on me."

"Check up on you? So you were living out here when my daddy was born and didn't even know it?"

Johnny bit his lip. "Your daddy's mother married someone else when she was still pregnant with him. Imagine she didn't feel too good about the situation. Found a man willing to let her put it behind her and that's what she elected to do."

Johnny stopped to let a group of tourists on rented bicycles pass in front of the car. He swiveled around toward the back seat.

"You know, Eloise, it's kind of hard to drive and answer questions at the same time. And right now I'm driving. We're going to have a lot of time to talk once we get to St. Augustine. Thing is, before we can do that I need to focus on the road. So I'm going to ask you to be quiet for a little while. Let me do what I got to do. Think you can do that?"

He turned back around and waited for the tourists to make their way across the street.

"I didn't mean nothing. I was just asking. Just curious."

"It's all right."

He started driving again, past a row of houses on stilts, another fish shack, and another motel.

"Just seems kind of mean for nobody to tell you something like that," Eloise said. "I mean, imagine if you had stayed. He might have wound up in your class. Your own brother sitting right in front of you and you wouldn't have even known it."

Johnny leaned forward and switched on the radio. An ad came on for Dawson, and Johnny got to hear the mantra of his new campaign: "Everybody deserves a chance, so that's what I aim to give people—not a second chance, but a real one."

"Mama says he's a crook," Eloise said.

A few minutes later he pulled into a parking lot next to a small municipal playground set off from the rocky shoreline by a low wooden fence.

"See? What did I tell you?" He nodded toward the water. "Better."

Eloise shrugged. "Looks the same to me. Same water, same sand. And I don't see any snow cones."

"Yeah, but we got the fort." He pointed to a crumbling stone wall rising out of the weed-covered hill that made up the northern edge of the beach.

"We?"

"You know what segregation was, don't you? Back in the day they didn't let us go to that beach back there. This was our beach. But I'll tell you the truth, I never wanted to go to that beach anyhow. Our beach was better. We had the fort."

He looked out at the water and smiled. For the first few years he taught in Lehigh, he'd used his own money to rent a bus to bring his students out here for Juneteenth celebrations. Justified the expense as a necessary part of his lesson plan for the upcoming school year, a means of demonstrating what he'd believed was the most important thing he could teach his students: that knowledge is like a fort. A shore of strength, a line of defense, and regardless of the subject matter, something no one could ever take away from you. A fort that looks out across the ocean, which for him of course represented the endless possibilities of the mind. He'd been a different man back then. Young, idealistic, and inspired by reports he'd read in *The Crisis* about peonage practices on sugar plantations in rural Florida, he'd truly believed he was going where he was needed most. Whether or not the things he said made much sense to his students, they seemed to enjoy the day at the beach. When the school year started up again in the fall he taught them math and tried to make them memorize the names of great black inventors. And when they finished his class they shook his hand and thanked him for all that he'd tried to do for them. Then one by one they went right back to work the fields of one of the surrounding plantations.

He turned to his niece. "You want to go swimming?"

"I don't swim."

"Then what did you want to come to the beach for?"

"I didn't want to go to the beach. I wanted a snow cone."

Johnny reached for his wallet. He pulled out a five-dollar bill and nodded toward the convenience store across the street. "I bet they sell Popsicles in there. Go and get yourself one. I'll meet you back here."

"Where you going?"

"I want to check out the fort. I don't get out here too often. Who knows when I'll get another chance?"

"I don't get out here too often either. I want to check out the fort too."

Johnny nodded. Somehow he'd imagined she'd wait in the car.

"Suit yourself."

He grabbed his shovel from the trunk and started walking, Eloise following him across the sand, hopping over crushed beer cans, cigarette butts, and clumps of seaweed that had washed up on the shore.

He looked up at the fort. He'd meant everything he told his students about the power of knowledge but after a while had started to wonder if circumstances did not dictate that more tangible efforts were required. So he started following them out to the plantations where they worked, paying attention to the details of how they lived. Came to understand how trapped they felt there, how few choices they had. He gave them a map, one that offered a bird's-eye view of their placement within it so that they could better see where they stood in relation to the things around them. He told them to study it carefully and then decide for themselves what to do with it. When a group came back and told him they were organizing a work slow-down and wanted to use his living room as a place to hold meetings, it had seemed like the least he could do. It was how he lost his teaching contract with the state.

It wasn't until reaching the stone path that one could see the hill was actually part of the fort, made out of stone almost the same pale color as the surrounding sand. Near the top was a narrow doorway that led to a small, damp room with a single high window that looked out on the Gulf. Johnny took two steps toward the window, then hoisted his shovel and started digging.

"What are you doing?"

"Left something. Just checking to see if it's still here."

"Why'd you leave it here?"

Johnny shut his eyes, trying to channel patience. "Sometimes, when I visit a place I really love, I like to leave something behind. That way I know I'll have to come back for it one day."

Eloise considered this for a moment. "That's kind of nice."

Johnny nodded.

"You know my daddy used to do like you. Hide things. Mama is still finding things he hid around the house before he died. But she says she likes it when she finds something because it makes her think of him. Is that a Ribkins thing? Something we like to do? Hide?"

"I don't know. Maybe."

She walked over to the window and looked out at the waves rolling in along the shore.

"You want me to help you dig?"

"No, I do not."

"You think if I help you dig then maybe you'd let me go back to that other beach and get a snow cone?"

"No, I do not."

After about ten minutes his shovel hit something slick and hard. He wedged the tip of the shovel underneath it and jimmied the handle until a black rubber bag popped out of the sand. He bent down, unzipped it, and pulled out a small diamond engagement ring.

"What's that?"

He looked down at it in his palm. "Conduct unbecoming to the terms of employment" was the reason he'd been given for why his teaching contract was not renewed. It wasn't until he lost his job that he understood how seriously he'd miscalculated his place in the community. After eight years, Lehigh had started to feel like home; but the truth was he had no family there, and very few friends, especially after he started receiving threats in the wake of his students' efforts to protest labor conditions on the plantations. He was labeled a troublemaker and an outside agitator and when the woman he'd proposed to gave him back the ring he was holding in his hand now, he realized that he no longer had the means or any reason to stay. And what had really broken his heart was the realization that a part of him was relieved.

Eloise reached down and touched the ring with her finger. "Pretty."

"Yeah." He closed his fist, slipped the ring into his pocket.

"I just wanted to see if it was still here," he said again, and without another word, he turned around and walked back outside.

He went to the car and put his shovel and the bag inside the trunk. Then he took her across the street and bought her a Popsicle.

They got back into the car. Johnny drove toward downtown, winding past a trailer park and a Popeyes. He cut over to East Dunbar where the car bumped and shook over potholes for a good ten minutes before they reached a small auto body shop. There were two ancient gas pumps in the front and beyond that three men in shorts and flip-flops sat on the porch sipping beers as they watched Johnny pull into the dusty parking lot. He put the car in park near the rusted hull of a pickup truck.

The girl's head shot up in the back seat.

"What now?"

"Getting some gas," Johnny said. He and Franklin had stopped here once on their way to Key West, shortly after what had been their first robbery together. The distance between the fort and the gas station was just a few miles but it had taken Johnny twenty-two years to get from the math teacher he'd been in Lehigh to the man he was when he first pushed through the station door with his brother. His life had taken several wild swerves by the time he found himself standing there, trying to negotiate a sale with Charles Avery, the wiry old man who owned the place. Mr. Avery had a side business fencing stolen jewelry, and disgruntled by how talks had turned out, Johnny had hidden a watch and a small stash of jewels underneath the floorboards of the man's storage room, telling himself he would come back for it later, when he and Mr. Avery could discuss things alone.

He opened his door. "Just eat your Popsicle and wait in the car. Nothing to see around here anyhow. I'll be right back."

He walked to the service station and tipped his hat to the men on the porch. A buzzer went off as he pushed through the door and found himself standing in the middle of a small convenience store. Bottles of cola and malt liquor lined the coolers along the back wall; shelves in the middle were stocked with dusty bags of corn chips, motor oil, and car air freshener. There was a woman behind a cash register, talking on a phone while a baby in a diaper straddled her left hip, its little hand lunging over her shoulder, swatting at the phone's cord.

"Help you with something?" the woman said.

"Looking for a man named Charles Avery. He still own this place?"

"Yeah, he owns it. Why? Whatcha want him for?"

"I'm an old friend."

The woman wheeled around and pointed to a young man in faded overalls and a tank top, leaning against the office door. The man shook his head.

"Mr. Avery say he don't know you. He say state your business."

"I meant Charles Avery."

The woman squinted. "That there *is* Charles Avery. Junior." She nodded to the baby. "This here is Charles Avery the third. Charles Avery *senior* been gone. For about seven years now. I imagine any friend of his would have known that."

Johnny frowned. He'd forgotten how much time had passed since he'd last been on this road. Old age seemed to require constant recalibrations on his part, the need to think on his feet. He took a deep breath and started again.

"Forgive me, ma'am, for being so misinformed. Truth is Mr. Avery and me weren't friends so much as business associates. Ran afoul of the federal government about seventeen years ago. Just got out of Valdosta last week."

The woman didn't say anything. He turned to Charles. "Can you imagine? Seventeen years? As nonviolent as I am? But I'm awful sorry to hear about your daddy. Didn't anybody tell me anything."

"Well, now you know," the woman said. She sounded frustrated. "So why don't you just be on your way?"

"I will do that. Just as soon as you give me what it is I came here for."

"Nothing here for you, old man. Trust me."

"Well, I hope that's not true." He smiled at Charles. "Your daddy wasn't doing nothing but holding something for me. I paid a flat fee for the service. He was holding stuff for a lot of folks who found themselves in my predicament. Told me the same as he told them, that it would be here waiting when I got out."

"Something wrong with your hearing? I just told you the man is gone," the woman said.

The buzzer chimed as two teenaged boys pushed through the door and headed toward the cooler. Johnny watched them fish out bottles of grape Fanta, then looked back at the woman.

"Ma'am? I'll tell you straight out, I don't much appreciate your tone. It's all right because, like I said, I'm what you call nonviolent. But when those others finish out their sentences and start showing up, they're going to tell you the same thing I'm telling you now, that they paid their flat fee and want their property. And when that happens, I suggest you remember that not everybody is as nonviolent as me."

He turned to Charles. "Then again, maybe you two counting on the fact that a lot of them might not ever get out. Maybe you counting on the fact that a lot of them are probably already gone. Maybe you figure you might just keep what they left here for yourself."

"Bullshit," the woman said. The two boys wedged their way around him and set the bottles on the counter. One of them reached into his pocket, pulled out a handful of coins and a crumpled dollar bill, and dumped them out in front of the woman.

Johnny shrugged. "It's none of my business. I just want what's mine. All you got to do is let me go around back to the storeroom, dig a little hole. Whatever you folks decide to do after that is up to you."

"Nothing in that storeroom, Charlie," the woman said. She scooped the coins into her hand and counted. The buzzer chimed as the boys pushed back out of the store.

Johnny squinted at Charles. "How much you know about your daddy's business anyhow?"

"Enough," Charles said.

The woman sucked her teeth. "Listen to me, Charlie. There's nothing in that room but junk. This man is trying to con you."

"Why would he do that? If there's nothing back there?"

Charles looked Johnny up and down. "Show me."

Johnny let Charles lead him through the office and back to the storage room. He removed the bolt lock from the door, then clicked on the light, and Johnny looked around a small airless room cluttered with cardboard boxes and industrial cleaning products. He pointed to a dirty floor tile directly under the light fixture and then watched Charles pull a pocketknife from his pants pocket. He jimmied the tile and it popped up, revealing a hard-packed layer of sand. Underneath it was a rusted tin box.

"What'd I tell you?"

"How I know that's yours?"

"There's a watch in there. My name is on it. See if it don't say H. P. Smith."

Charles opened the box. There was a thin fold of bills tucked inside a money clip and a gold watch. He pulled out the watch, turned it over, and saw the name of the man Johnny had stolen it from engraved on the back.

"How long has that been there?"

"About twenty years," Johnny said. "Crazy, huh? Who knows what else your daddy got stashed in this room, just waiting for somebody to come claim it." He shook his head. "Money, jewels . . . No telling what you might find if you dig deep enough."

He held out his hand. "Just give me my property first."

Charles gave Johnny the box.

"Thánk you, son. I feel better now." He slipped the watch on his wrist and tucked the box under his arm. "I always feel better when I know what time it is."

When he passed back through the store the woman was still standing behind the register, glaring at him.

"Satisfied?"

Johnny shrugged. "I just wanted what's mine."

"I know. You and everybody else. You think you're the first old man to come through here talking about some crazy deal they had with Charlie's crazy daddy? Man wasn't nothing but a thief and a con, but somehow Charlie got it in his head his daddy meant to leave him something more than what you see here."

Charles walked back through the store, cell phone pressed to his ear, yammering excitedly to whoever was on the other end. He disappeared behind his office door and a moment later he came back out carrying a sledgehammer.

The woman sighed. "Somehow all it ever leads to is something getting torn down."

Johnny turned around and realized Eloise was there too now, wandering through the candy aisle.

"I thought I told you to wait in the car."

"I needed to use the facilities," Eloise said.

The woman reached under the counter. She brought out a key tied to what looked like a table leg, and as she handed it to Eloise, Johnny could hear the banging of the sledgehammer pounding against the storeroom walls.

"Go on around back, honey. Up the stairs, first door on the right."

Eloise walked to the counter, reached for the table leg, and disappeared up the stairs. The woman turned away from Johnny and went back to her conversation on the phone. The baby on her shoulder looked up at Johnny and smiled, revealing a single tooth.

Something about that child's stare made Johnny feel real bad all of a sudden. He thought about the man he'd been back when he'd taught school in Lehigh, how that man's life compared to what he was now: standing in a run-down convenience store, trying to con some drooling baby's daddy out of a rather piddling sum, while his niece watched. After all that work he'd done over the past decade, trying to remember what it meant to be a good man, was this how he wanted his niece to know him? Was it all he had to teach her?

Then a toilet flushed, followed by the sound of someone ripping down paper towels. The girl came back downstairs, grabbed a bag of Funyuns and a grape Fanta, then pushed right past him to the counter without even asking if it was okay. He watched her reach into her pocket for the money Meredith had given her and clucked his tongue.

"Put your little money away," he said. "What, you think I'm not going to feed you?"

He reached into his wallet and set a twenty-dollar bill on the counter. Eloise took the chips and soda and, without a word, walked out to the car. Johnny waited for the woman to give him his change, then followed her outside.

"You all right now? Got everything you need?" he asked as he climbed back into the driver's seat.

Eloise didn't answer.

He sighed. "Look, girl. I know this is all kind of sudden. You don't know me and I don't know you, right? Yet here we are in this car. But Franklin was indeed my brother and you are my brother's child. We're family, understand? And I always take care of my own; that's just the kind of man I am."

The girl gave no response. Through the window in front of him he could see Charles rushing back into the store, still gripping the sledge-hammer and covered in plaster as he started talking excitedly to the woman behind the counter.

"Maybe you're thinking I should have come around sooner. I'm just guessing about that because you're not saying anything. But I didn't know you were there—that's just a simple fact. If I had known, things would have been different. A whole lot of things."

He sighed.

"You might even have fun with me, ever think of that?"

She looked up. "It's not that. It's just . . . about those cans. They *do* know. My friends, I mean." She shook her head. "I don't know what my mama told you, but the only reason Bobby was doing that was because I asked him to. I wanted you to see what I can do."

"Why?"

The girl shrugged. "I thought you were like me."

"What are you like?"

She bit down on her thumb and then turned her head and spit out the window.

"A Ribkins," she said.

He started to ask her what that meant but then realized there was no need. He'd heard for himself how easily the word "peculiar" rolled off Meredith's tongue the day before. That, no doubt, was just the subject heading for any number of misunderstandings and out-and-out lies the girl had probably heard about her people over the years.

When the truth was most Ribkins were fine, respectable people living relatively clean, easy lives.

Unlike him.

He put the key in the ignition.

"Don't spit in my car again," he told her. "It's nasty."

He started the engine.

"Where are we going?"

"I want to show you something."

"Thought you needed gas."

"It can wait."

3

VIGILANCE

An hour later they entered Sarasota. They got off the interstate and took Cattleman's Road to Tamiami Trail, then kept going until they reached the stone pillars that marked the entrance to Cherokee Estates. They wound down quiet, tree-lined streets for twenty minutes before coming to a stop in front of a large white colonial-style house. On one side was a swimming pool boxed inside a gray screen, and on the other, an enormous flower garden where an old man in green overalls was crouched in front of a yellow azalea bush, a coil of water hose slung across his forearm as he tended to Johnny's cousin's twittering blooms.

"Is this it?"

Johnny smiled. He took one look at his niece's face in the rearview and felt nothing but relief to have finally reached Simone's. Somewhere between East Dunbar and Sarasota he'd decided Eloise was going to stay with his cousin until he got his errands finished. After he reclaimed the money he'd stashed in Simone's yard, he figured it wouldn't take him more than a day or two to dig up the rest of what he needed; while he was doing that, this was what he wanted Eloise to look at—not just the people who lived here, but the things they'd gathered around them. Respectability, stability, large homes nestled in nice, clean suburbs. Proof that all things were possible. So when he told Eloise there were many Ribkins living many different lives, she would know he was telling the truth.

"Come meet your cousins," Johnny said, and climbed out of the car.

He walked up the short brick path to the front door, Eloise trailing so close behind him that he could feel her shivering against the back of his jacket as he reached forward and pressed the bell. A series of chimes rang out, playing the first notes of a lullaby, a sound gradually replaced by the metronomic swish of slippers sliding across a hard floor. A woman's voice called "coming" followed by a loud "look who it is" shouted through the peephole. Locks were pulled back, the heavy door swung open, and a petite elderly woman appeared before them, dressed in a dark green pantsuit and gold lamé slippers.

"Johnny Ribkins? Is that really you?" His cousin blinked at him with enormous brown eyes. Simone leaned forward, gripped him to her chest, and then reached for his hand. When she took a step backward and looked him up and down, he could only imagine her thinking some version of what he did looking at her: *damn, you got old*. Aside from that she looked pretty much as he remembered: Large head, full of thick auburn curls, balanced atop a slim, birdlike frame. Skin the sun-glint shade of a new copper penny. Face composed of prominent features— long nose, small mouth, jutting chin—that somehow came together to startling effect. He glanced at Eloise and wondered if he should have explained about his cousin beforehand, given the girl a chance to step outside of the effect and thereby something to marvel at. Simone was possessed of a particularly potent power of illusion and could, at will, make people think they were in the presence of the most beautiful woman they'd ever seen. "Why didn't you tell me you were coming?"

"Just passing through," Johnny said. "And that so rarely being the case, I just had to stop and say hello."

"Passing through? Passing through what?"

"Down at my brother's place," Johnny said. "You remember my brother."

"Who? Franklin?"

"Look who I got with me."

Johnny reached around, gripped Eloise by the shoulder, and pulled her out in front of him. "This is Eloise, Franklin's child. She's spending the summer with me."

Simone squinted at the girl and then back at Johnny. After a while, she smiled.

"What a nice surprise," she said, and welcomed them both inside.

They made their way to the living room, a large, cavernous space illuminated by the light coming through the windows that looked out on Simone's garden. Potted palms had been placed in each corner of the room, their top branches growing wild and curving against the high ceiling, shading a series of small wood-framed portraits mounted to the walls. Nestled inside all the foliage was a beige leather sofa and two matching love seats, arranged in a curve to face an enormous flat-screen TV. A teenaged boy in a blue polo shirt and khaki pants was sprawled across one of the love seats. At first glance, Johnny mistook him for one of Simone's two sons.

"That's my grandbaby, Andre. He's staying with me while his father's working out in Los Angeles. Dre, turn that mess off and say hello to your uncle."

The boy put the TV on mute and, with great effort, swiveled around.

"Hey," he said.

"Nice to meet you," Eloise chirped back.

"You two make yourselves at home," Simone said.

Johnny looked around the room. The last time he'd come to visit it hadn't been like this. Simone and her third husband, the Judge, had just moved in, so half their belongings were still in boxes, the yard outside a rolling hill of dirt and sand. He remembered staring out the window while Simone described her plans for a glorious flower garden. He'd been in a bad mood at the time but at some point felt her hand on his shoulder and realized she was telling him that everything would be okay, explaining some theory of why things could only get better in time. So he'd nodded and tried to smile at her imaginary landscape—when in truth all he'd seen when he looked out her window was a good place to dig a hole.

"You want some lemonade?" Simone smiled at Eloise. "I bet you like lemonade." She spun around and hustled off to the kitchen.

"Is that Auntie Simone?"

Eloise was standing in the middle of the room, staring at one of the photos on his cousin's wall: a picture of Simone back in the early 1980s, up on a wooden stage, wearing a short red dress and clutching a microphone as she smiled and waved to an unseen crowd.

"Cousin used to do some acting and modeling and . . . other things."

"Grandma was hot!" Andre said.

The picture must have been taken after the Justice Committee disbanded, when she'd left New York and spent the next few years in LA determined to put her natural charisma to use in Hollywood. There'd been a few commercials and a couple of low-budget thrillers, one of which had surprised everyone by managing to draw enough of an audience to merit talk of a sequel. Nothing had come of it but for the next few years he half jokingly referred to her by her character name: the Siren—a hardhearted, gun-toting, Afro-wielding woman, tearing her way through the desert on a motorcycle.

"What's this one?" Eloise pointed to a smaller, unframed Polaroid that had been tacked onto the wall next to it: a group of five young men and women crowded together on a small floral sofa. It had been taken so long ago that it took him a moment to recognize himself sitting in the center, Simone's arm draped over one of his shoulders. After leaving Lehigh he'd gone to New York to visit Simone, who was living there at the time. He wound up sleeping on that sofa for the next three years.

"That's that group I told you about. The Justice Committee."

"I put that up there," Andre said.

"Were you an actor too?"

"Not actors. Activists. These were my friends, back when I lived in New York. Had a job making maps for black drivers trying to navigate through the South on the interstate roads, telling them where to go if they needed gas or supplies. Things were different back then. Segregated. And the last thing you wanted was to be driving some place and run out of gas. Just being black, trying to get from one place to another without bothering nobody, seemed like a provocation to a lot of folks, so you had to be careful where you pulled over. Gas company paid me to make them. They owned the only national chain of service stations catering to black drivers and wanted to be sure everybody knew where to find them. That's how I met Flash. We used to work together." Johnny smiled at the picture. "One night after work we were sitting together when a story came on the news about a man who'd decided to walk across Florida on the state roads unaccompanied and unarmed. I guess Flash and I thought the same thing, how much we admired that man. Talked to Simone and Bertrand about it and we all decided to go down there together, see if there was anything we could do to help keep him safe. That's how we got started. And that's pretty much what the Justice Committee was. A group of people trying to do what they could to keep their heroes safe."

"That's real funny, Uncle Johnny," Eloise said.

"What?"

"I've never heard anybody say that before, that heroes might be the people who need saving. I don't think most folks think about heroes like that."

"I don't know what most folks think. That's how we felt about it. Felt like we needed heroes. We just wanted them to keep going."

Eloise nodded. "That's what you meant by the freedom-of-movement movement?"

"That's right."

He looked at the picture, thinking about those maps he'd made for that gas company. He'd had to give up his job in order to take that protest walk through Florida, which was a shame because for a while it felt like he'd finally found an occupation for which his talents were perfectly suited. But he'd also always known that the job couldn't last forever. In their insistence that green was the only color that mattered, the very existence of those maps was mediated by the contradictory demand to render themselves obsolete.

He looked at his niece. "You know who that man was, don't you? The one we saw on the TV that night? The one who had us so inspired? None other than J. D. Thompson."

Eloise blinked.

"J. D. Thompson? You don't know that name? What the heck they teaching you in that school?"

"Maybe we just didn't get to it yet."

"He was a genuine hero, from right there in Lehigh. Turned out one of his brothers was in my class."

The kitchen door swung open.

"Cousin? I could use some help. Get your boney ass in here. Now."

Johnny smiled at his niece, trying to shrug off the salt of his cousin's voice. But Eloise hadn't heard it. She'd gone back to staring at the picture of Simone with the microphone, eyes just as glittery as the dress Simone had been sweating in when the picture was snapped. "Why didn't you tell me my aunt was so beautiful?"

He found Simone leaning against a white marble counter in a bright yellow kitchen, already glaring as he pushed through the door.

"What?"

"Who is that girl?"

"I told you. Franklin's daughter."

"Why is this the first I'm hearing it? You never told me Franklin had a child."

"I didn't know myself until yesterday. Believe me, I was just as surprised as you to realize that woman had the girl with her."

Simone frowned. "Now you listen here, Johnny Ribkins. This is me, remember? I know you, so you might as well tell the truth. Is that really why you're here?"

He stared at her. Unlike Meredith, Simone was smart enough to know when he was outright lying. So he reminded himself not to do that.

"It's absolutely why I'm here now," he said. "She wanted to meet family, and I figured, well, you count. Thought I'd let her get to know some real Ribkins. I don't want her getting the wrong ideas about what kind of people we are and how we live, out in that swamp."

He watched his cousin consider the reasonableness of this explanation. After a while, she sighed.

"Fine, Johnny. You don't have to tell me anything if you don't want to. I'm happy to see you, whatever the reason. You know I'm always here for you."

Johnny nodded. Bullshit, he wanted to say, but didn't. He knew very well that if he told her what was in her yard she'd just claim it for herself. Tell herself she was trying to teach him a lesson when the truth was if it was in her yard it was hers. So far as he knew there wasn't a Ribkins who'd ever been born not knowing instinctively that possession is nine-tenths of the law.

"Actually, Simone, I do have a favor to ask."

"Anything."

"Like I said, the girl was a surprise. And don't get me wrong, I'm real happy to meet her, got some things I want to show her back in St. Augustine. Unfortunately she kind of caught me in the middle of something; I got some business to take care of before we head back. I was wondering if it would be all right for her to stay here for a couple days while I'm finishing up."

"What kind of business we talking about, Johnny?"

"Just something I got to do. Doesn't mean anything to her except a lot of riding around in the car. Figured she might have more fun with you."

She pursed her lips and frowned. "Look at you, Johnny. Still running and scheming, at your age. Don't you ever get tired? As happy as I am to see you, I can't imagine it."

He opened his mouth to say something but whatever he wanted to tell her got stuck in his throat. For a moment it was like she could see right through him to all the things he would not allow himself to say: he *was* tired.

She handed him a glass of lemonade. "Of course the girl can stay. That's not even a question. You go on, take care of your business."

"Well, thanks."

"You know, a part of me was always upset with that girl's father for setting you down the road you're on."

Johnny shook his head. "Your timeline is off. Mistaking cause for effect."

Whatever road Johnny wound up on he'd already been heading toward it when his father told him he had a brother. The proof of this, he might have told her, was right there in her yard. When he dug that particular hole he hadn't even met Franklin yet.

"Say what you want," Simone said. "I may not know what you're playing but I know you. Don't forget that."

She patted his hand and walked back to the living room.

Johnny stayed in the kitchen for a moment, trying to absorb the enormity of his fatigue. All she'd done by pointing it out was make him aware of it. He squinted past the lace curtains on his cousin's window, saw a plastic lounger floating aimlessly in the pool. He reminded himself that whatever else happened, by the end of the week, this would all be over too.

When he got back to the living room, Simone was standing in front of the bookcase, sliding out an old leather photo album, while behind her Andre leaned over the armrest of the love seat and whispered something to Eloise, who blushed. Then the boy looked up, saw Johnny standing there, and had sense enough to turn back around.

Johnny narrowed his eyes. There was something about the boy's look that was familiar, yet inspired an immediate distrust. Before he could figure out what it was, Simone grabbed his hand and led him across the room with her leather-bound book. She sat down next to Eloise on the couch.

"This really the first time you're meeting your uncle? Now, that's a shame. Ribkins, you should know, are a close-knit family. Generally speaking. A proud and loyal people. Going back to the first, the family patriarch, your great-grandfather, the Rib King."

She opened the book and pointed to a yellowed newspaper advertisement for Rib King™ Barbeque Sauce, featuring an exaggerated cartoon portrait of a smiling black man, with a pair of bulbous eyes, a wide nose, and white teeth. There was a crown on his head but it had been drawn to curve over at the points, making it look like a jester's cap. At the bottom was the caption, "Dat Eats Like a King!"

"Your legacy," Simone said.

Johnny winced. It was a caricature so familiar from his childhood that he'd forgotten how obscene it was.

"Him we don't have any actual pictures of, save what they put on the can, and of course that don't capture the true essence of the man. He didn't do much smiling in real life."

Johnny glanced at Eloise and realized he had no idea what she saw. But part of growing up in that family had been learning to read between lines, acquiring the ability to squint to see. The Rib King's descendants had inherited no other likeness and so embraced this one—as a testament to all he had accomplished in spite of it.

"People say my father looked just like him."

Simone flipped the page and pointed to a picture of Johnny's uncle Freddy, the eldest of the Rib King's three sons. A tall, angular man seated in a high-back velvet chair, looking regal in a gray suit as he stared face forward and, pointedly, did not smile. His wife, Josephine, in a long white dress with her hair pulled back in a neat bun, stood to the left and slightly behind his chair while Simone, still just a radiant, apple-cheeked baby, grinned contentedly on her daddy's lap.

Simone gave Eloise a few moments to absorb the dignity of the man, then flipped the page, stopping when she came to a grainy photo of all three of the Rib King's sons as very young men: Uncle Freddy, Uncle Bart, and Johnny's father, Mac. They were standing next to an old car in the yard of a small wooden house. The eldest, Uncle Freddy, stood on the left with his arms folded in front of his chest. The youngest, Uncle Bart, stood on the right with his foot propped up on the car's runner. Johnny's father, Mac, stood between them, hands tucked behind his back as he looked at something on the ground. They were all wearing matching suits.

"The Rib King doted on his boys, worked day and night to make sure they had everything they'd need in this world. But he also made sure they understood what was required of them, that they would always have to be at least twice as good at whatever they did to get half the credit. The Rib King expected nothing less than excellence from his children, and because of that expectation, one son, my daddy, made it through medical school, became the first black man accepted into the American Medical Association. Your great-uncle Bart became a justice of the peace."

Johnny snorted. The part about Uncle Freddy was perfectly true, but Uncle Bart was a gangster. He had been an ambitious bootlegger by the time that photograph was taken and thereafter ran an illegal distillery for years. The man's true vocation was making money; the justice-ing that seemed to go along with it was just a hobby.

"What about my grandfather?" Eloise asked.

Johnny smiled. "Your grandfather was a painter."

"Oh, yeah, that's right," Simone said, as if she needed help recalling the fact that had ruled Mac's life. The man had been obsessed with colors no one else could see: that was his talent. Before he moved to St. Augustine and bought his shop he'd earned his living painting houses in order to afford canvas for all the abstract oils he painted in his free time.

Simone flipped the pages until she came to a photo of the next generation of Ribkins: Simone, Johnny, and Uncle Bart's son Bertrand at ages ten, fifteen, and eighteen, standing together on the front steps of a church.

"That's me and Johnny and Cousin Bertrand. Now, I didn't know your daddy so well, but Johnny and me? We pretty much grew up together."

This was simply the truth. Until he and his father moved to St. Augustine when Johnny was sixteen, his uncle Freddy had made sure Johnny went to church with him every Sunday. Johnny had been so grateful for an excuse to get out of his father's house that it had taken years for him to understand that this was, in fact, a rebuke.

She smiled at the picture. "I remember him like this, when he was a little boy. Remember when his father took him up to St. Augustine. Remember when he went down to that town where you live, to be a teacher. Should have seen him back then. They didn't call him Johnny the Great for nothing. He was smart, smarter than the rest of us put together, and that's saying a whole lot. When he graduated college, he could have been anything he wanted to be in this world, but that was his choice: go down to that rinky-dink town where you live to teach a bunch of ignorant, know-nothing children math and poetry. Isn't that interesting? I respected it," Simone said.

Johnny smiled. "Don't lie. You didn't respect anything."

"Not true," his cousin said. "May not have always understood it but I respected it. Daddy did too. He thought you had character." She turned to Eloise. "Now your grandfather on the other hand, Uncle Mac. He *was* a character. You see the difference? Yet we got to be grateful for it because it's how a lot of things come to be. If Johnny hadn't been who he was he wouldn't have gone down to where you and your mama live, and if Uncle Mac hadn't been who he was he wouldn't have gone out to visit him, and Franklin wouldn't have gotten born. And you—"

"I think she gets it," Johnny snapped.

"I'm just saying. Character. It's what makes the man."

She looked at Eloise. "You know why I'm showing you my book, don't you? Because you are a Ribkins and you need to know what that means. All these fine people you see here? I want you to know you are just as fine. You got that same greatness in you, that same talent. Understand?"

"Yes, ma'am."

"Plus you're a woman, so I'm sorry to say but that makes it doubly important that you know your worth. Because ain't nobody else going to tell you. Quite frankly, there's no such thing as a black woman who ever amounted to anything walking around like they got something to apologize for. You've got to stand tall, child. Got to go out there and be strong no matter what. Hear me?"

"Yes, ma'am."

"All right then."

She flipped the page. Johnny stared down at a picture of Simone at thirty-eight, standing next to the Judge on their wedding day. Twenty-five years her senior, the Judge was already a dour old man with a puritanical air and a penchant for dark suits when she met him. Tucked inside those suits, however, were pairs of very deep pockets, and it had taken no time for Simone's unique charms to turn them out. The man had lived with his first wife for thirty years in a small one-bedroom house; Simone had gotten the mini-mansion as a wedding present and, over the next decade, used what was left of the man's money to buy up at least a quarter of the city's north side. In the photograph, Simone was just a big-eyed, innocent-looking woman in a sheer pink dress. She had one hand pressed against the Judge's chest, body turned away from the camera and smiling so brightly it was difficult to say whether she was trying to hide her small but visible baby bump or simply show off the dress's open back. The Judge stood stiffly and stared straight ahead, one wrinkled hand resting uneasily on his wife's hip. He looked mystified, or stunned.

"My husband," she said proudly.

For the next half hour Eloise was made to look at pictures of Simone's branch of the family tree while she listened to Simone's droning narration of their various accomplishments over the years: Andre's father worked for a law firm out in Los Angeles; the other son was a successful oral surgeon in Tampa . . .

Johnny checked his watch. He'd already heard these stories and had known the Judge personally, so he only half listened, aware of how much she was leaving out. He wondered if Eloise noticed how the photos in the album seemed to glide over the long stretch of years from Simone's childhood to her third marriage. The album contained not a single image of the Justice Committee and, except for a few airbrushed headshots, no mention of her Hollywood career either. This meant that vast parts of her life, of her being, remained undocumented.

He squinted at the sweet, elderly woman sitting next to him on the couch. She'd worked hard to cultivate a veneer of domestication but he remembered her too. Remembered how headstrong she'd been at twenty-three, when she'd helped him start the Justice Committee; how wild-eyed at thirty-two, when she went out to LA, determined to be a movie star; how calculating at thirty-seven, when she moved back home and set her sights on snagging the married judge. Ribkins could be pretty ruthless when they felt they needed to be, when it came to getting what they wanted or thought they deserved. How did he imagine a woman like that was going to react when he tried to dig up her precious flowers?

He stood up.

"Where do you think you're going?"

"Left something in the car. You just keep doing what you're doing, Simone. I'll be back."

He went outside, stood on the porch. His cousin was doing well for herself. By hook or crook she'd moved up in the world, made it so her sons were able to achieve a level of social mobility that had once seemed a distant dream. Under other circumstances it might have made more sense to just tell her about his situation, to ask her for the money he needed, seeing as how he was sure she had it. But every time he pictured himself asking, the Judge's face would appear in his mind, shaking his head as he told Johnny that the shame was not in asking for help but in needing it in the first place. And then he knew that he'd rather dig a thousand holes before he asked his cousin for help.

He looked out at the large houses surrounding him. Everything around her now seemed so calm and complacent that when he heard the deep rattle of a thumping bass line, at first he just assumed it was coming from the open window of a passing car, the sound of more lively people on their way to someplace else. It took him a minute to realize it was coming from the open window of a dusty yellow Camaro parked at the end of the block. The car looked out of place there, surrounded by all the gleaming luxury vehicles parked in the driveways. But what caught his attention was the familiar logo on the bumper sticker: MELVIN MARKS INVESTMENT AND PROPERTIES.

Johnny frowned. He hadn't considered that Melvin might be paranoid enough to actually send people out to follow him. He walked to the corner, rapped his knuckle on the driver's window, and waited for the glass to slide down. There was a skinny man in his twenties sitting in the driver's seat, with a container of fries balanced on his lap. A tall, heavy-set man was pinched into the passenger seat next to him, arms folded in front of his chest as he stared straight ahead.

"Yeah?" the driver said.

"Help you with something?"

"Do we look like we need help? Just go on about your business, Johnny. Act like we not here."

"I thought I had until the end of the week."

"Yeah, we know," the driver said. "It's just you took off pretty fast, didn't you?" He pinched the tip of a packet of ketchup between his fingers, trying to squeeze it open. "Melvin didn't want you to get confused is all, start thinking he'd actually turned you loose. Because you not going anywhere until you pay the man back. Understand? Kind of just rolling around until the end of the week."

Johnny nodded toward the house. "You probably noticed I got someone riding with me."

"Yeah, we noticed."

"Is that a problem?"

"You tell me."

"I need to know. Give me an hour and I can send the girl home."

The driver stared at him.

"You know the difference between fucking up and not fucking up?"

"I do indeed."

"And can you tell time? As long as you don't fuck up and keep track of the time then you're not going to have a problem with us. You got until the end of the week, just like you said." The driver popped a French fry into his mouth. "Go on ahead and spend it with your loved ones. That's what I'd do. And don't even ask if I'm telling you the truth because, believe me, I got no cause to lie. Matter of fact, something change, I give you my word we'll let you know in advance. Give you enough time to send the girl home."

Johnny winced. He knew how old and harmless he must have looked to these two men. If hiring someone to follow him seemed excessive to Johnny, it could only have seemed more so to them. Where was Johnny really going to go if he tried to get away? Quite frankly, if it came to that, how fast could he even run?

"I thought Melvin was the big man now, thought he had a business to run."

"So?"

"So why is he so worried about me?"

"Fuck if we know." The driver licked his fingers. "I guess it means he cares."

The man in the passenger seat leaned forward. "Little girl probably looking for you. Go on back inside."

Johnny turned around and walked back to the house. He wondered how long the men had been following him, how much Melvin was paying to have them do it. Not that the man couldn't afford it. Things had changed since Johnny met him. Melvin had just shown up at Johnny's house one night, shortly before Franklin passed, claiming to be his brother's friend. It turned out Melvin had once been a successful lawyer but had fallen on hard times; for the first few years that Johnny made maps for him, he'd been paid with a crumpled mix of denominations tied up in a rubber band; now everything was crisp. Not just the bills he used to pay Johnny, but also his suits, his smile, even the tone of his voice. In fact, if Johnny were to judge a man simply by the way he carried himself, he had to figure that Melvin was more successful now than he'd ever been before he lost his license to practice law. And somehow Johnny was partly responsible for that. If Melvin was a threat, he was one Johnny had helped create by selling him his maps.

He tried not to think about that and looked out at his cousin's yard. Somewhere out there was a bag full of money, one that would go a long way toward finally paying off his debt and putting his association with Melvin behind him once and for all. He walked around to the side of the house, trying to remember where exactly he'd stood when he dug the hole, then stopped when he saw the yardman crouched over a hedge outside the living room window, sheers in hand.

"Something I can help you with?" the man asked.

Johnny shook his head stiffly. "I don't think so."

He walked back around to the front of the house. Clearly, he was going to have to find a time when the house was empty, when he could be alone.

Back in the living room Simone and Eloise were still sitting on the couch but they weren't looking at the book anymore. They were talking.

"So it's just the two of you now?"

"That's right. That's how it always was before."

"Well, you ask me, you did right, getting him out of there. Still, I can't imagine it's easy living like that, just you and your mama."

"Actually we're very happy."

In the brief interim since he'd left the room, the girl's entire demeanor had changed. Her voice had taken a gentle, confessional tone and she seemed relaxed, perfectly at ease talking to Simone. It had been so long since he'd been in his cousin's presence that it took him a moment to remember that this was just one of several ways Simone's power affected people. Whatever they saw when they looked at her made them feel so safe and comforted that they wanted to sit down and confess the truth.

"Reminds me of another child who had to make their way without their father," Simone said. "Didn't have any money, had to walk this world with nothing but faith. Yet somehow he did okay."

"You talking Jesus again, Grandma?" Andre called from the love seat.

Simone frowned. "I'm talking about your great-great-grandfather, the Rib King." She smiled at Eloise. "See? His people owned a lot of land once. He had a whole community around to take care of him when he was born. But the land got taken away, town burned down, his people run out and scattered to the winds. By the time he was your age he was pretty much on his own. Yet he never forgot who he was, where he came from. And that knowledge was what sustained him through all the hardships and trials he faced just trying to survive."

Johnny stood by the window, watching the Camaro.

"Why are you just standing there, hiding in the corner, Johnny?"

"What difference does it make to you? All you're doing is bragging about the Judge. I can hear you just fine from here."

Simone turned to Eloise. "Honey? Why don't you go and watch TV with Andre for a moment? Let your uncle sit next to me, so we can talk."

The girl scrambled off the couch and Johnny took a seat next to his cousin.

"Why shouldn't I brag on the Judge? Man was my husband, wasn't he? Anyhow, what you call bragging is just me trying to give that girl something to aspire to. Let her know she might set herself to a higher standard if she wants to. Isn't that why you brought her here? It's what you said. Let her know the world has got more to offer than whatever gallery of rogues she might happen to be looking at now."

"Right now she's looking at me."

"Yes, Johnny. I realize that."

Johnny nodded. "What was she talking about?"

"Just some boyfriend her mama had living out there with them. Sounded like a real loser. Girl said she finally had to make her mama put him out."

"When was that?"

"I don't know. Couple of months ago . . ." Simone squinted. "You don't know a thing about that child, do you? How she's been living?"

"I told you. I didn't even know she was there."

He looked at Eloise, sitting next to Andre, the two of them staring at the TV screen. For the first time, he noticed she was wearing the same outfit she'd been wearing the day before.

Simone sighed. "Well, look, if it's any comfort, you're not the only one. You see Andre? Why do you think he's here? Mama not stable, daddy working all the time. The boy was just running wild out in Los Angeles. That's why it's good I'm here. It's why it's good I got something too, so the child had someplace to go. Understand? Because you can't give nobody nothing if you don't have nothing to give."

She reached for his hand. "You hear me, Johnny? You got to have something before you can give it to somebody else. Now, I'm not judging you. I'm trying to help. Right now I'm going to make dinner and while I'm in the kitchen I want you to sit here for a minute and relax. You look tired, old man. But you are home now. We are family. I want you to remember yourself and what that really means."

She stopped, distracted by something on the TV. It was another campaign ad for Dawson.

"That's your friend, right?" she asked.

"Not my friend. No."

"But you used to work for him? You and Franklin? Bertrand told me that."

"What's your point, Simone?"

"Just trying to make you feel better. Because he's making a comeback. Isn't that something? Old as dirt and here he is, coming back. It just goes to show that it's never too late to turn your life around. Never too late to get yourself back on track."

She stood up and walked to the kitchen.

Johnny stared at the TV. Dawson, it seemed, was doing surprisingly well in the polls. The image on the screen showed him making his way through an enthusiastic crowd, smiling and shaking hands while the voice of an unseen commentator spoke.

"I think most pundits are pretty surprised to see these kinds of numbers, given the scandals that plagued his last run for office. But maybe what it comes down to is everyone loves a comeback. And the man does have heart, you have to give him that. Somehow he just keeps going . . ."

He looked at his niece sitting beside Andre on the love seat. "Eloise? Come sit by me for a minute. I need to talk to you."

She plopped down next to him on the couch.

"You having a good time?"

"You kidding me? This place is crazy."

"Well, now you see? I thought you'd like it here."

"Does that mean we can stay for a little while?"

"We? Well, here's the thing. I still got a couple errands to run. But I was thinking maybe, if you want, you could just stay here with Simone until I'm finished."

"You mean without you?"

"It's just for a couple of days."

Eloise frowned. "If that's what you want to do, then okay. I really don't care."

"You just said you loved it here."

Eloise shrugged. "It's all right. Really, I think I'd rather just go home."

Now her lower lip was quivering.

"Don't do that. Hear me? You taking it wrong."

"I'm fine."

"You're not though. But I'm telling you, you got no cause to be upset, because of course you don't have to do anything if you don't want to." He sighed. "Never mind. We don't have to talk about this now. Why don't you go see if Simone needs any help in that kitchen. Just relax."

He watched her stand up and walk to the kitchen. It was not at all the reaction he'd expected. He wasn't Simone, didn't really know how to talk to the child. It seemed like it was just too easy to say the wrong thing.

When he turned his head, Andre was still in the love seat, grinning at him. He forced himself to smile back.

"How's your daddy doing, anyhow?"

"Fine. Just got a big promotion at his firm. They made him the head of the tax litigation department."

"Tax litigation? What happened to drug policy?"

"Drug policy? Oh, man. I forget you been out of the loop a long time. He told me about all that social aid, pro bono stuff he used to do. Said he had to give up on that just as soon as he realized he actually had to pay back his student loans."

"Shame. I remember how much he used to want to help people."

"He's still helping people. Just doing it a different way."

"What way is that?"

"I told you. They just made him the head of tax litigation. First black man to have that position. He's setting an example. Giving folks something to aspire to."

"Okay," Johnny said.

Andre was still smiling. "What about you, Uncle Johnny? Got something you need help with?"

"What do you mean?"

He nodded toward the window. "Car out front. The two men sitting inside it. Ones playing all that music. Ones you keep watching through that window."

"What about them?"

"Couldn't help but notice they showed up right when you did. And they're parked in front of my grandmama's house. I don't want any trouble in front of my grandmama's house."

"There's no trouble. What are you talking about trouble for?" Johnny squinted. "What do you even know about trouble?"

"I know enough."

"Not going to be any trouble unless you start some. Hear me? Those men aren't bothering you. Just let them alone."

"If you say so." Andre shrugged. He picked up the remote.

Johnny stopped staring out the window. Instead he looked straight ahead at the pictures on his cousin's wall.

After a while he found himself doing exactly what Simone had asked: he remembered himself. Remembered a time when he was still young and free of debt. When what he had to offer was something he never had cause to question because he was still Johnny the Great and always followed his own path.

He shut his eyes and remembered. The Justice Committee, circa 1965. Simone had been part of the group. So had Cousin Bertrand, although back then they called him Captain Dynamite on account of the fact that he could spit firecrackers. Then there was Flash, so called for both the speed with which he ran and the sheer wattage of his dazzling smile. After their first year together they were joined by a woman they met in Birmingham, Alabama, whom they all called the Hammer because she had one really strong hand. And finally there was Johnny—he was the one who mapped out their routes. After they'd finished their walk with J.D., they wanted to do more. So they kept going, wound up spending the next seven years traveling all over the South, following the progress of the civil rights movement. Staging minor interventions, doing whatever they could to help ensure the freedom of movement of people they considered heroes. No one asked them to do it. They'd had no particular training or facility for it before they started out. Just a feeling that it was right and therefore necessary, that it was what they had been called to do.

He leaned back on the couch. Who was Melvin Marks to stand in judgment of Johnny's life? What had Melvin ever been a part of that could compare to the Justice Committee? And maybe it was a long time ago and maybe they hadn't accomplished as much as they'd hoped. But the point was they had tried, had been willing to stand up for what they believed was right. What had Melvin Marks ever stood for? The man might look impressive now, might have a nice office downtown with a sign on the door that made him sound like he was in charge of something stable and permanent: MELVIN MARKS, INVESTMENT AND PROPERTIES. But when you came right down to it, who was Melvin really? Just another hustler in a business suit, using Johnny's maps to chase down one convoluted money-making scheme after another. Johnny just assumed they were all different versions of whatever hustle he'd worked before. After Melvin had been caught embezzling funds and lost his license to practice law, he didn't actually go rogue. He went freelance.

"Got you now."

Johnny's eyes snapped open to the jarring sound of Andre shouting curses at the TV screen.

"Oh no you don't! I got you!"

He sat up, disoriented, and realized he must have dozed off.

"Die motherfucker!"

The kitchen door swung open.

"Turn it off," Simone said.

Andre pressed a button and the screen went dark.

"Sorry about that, Cousin. He bothering you? Told you he gets a little wild sometimes. Forgets who he is, forgets where . . ."

She pursed her lips and frowned.

"Andre? We've talked about this. And you know I've worked very hard to make sure you are comfortable while you're here. Bought you all those new clothes. Put up with all these damn video games. I'd like to think you appreciate it. Like to think it means something to you, all the sacrifices I've made trying to keep you happy. You know I expect more from you."

"Yes, Grandma. I'm sorry."

"Don't disappoint me, Dre. And don't put your feet on my furniture." She went back into the kitchen.

Johnny looked at Andre, now just sitting there, hands folded on his lap as he stared at a dark screen. Simone clearly had the child mystified, was trying to control him with the seductive power of guilt. Then Johnny noticed the fading light coming in through the windows and it occurred to him that he had no idea how long he'd been sitting there, remembering himself, just like she'd asked him to. He started to wonder if she hadn't worked some kind of mojo on him too.

"I keep forgetting Grandma don't like a lot of noise," Andre said. "She's old."

Johnny nodded.

"What was she like before?"

"Before what?"

"Back in the day. You know, when you all were my age. Sometimes I look at pictures and it's like looking at another world. Everybody just looked so different."

"I guess everybody did," Johnny said.

What had Simone been like then? A woman who wanted to be free and independent and was willing to fight for the chance is what she would have said. It's pretty much what they all would have said, although looking back he wasn't sure anybody really knew what it would take to get there. At some point, he imagined, Simone must have settled on the answer that, in truth, had seemed the most obvious all along.

Money.

4

FAMILY VALUES

It's what Johnny was after too. He waited until after the yardman had finally finished whatever he was doing in the yard, until after they'd eaten dinner and then at long last said goodnight and went off to bed. Then when the house was quiet, he crept back downstairs.

He looked through the living room window, saw his cousin's blooms flashing white and gold along the side of the house. He had to admit they were a beautiful sight. He could sense how much work had gone into that garden, how many years it must have taken to cultivate. In truth he'd never thought she'd stick around in that house long enough to do it. Thought the Judge was just another in the long line of men she'd already run through like useless details.

But that was the thing about Simone. For all her vanity and manipulations she was nothing if not a strong woman who could be very loyal when she wanted to be. She'd stayed with the Justice Committee to the very end, even after Flash got arrested, even after Bertrand left to start his own group as a consequence of Johnny's maps getting, in Bertrand's words, "too weird." At some point Johnny's routes had begun getting more circuitous, his maps more theoretical and therefore, on the surface perhaps, confused. The Justice Committee had seen a lot of violence and chaos in the four years they were together and the more time went on the more Johnny felt forced to weave his way around the nagging suspicion that they weren't really getting anywhere. Just shuffling back and forth, helping to remove one obstacle to the goal of free and unfettered movement only to find that two more had popped up somewhere else. He'd begun to suspect that maybe the reason they weren't making more progress was that they were not addressing real sources of power.

It was a suspicion that had developed naturally enough out of experience. For example, it was just a fact that the group could not be everywhere at once. Yet, at the time, there were protests going on all across the South, often simultaneously and so throughout the Justice Committee's existence, their movements were determined by a set of priorities that Johnny used to calculate when and where it would be best to conduct their various interventions. A set of priorities that, when enacted as movement, was of course just another map. When they arrived at each location Johnny would make a smaller map outlining what they would do there. But these maps were always secondary considerations, straightforward in their aim and therefore relatively simplistic in their design. The primary map was entirely different: complex, constantly evolving as it was constantly elaborated upon. It was also always inexact. In many instances it would have taken a lifetime to properly quantify the value of a given route over another and because of that they'd often wound up doing things for expediency's sake alone, operating under the assumption that it was always better to do something than to do nothing. And yet it remained true that anyone trying to anticipate their next move would have a hard time doing so without recourse to at least a basic outline of this primary map.

At some point it occurred to Johnny that if their own pattern of movement was determined by a set of coordinates representing a conceptual hierarchy rendered inexact due to expediency, then was it not possible that the opposite was true as well? After all, he was not the only mapmaker in the world; what if their interventions were in fact doing little more than disrupting the secondary manifestations that emerged from the calculations of another mapmaker, another map altogether, a set of hidden priorities the existence of which he could only speculate upon, because he had as yet never seen it? Because if it did exist, then it meant that in order to be an effective mapmaker, Johnny had to do more than simply trace routes. He had to be able to chart actual corridors of power and, furthermore, figure out how to anticipate movement through those corridors. Which meant that any map worth its salt would have to have a fourth dimension: time.

He looked out the window. That was the part that had made things complicated, the part that had ultimately proved so hard to explain. But, really, that was all Johnny was trying to do with the Justice Committee toward the end: map time.

"What are you doing standing by yourself in the dark?"

Johnny turned around. Simone was standing behind him in a long floral bathrobe, holding a cup of tea.

"Thought you were asleep."

"I don't sleep," Simone said. "I'm old, ain't you heard? Just putter around all night. You?"

"Same." Johnny forced himself to smile. "Just admiring your garden. Remembering how different it looked before. Made me realize how long it's been."

"That it has."

He nodded. "Nice to see you doing so well, Simone. You've got a real nice family and a beautiful home. Almost hard to picture back in the day."

"I know it." Simone sipped her tea. "All that wildness. I wasn't happy back then. Not really."

"What about now?"

"Happy? Oh, I let go of that a long time ago. Stopped worrying about it and it just stopped bothering me. What I am is content. What about you? When you planning on settling down?"

"I'm working on it."

"Yeah? Well, that's something, I guess."

She sighed. "The Great Johnny Ribkins. Do you know how much I used to look up to you? When we were younger? Have you got any idea? There was a time when I would have followed you to the end of the earth, a time when you could have been anything you wanted in this world. Doctor, lawyer, Indian chief, you name it." She shook her head. "Instead all you are is a damn shame."

Johnny frowned. It had been so long since he'd been to visit and only now he remembered there was a reason for that, a reason why he'd stayed away. The Judge was a part of it but not the only reason. She acted like she'd all but forgotten that part of her life but he knew that in truth she still blamed him for the breakup of the Justice Committee. He was the one who mapped out their routes; if anybody should have known where they were going, it was Johnny.

"All that talent just wasted," Simone said. "What happened to you, Cousin? How did your life get so turned around?"

Now her eyes were welling up with tears. Droplets slid down her cheek, seeming to drag the left side of her face with them. Johnny winced as a long, gnarled welt appeared on the side of her face, stretching from the corner of her left eye to just below her chin. She must have been upset because she was showing him her true face, which he already knew was riddled with scars.

"When are you going to start doing right? Start living right? Remember who you are?"

"Believe it or not I've been trying."

"That right? That why you show up out of the blue like this? Why you so busy taking care of some business you don't even want your niece to see you doing? See, I know you."

"It's complicated."

"It's not though. Either you're right or you're wrong."

She leaned forward and reached for his hand. "Don't be mad, Cousin. You know I love you. But somebody's got to tell you the truth. You've got to get yourself together before it's too late. If you can't do it for your own sake, then do it for that poor, pitiful child. Because it looks to me like you're pretty much all she's got."

She stood up, kissed him on the cheek, and shuffled back to her bedroom. Left him alone to think about the choices he'd made, how in truth most of them hadn't felt like choices at all. After losing his brother, the dissolution of the Justice Committee was the most painful passage of his entire life; he would have done anything to hold the group together but at the time hadn't seen another way except to keep doing what he was doing. Because there *was* another map. He still believed it was true and nothing he had seen or done in the years since he stopped trying to pin it down had convinced him otherwise. He'd just wanted to see it; all he'd needed was one quick, clear glimpse of that other map and then he could copy it, offer up his map of time in response, and everything would change. They would have a clearer picture of what they were fighting for because they would finally know what exactly they were fighting against. The only problem was access and it was in the process of trying to work that out that everything seemed to fall apart. Because somehow he'd gotten it into his head that in order to access the hidden map and thereby make it possible for him to complete his own, they needed money. If no one would give it to them, they would just have to take it.

He shook his head. It seemed strange now but when he tried to retrace the patterns his mind made when he'd dug the hole in his cousin's yard, he knew that because of the group's efforts to finance his map, when he showed up at Simone's house all those years ago he was, technically, already a thief. Somehow this hadn't even occurred to him at the time. Until the Judge pointed it out.

You think you are above the law? You think anyone cares about your motives? A man is defined by his actions, Johnny. No more and no less.

The Judge had been right, of course. Most of the money the Justice Committee had raised to finance the implementation of his map had been stolen. It's just that the money wasn't for Johnny. It was for the Committee, for something much larger than himself. At the time, that seemed to make all the difference.

He waited for the light in Simone's bedroom to click off and then he stood up and walked back down the hall. He had his hand on the front doorknob and was about to pull it open when a voice called out to him.

"Careful, Uncle. She put the alarm on."

Johnny wheeled around and saw a pair of eyes like those of a six-foot-tall cat glowing back at him.

"Andre?" Johnny squinted. "You can see me, can't you?" His father's eyes used to shine the exact same way.

"Oh, I see everything. Haven't you heard? I just figured it was something you already knew."

Johnny nodded. Seeing in the dark was one of the most common traits to show up on the Ribkins family tree and Johnny knew from experience how dangerous it could be. "You should be careful with that."

"I'm careful," Andre said. Johnny felt an arm move in front of his chest as Andre reached for the wall behind him and typed in the numbers to turn the alarm off.

"See? Very careful."

Andre opened the door.

"Where you going?" Johnny asked.

"Got to meet some friends of mine."

"Yeah? Well, you make sure you mind what I said. Leave those men on the corner alone."

"All right, Uncle. Whatever you say."

Headlights slid across his nephew's face as a car pulled up to the curb and Andre walked out the front door. As he watched his nephew climb into the back seat, it occurred to Johnny that he'd misread at least part of what was going on in his cousin's house. The alarm wasn't to keep danger out. It was part of a failed effort to keep Andre *in*.

WEDNESDAY

5

COVER

Johnny woke up in the guest bedroom at dawn, the tatters of a long dream still fluttering in his mind. Something about his ancestors watching over him, their vigilance a map of stern looks, loud laughter, and wide smiles. It felt so good that he let himself lay there for a long time, in the warmth and comfort of his own lethargy. Then he went downstairs and made his way through the silent house. When he looked out the window the Camaro was gone. He realized he was finally alone.

He went to the kitchen, poured himself a cup of coffee, then took his cup and pushed through the front door. He walked around to the side of the house, looked at that bright yellow azalea bush nestled against Simone's living room window.

The hole he was looking for was all that was left of the money the Justice Committee had raised to finance the implementation of his map. In the process of trying to obtain these funds Bertrand had quit the group and Flash had been arrested; most of what they'd gathered wound up going toward Flash's legal defense. The group went on hiatus not long after; having nowhere else to go, Johnny took his map and what was left of the money and drove to his father's house, telling himself he just needed time to figure out his next move. He ended up staying there for the next four years, helping his father around the shop, not answering his phone, and not knowing what to say whenever his father asked him what had happened, what was going on, why he wasn't acting like himself.

Because Mac *was* acting like himself. Still stumbling around the house with a paintbrush in his hand. Still making his pictures, spinning out his abstract oils, trying to show the world colors no one else could see. Mac never had any useful advice to give Johnny when it came to trying to navigate the real world. He lived by his own obsessions and therefore the best he could do was stand there and absorb Johnny's choices with a bruised silence, a numb confidence that somehow his son would figure something out, some way to survive.

Then one night over the course of an evening playing poker with a circle of old men, Mac, in an effort to cheer Johnny up, let something slip about having another son, back in Lehigh Acres.

You think you got it bad? How you think that boy feels?

The information was appalling and pitiful, another something to add to Johnny's well-seasoned disgust for his father's lack of judgment. Yet in retrospect Johnny realized that Mac had given him exactly what he needed at the time: a brother who needed him, a renewed sense of urgency, a reason to get back on his feet.

A new map.

And somehow, on the way to find his brother, Johnny had decided to stop here.

Now he set his cup down, took a deep breath, and tried to wedge his way back inside. He stepped over a tangle of roots, shoved his body forward, took two steps to the left, and twisted around so he looked back out at the yard, trying to remember what it had looked like when he dug the hole: a broad patch of dirt balanced beneath the blank blue sky. He crouched down, put his hand out, gripped a slender branch. He clamped his fist around it and pulled.

"What do you think you're doing?"

Johnny whipped his head around and felt a patch of thorns slap him across the cheek. He looked up and saw the yardman standing over him.

"Dropped something . . . out the window . . ."

The yardman frowned. He reached in, grabbed Johnny by his arm, and pulled him back out.

"Why didn't you just ask for help?"

Johnny blinked. "I didn't think anybody was home."

An hour later he was sitting at the kitchen table when he heard the front door open. Simone walked in and the first thing Johnny noticed was the glare coming off her.

"Where have you been?"

Simone shook her head. Her jaw was clenched tight and it was only with great effort that she was able to force out the words, "Shot in the foot."

"What?"

Then Eloise came in after her, followed by Andre, wincing as he limped on crutches.

Simone took a deep breath and started again. "Boy was out there, running around in the street last night. Got himself shot in the foot."

"It wasn't my fault, Grandma. Just happened to be in the wrong place at the wrong time."

"Oh, you were in the wrong place all right. Seeing as how you were supposed to be in bed sleeping. The rest of your story I'm not so sure about."

"It's the truth." Andre winked at Johnny. "Just trying to help out a friend."

Johnny glanced out the window. The Camaro was still gone. He squinted at Andre.

"Maybe your friend didn't need any help. Maybe you would have been helping your friend more if you'd just stayed out of it."

"Your uncle's right. Because any friend who got you coming home like this is a friend you don't need to have."

"I'm telling you it's not a big deal."

"No big deal? Do you know how crazy you sound?" Simone turned to Johnny. "You see what I'm dealing with now, don't you? Got a grandson under the impression that any trouble he gets into, so long as he manages to limp away from it somehow, is no big deal. I keep trying to tell him that as long as you doing wrong, whatever little chump change you might be able to pick up in the meantime don't count nearly so much as your good name."

"Chump change?" Andre snorted. "I don't know what you think I was doing last night but I'm telling you, you got it wrong. I really was just trying to help a friend. Besides, if I did do something for money, you can be sure it wouldn't be chump change. Because I do know how to count zeros, Grandma."

"You so busy counting zeros you're missing the point. People judge you on what you show the world. Stop showing your ass," Simone said. "It's just sad is all. In the old days, when we were coming up, we knew who we were and we knew what was worth fighting for. These days it seems like you kids just stumble around in a state of confusion. Ain't got nothing, ain't got nobody. So busy chasing after nonsense you don't even seem to realize that's all it is."

"Well, now you see? You just said it yourself, times have changed."

Simone frowned. "That's the *opposite* of what I said. Ain't nothing changed, boy. Not really. Not since my day, not since the Rib King's. You got to know who you are in this world, decide for yourself what you want the world to see, then make sure everybody else sees it too."

She turned to Eloise. "You ever tasted Rib King sauce? It's delicious. That's why they still make it to this day."

Andre shook his head. "They don't. Those discounted cans you found at the A&P that time were already ten years old."

"It's delicious," Simone said. "Go on. Take your cousin out back and show her. I know I still got some of those cans in the deep freezer. Then find someplace to lie down and rest your foot."

Andre got back on his crutches and led Eloise out of the kitchen.

Johnny looked at his cousin. "You all right?"

"No. Not really. You think it's easy trying to deal with something like that? The boy has got no common sense."

Johnny tried to smile. "Well, the foot doesn't look too bad."

"Oh, he's just all hopped up on painkillers right now. Wait until they wear off, then he'll really start to feel it."

"You'll figure it out. Find a way to get through to him." He reached for her hand. "One day he'll look back on all this and realize how lucky he is to have you."

"That's nice of you to say."

"It's the truth."

Simone sighed. "Listen, Johnny. I know I said some things I probably shouldn't have last night. I want you to know I didn't mean it the way it sounded."

"Don't lie. You meant exactly what you said."

"Yes, but not the way it sounded."

She shook her head. "Brady told me he caught you out in the yard this morning, digging around in my flowers. And the girl told me about how you came to her house, what you were doing there. You need to know you've got no cause to dig up my azaleas, if that's what you're gearing up to do. Your money isn't there."

Johnny stared at her.

"You heard what I said? The azaleas? The money? All gone."

"I heard you. Where is it?"

"I used it to help pay off my mortgage. Took what was left and made some investments, put a down payment on some additional properties . . . "

She reached for his hand. "Try to understand, Johnny. You got to see it like it was, at the time. It was, what, twenty years ago? Right after the Judge had his heart attack. I came to visit you in St. Augustine, remember? The bills were just piling up and I didn't know what I was going to do. When Andre's father dug that money up I was so grateful to have it that I didn't question where it came from. Never occurred to me you might be coming back for it after all this time."

She kept talking, seemed to have a lot more to say, but after a while Johnny couldn't hear her anymore. He could see her lips moving but it was like she was drifting away from him, pushed back by the pressure building in his chest. He realized Simone probably knew from the moment he walked through her door what he was there for, just like she'd known he wouldn't find it. All he could think about was the time he'd wasted sitting on her couch, looking at old photographs, remembering himself, and then listening to her tell him he was a damn shame. And somehow it still wasn't over. Somehow he was still sitting there, still wasting time, listening to his cousin try to explain.

"I'm not cold-blooded, Johnny. I can cut you in for ten percent. You hear me? Give you one of my green acres for your very own. You don't even have to ask for it, it's already done. Now you got something, if you want it. Someplace permanent to call home. For when you finally decide it's time to settle down."

Then he became aware of another sound, soft at first but gradually growing louder and more distinct. It was the sound of a child's laughter.

"Where's the girl?"

"Never mind, Johnny. She's all right. Just listen to me for a minute. Here, let me hold your hand."

He pushed back his chair. "Where's Eloise?" He stood up from the table.

"Cousin, calm down. You're getting agitated and I'm trying to explain to you why you got no cause—"

He walked away from her, stumbling toward the sound of that laughter, and a voice:

"I see everything. That's why can't nobody hide from me—"

Not the girl's voice but Andre's. It led him through the house and out the back door.

"The only time it's actually dark is when I shut my eyes."

He found his niece in the garage with all the lights turned off. She was standing next to the deep freezer while Andre stood on the other side of the room, leaning on his crutches and smiling. There were two cans of barbecue sauce in her hands, each one bearing a twin image of his grandfather's cartoon smile.

"We just playing, Uncle Johnny."

Johnny looked at his grandfather.

"That's enough. Get your stuff together, Eloise. We're going."

"But I thought you said you wanted me—"

"Changed my mind." He snatched the cans from her hands. "You better off sticking with me."

Eloise ran out of the room. Johnny waited until she was gone and then turned to Andre. "You were out there bothering those men on the corner, weren't you?"

"They gone now, aren't they? Thought you'd be happy."

"I look happy to you?" Johnny shook his head. "One day you're going to realize that seeing everything is not going to do you much good until you learn to listen too. I told you to let them alone."

Andre frowned. "That's all right, Uncle Johnny. You don't have to thank me. That's just what family does for each other. What they can."

Johnny turned around and walked back to the kitchen.

"We're leaving," he told Simone.

"Now, Johnny, don't be like that. You know I love you. Don't leave here mad."

The girl came downstairs with her backpack. She kissed Simone and told Andre goodbye and Johnny led her out to the car. As he backed out of the driveway he saw Simone watching him from the kitchen window. But Andre was the one who stuck his head out and smiled.

"Nice to see you, Uncle. Come back any time."

He started driving north.

"Why did we have to leave like that?"

Johnny didn't answer. He pressed his foot on the gas, trying to get some distance between him and Simone.

"Aunt Simone said I should be careful around you. She said you were a good man but I shouldn't follow you too closely, shouldn't ever forget to think for myself."

"Sounds like good advice. Hear me? I got no problem with it."

He was mad.

"What happened between you two? How come you stopped being a team? She said you abandoned her."

"That's what she said? It's not true and she knows it. I tried every-thing I could to keep the group together. Even after Flash got arrested, even after Bertrand went off and started his own group. Even after J.D. . . ."

"What?"

"J. D. Thompson. The man from Lehigh, the one I was telling you about—man who inspired us to get together in the first place. He didn't make it."

He found himself searching for her eyes in the rearview. "It's not a secret. Imagine when you do get around to reading about him in school they'll get to that part too, although I bet you five dollars they get the details wrong. Group of white vigilantes shot up his house. He was up in bed sleeping when it started. Anybody try to tell you he was armed don't know what they're talking about. Hear me? That's a lie."

Johnny shook his head. "The point is I should have been there. Instead I was back in New York at the time, working on a map. Called myself trying to do something important. World don't stop spinning just because you trying to do something. That's what I learned. You got to hold on tight to what you got, otherwise things can start spin-ning out of control. Look up one day and Bertrand was gone, Flash gone. Come to find out J.D. gone too. I'm still sitting up there trying to make a map for the Justice Committee and realize there wasn't a Justice Committee anymore. But see, Simone didn't care. Just expected me to keep going, no matter what."

"Maybe you were her hero," Eloise said.

"What?" He remembered what he had told her about heroes. "No. That doesn't sound right." That didn't sound like Simone at all.

They kept going.

"Andre can see in the dark," Eloise said.

"Yes, I know. What were you doing with him anyway?"

"He was trying to teach me to catch in the dark."

"Why?"

"What do you mean, 'why'?"

"I mean, what do you need to catch in the dark for? Why can't you just have sense enough to stay in the light where you can see?"

Eloise was quiet for a moment.

Johnny sighed. "Look, girl. Your grandfather was like that too. Seems to be a pretty common trait in this family. But you spend enough time around someone like that and you start to realize it's not just some neat trick, that maybe sometimes it's dark for a reason. Because really it just leads to a whole lot of confusion."

"Maybe. Still, it was nice to meet somebody else who had something like that, something that made them different. Sometimes, back home, I feel like I'm the only one."

The car went up a hill and back onto a lush, shady stretch of the Tamiami. They rolled past the short strip of boutiques, cafes, and art galleries that made up downtown.

"Has everybody in the family got something like that? Something worth remarking on?"

"I don't know everybody. But why not? Stands to reason."

"What about my daddy?"

"What did your mother tell you?"

"She told me he could climb things. She said he might have been scaling mountains, been an Olympic mountain climber, in another life."

"They don't climb mountains in the Olympics, girl."

"Why not? They play Ping-Pong, don't they? Why do they play Ping-Pong and not climb mountains?"

Johnny shook his head. But he did wonder why mountain climbing had never occurred to him back when he and Franklin were together. All he'd ever seen his brother scale were walls.

"All I know is your daddy had an awesome talent. Beautiful to see. You too, what you can do, that catching thing. It's beautiful." He said it automatically, without thinking about whether or not it was true. Really, what he'd seen of her talent so far had disturbed him more than anything else.

"We just got to find a way to showcase it properly."

"What does that mean?"

"Showcase? Well, for one thing, it means I don't want you letting people chuck cans at your head again. Understand?" That seemed real basic. He might not have known what her talent was good for, but he knew it wasn't that. "You've got to cut that out. Didn't your mama ever think to put you on a softball team or anything?"

"Softball? You think so?"

"I don't know, girl. Maybe." He climbed onto Interstate 75. "Just got to figure it out. Find your place. Where you need to be, to be happy."

"You can help me do that?"

"I can try."

It was ten in the morning when they rolled over the Skyway Bridge, bright sunlight and a broad view of the Gulf flashing between its yellow support beams. As soon as they touched down he made an immediate turn onto a small beach next to a dilapidated condominium complex wedged between the interstate and a view of the water.

"You really think I might be good at softball?"

"Girl, I don't know. Maybe. Sure."

He put the car in park.

"Be right back."

He got his shovel, then walked down a brick path until he reached a small fenced-in pool bordered by condos on three sides and the rocky shoreline on the other. He walked around the fence and stood on the beach, looking for the largest palm tree. When he found it he counted out ten paces and stopped.

Simone had left him in a real bind. None of the other holes he still had out there were anywhere near as large as the one he'd left in her yard. He figured he'd have to dig up at least a dozen more just to come close to making up for what she'd taken from him. Yet, as disappointed as he was in how things turned out, he knew he couldn't blame her for his situation; she was just being herself, had done with the money exactly what he'd known she would do if she ever found it. The only reason he left it there was because he'd wanted to get rid of it. Didn't want to think about the Justice Committee or that map anymore; told himself he was putting that part of his life behind him. It had never even occurred to him that he might actually need it someday.

No, this was his fault and there was no sense pretending otherwise. He never should have let things go on with Melvin for as long as they had, should have quit while he was still ahead instead of simply wait-ing to get caught. Instead he'd taken Melvin's money, then kept right on taking it, and deep down he knew the only real reason he had for doing it was because he'd wanted to. The wealthier and more powerful Melvin became, the easier one could see how potentially dangerous the man was, but somehow that just made Johnny feel more conflicted about the role he'd played in how all that wealth and power had been acquired. Taking some of it back seemed to soothe his grief, made his situation seem more tolerable. Like maybe if he took it and tried to do something useful with it, he could tell himself that there had been a reason for it, that all the maps he'd made for Melvin had served some purpose. That's all taking Melvin's money had really done: given Mel-vin a purpose.

He had his back to the Gulf but he could still feel the cool breeze coming off the beach, still hear the rush of waves as he dug. It was a soothing sound interrupted periodically by the whizzing drone of passing cars. After a while he got lost in the rhythm of his digging, lost track of time.

He dug a very deep hole, then reached in and pulled out a rusted tin box.

"You were gone for like an hour you know," Eloise said when he got back to the car. She had both doors open and was sitting in the driver's seat with her shoes off, tips of her toes resting in the sand. "What was I supposed to do out here by myself?"

Johnny put the box in the trunk.

"I thought you were going to take me to play softball or something."

"I'll take you to play softball. Later. When I'm finished. Told you I had to run some errands first. Sooner I finish, sooner we can start having fun. So just let me concentrate on what I'm doing."

He started the car. They took the Twenty-Sixth Avenue exit into St. Petersburg, rolled past a series of small brick houses set off from the boulevard by palm trees and scrub grass lawns, several of which were decorated with VOTE DAWSON signs. He dug a hole in the abandoned lot behind Bethel Community Baptist Church and another near a drainage canal near Lake Maggiore. Then he got back in the car and turned down Sixteenth Avenue, past a series of chain-link fences, cracked roofs, and splintered porches that nevertheless shined golden in the dappled light falling through the branches of the surrounding trees.

When he reached Ninth Street he pulled into the parking lot of an apartment building and dug a hole next to a Dumpster. He pulled out a Glad bag inside of which was a briefcase, price tag still on it, that contained a display case full of watches.

When he got what he was looking for he walked back to the car.

"I want to go home," Eloise said.

"Yeah? Well, you can't." He was tired. His hands hurt from gripping the shovel and he could feel blisters on his palms. "Mama's already gone and I'm not taking you back to an empty house."

"What's the difference? I'm alone here too."

"Difference is, so long as you sitting in the car I know you're safe."

"I don't need you to be safe. That don't even make sense, seeing as how I just met you. I got along just fine this long without you worrying about me. Imagine I'll be all right for another week, until my mama gets back home."

Johnny said nothing.

"I'm serious, Uncle Johnny. Nobody is going to bother me. I can handle myself, and anybody come to my house know they have to act right. Or else they have to go."

"That what happened with your mama's boyfriend? Man you run out of there? I heard you talking to Simone. Did he ever try to bother you?"

"He was annoying. Talked too much. Always left the toilet seat up in the bathroom."

"That's not what I meant."

"I know what you meant. No, he never tried to bother me. I just wanted him out of my house."

Johnny nodded. "I'm not taking you back home until you actually got someone there to look after you. Now put your shoes back on, you coming with me this time."

"Why? Are we finally going to do something fun?"

"Maybe."

He drove her to a pawnshop downtown. They pushed through the door and found a wiry-haired man in a dark blue cardigan sitting slumped behind the counter.

"Can I help you?"

Johnny reached into his pocket and pulled out a jumble of jewelry and baubles that included four of the watches, two money clips, and the engagement ring from the fort. As he set them on the counter he could feel the man watching them, trying to figure out what pitiful hard-luck story had led the old man in the rumpled suit and his granddaughter to him, selling off the family jewels. The man dipped his finger through the pile, every now and then scooping a ring out by looping it over his pinkie finger, squinting at it for a moment and then setting it aside.

When he was finished, he shook his head and frowned.

"I'm sorry," he said, and all at once Johnny realized his mistake. Because of course, aside from the engagement ring, a lot of that jewelry was fake. Gold-plating, cubic zirconia, a couple of rhinestones. One or two of the more anonymous-looking were actually the most valuable, and in the end the man offered them fifteen hundred dollars for the whole pile.

Eloise looked down at how the man had sorted the jewels into two groups, a smaller group for the ones he deemed authentic and a larger one for those he claimed were fake. She reached into the fake group and pulled out a large gold ring encrusted with what appeared to be rubies. "What about this one?"

"What about it?"

"You put it in the wrong pile. Go ahead and look again."

The man glared at her. "Are you calling me a liar?"

"I wasn't. Really, I don't know what you are. I'm just saying I think you made a mistake. If I'm wrong about that we might as well just keep it, seeing as how it's not worth anything."

The man cocked his head and squinted. "I'll give you another five hundred for it, but that's all."

When they got back outside, Johnny asked, "How did you know that one was real?"

"I didn't. But I was watching how he was sorting them. He did the same thing to that one that he did to the real ones, but then he set it down on top of the ones he said were fake. I thought maybe he got something confused."

She shook her head.

"Can I get something to eat now?"

"I'm about to take care of that."

First he drove out to Mirror Lake and dug another hole. When he was finished they went across the bridge to Tampa and he took her to a busy restaurant downtown, full of professional-looking men and women in suits, talking loudly. They found a table in the back and he ordered Eloise a cheeseburger and chocolate milkshake. He ordered a beer for himself and when that was finished, an iced tea. Then he excused himself to use the bathroom, slipped out through the kitchen door, stood under the shade of a small ash tree at the edge of the parking lot, and dug a small hole.

When he got back Eloise was still sitting slumped in the booth where he left her. He eased into the seat across from her.

"You all right? Listen, I should thank you for catching that thing with the ring back there. It's not like me to—"

"I want to go home."

"We've already been over that."

"Yeah, but I don't think you're hearing me. I tell you I can handle myself. Don't need you to protect me."

"You know you talk a lot about handling yourself for a little girl. You sure there's not something more went on with that boyfriend you not telling me?"

"Well, first of all, I'm not a little girl. Second of all, why do you keep asking about him? I told you he was gone. Went back to where he came from and I know for a fact he's not coming back."

"Where he came from? You mean he wasn't from Lehigh?"

"No, mama knew him from before."

Johnny winced at the sound of that. He knew what Meredith's before was like and could only imagine what that meant. Just thinking about it made his stomach tense.

"Also he wasn't her boyfriend. Just a friend. She said he was real good to her back in the day. That's why she was trying to help him get back on his feet. But you see, it didn't do any good. He wouldn't even look for a job, just sat around the house all day, drinking beer and talking on the phone. Then when mama came home he had the nerve to ask her what's for dinner. He was annoying."

"Your mama should have had more sense than to let somebody like that around you. When we get back I'll tell her so myself."

Her head shot up at the sound of that and he realized that he'd said too much.

"Who are you to be telling my mama anything? You weren't there. I told you she was just trying to help."

"You the one wanted him out of your house."

The girl was quiet.

"Eloise? I'm not saying you can't handle yourself. I'm saying you shouldn't have to. And maybe the reason I keep asking about that man is because I feel bad. Feel like I should have known what was going on with you and didn't even know you were there. But see, now I know. And you might think you are alone with me, but trust me, you're not. I'm right here. And you're safe with me. Might just be around the corner or up the block . . . But the point is nothing will happen to you and nobody will hurt you so long as you riding with me. Understand?"

"Yes."

"Good. Now clean that up before we go."

She'd dumped all the salt from the shaker onto the table and was poking at it with her finger, tracing swirling loops that spelled out her name.

"You've got to act right in a restaurant, Eloise. Leave a mess like that and somebody liable to spit in your food next time you come back."

"Are we coming back?"

"Clean it up anyway," he said.

It was ten-thirty at night by the time they pulled into the parking lot of a motel in Clearwater. Over the course of a single day he had dug up a dozen holes. When he counted his money he realized that, if he included what he got from selling the jewelry he'd dug up, he'd raised almost half of the $20,000 he needed.

He paid for their room, helped her carry her backpack up the stairs, then stepped into a gray room that smelled of mold. There was a wooden table with a TV set on top of it, a single chair by the window, and two twin beds covered in matching plaid quilts.

Besides that it just looked small.

Standing at the front desk with his credit card, he'd not been able to properly gauge how odd it would feel to be sharing a room with the girl. Now he wished he'd gone ahead and paid for two rooms.

"Pick the bed you want and I'll take the other one. It's just for one night."

He collapsed into the chair by the window and, not wanting to make her uncomfortable, tried not to look in her direction.

Eloise put her bag on the bed nearest to the door. She unzipped it, pulled out a toothbrush and an armful of clothes, and disappeared into the bathroom. When she came back out she was wearing a gray sweatshirt and a pair of cutoff shorts. She sat cross-legged on her bed and started braiding her hair.

"You really think you can help me figure out what to do with my talent? Like you helped my daddy with his climbing?"

"Your daddy didn't need any help to climb."

"He ever tell you why he liked to do it so much? Was he always like that? Or did it kind of just sneak up on him one day?"

"I wasn't there, so I don't know." He smiled. "I mean, I know what he said. Said he climbed because he couldn't fly. Said his first memories was sitting in the grass with his mama somewhere, looking up at all the birds moving around in the sky, thinking about how happy and free they all looked up there. Said somehow he got it in his head that if he couldn't do that, then it meant he was just going to have to climb."

Johnny chuckled to himself, thinking back to that conversation. "Wasn't exactly the answer to the question I'd put to him. So I asked him to explain, you know, clarify. Was he saying he started climbing because he wanted to be a bird? Or had he been climbing before that and seeing those birds was how he made it make sense to himself? He said he wasn't sure because seeing those birds were his first actual memories. Said all he knew was that somehow the will and the want and the way all worked out to be the same thing, and that that was how he knew he was blessed." He looked at Eloise. "Your daddy was kind of crazy like that. I mean in a good way. Talked crazy, acted crazy too sometimes. Well, a lot of times. Thing is, he was real smart. It was just that when he talked you had to sit for a while and think about the things he said if you wanted to make sense of them."

"Guess you two had that in common."

"Maybe."

She gave him a serious look. "I'm going to apologize to you for any misunderstanding we might have had before."

"Are you now?"

"I am. I know you're busy. You didn't have to bring me with you. But Auntie Simone is right, it's important to know who you are. And I do want to find my place. So long as you're really going to help me do that I guess I don't mind all this riding around in your car, if it's just for a couple days."

Johnny nodded. His whole body ached by then and his left hand was so swollen he had a hard time making a fist. "Why don't you just relax? See if there's something you want to watch on the TV."

She reached for the remote and started flipping channels. Johnny sat in the chair, massaging his left hand with the pad of his right thumb while he stared out the window at the lights shining from the Applebee's across the street.

After a while Eloise put her head down on her pillow and shut her eyes. He waited until he was sure she was asleep and then crept back downstairs.

He walked out to his car and unlocked the trunk. He reached for his shovel, carried it to the patch of piney woods that marked the boundary between the interstate and the motel grounds, looked around him at the highway on the other side of a chain-link fence where a long row of headlights was burrowing through the darkness. He counted five of the tallest trees, swung his body to the left, and walked seven paces. He hoisted his shovel and started digging.

The last time he'd been here it was with Franklin, just a few months after he'd dragged his brother out of Lehigh Acres with the promise of, if not a better life, then at least a little adventure. Maybe he wouldn't have done it, maybe he would have just left Franklin where he was, pretending to be a farmer like his mother's people, if he hadn't been so convinced the boy was like him: gifted, blessed with a special talent, and therefore a true descendant of their grandfather the Rib King.

He'd been so impressed with his brother's talent, so determined to get Franklin out of Lehigh Acres that it wasn't until they were finally on the road that it occurred to Johnny he didn't actually know where they were going. St. Augustine was the obvious destination, but what would they do when they got there? As beautiful and brilliant as his brother may have been, he had no education, no money, and a criminal record by the time Johnny met him. What's more, he was wild: so busy partying and chasing after a good time that he couldn't maintain a relationship, couldn't hold down a job. He seemed to have no sense of consequence, no sense of scale with regard to his actions, and it hadn't taken long for Johnny to realize that the things that made him so beautiful and fearless moving up the side of a wall were also making it difficult for him to navigate solid ground. Up there, hanging off the side of a building, the man was simply unfathomable grace. Down here, with the rest of us, Franklin was hyper and dreamy eyed, so distracted by the manic pull of his imagination, the endless possibilities of his own mind that he had a hard time paying attention to what was going on around him. For Franklin, walls were not limits or constraints; they were something to hold on to. He was not intimidated by them, had no fixed notions of what they were supposed to represent. He interacted with them as if their sole reason for existing was to give him what he wanted most: something to climb.

None of this made Franklin the easiest person to get along with and it certainly had not made for the easiest life. By the time Johnny met him, all his brother had to fall back on was his own talent, a fearless need to climb, something inside him that wanted more. So that was what Johnny promised to give him: not a better life, but more of it. What that "more" meant he'd tried to keep vague. Once they were on the road, however, it became increasingly clear that Franklin had his own ideas about what more was.

Money.

This all you think I'm good for? Franklin had said after their first job together, the robbery of a man named H. P. Smith, a crooked preacher living in Ybor City, who'd once been friends with their father, and who, among other things, had been stealing from his parishioners for years. In proposing the theft all Johnny had meant to do was find a way to demonstrate how the two of them might work together, combine their talents to some shared purpose that, in Johnny's mind at least, was still undefined. Somehow his brother seemed to take it as an affront.

Why are we even bothering with this small-time stuff? I can climb anything, you said so yourself. You want to steal something? Let's go rob a bank.

That's what Franklin had been like in those early days. He'd spent the first twenty-five years of his life stuck in Lehigh Acres and now that he was finally set free seemed to assume that meant trying to get rich. He talked about rich as if it were less a state of being than an actual place and never tired of describing all the things he was going to buy and do once they got there. Which was almost sad at first because it was clear he had no idea how much anything actually cost. And every time Johnny tried to explain that part to him, tried to tell him how the world worked, he'd find his train of thought interrupted by his own lack of certainty as to whether or not he knew what he was talking about. After all the heartbreak and confusion caused by his map, all the mistakes he'd made, first in Lehigh and then with the Justice Committee, who was he to tell anybody what they should want? His brother needed a way to live but he was already beautiful. Who was Johnny to try to change Franklin? Change him into what?

If this is all you about, all you planning on the two of us doing, I might as well have stayed home . . .

Things got so tense between them during those first months together on the road that there were several times when Johnny thought about giving up, telling Franklin he'd made a mistake, turning the car around, and sending him back home. But he couldn't do that. Even if he couldn't tell his brother what to do, he would not leave him to suffer the consequences of his choices alone. He had to keep his brother safe.

All that shit you told me. I thought you were big time, I thought you were the man. The Great Johnny Ribkins . . .

Instead Johnny got in the habit of waiting until Franklin was asleep, then sneaking out to commit minor robberies on his own. It seemed to settle his nerves at the time, but aside from that, he wasn't sure why he did it. Maybe he was practicing, without being fully conscious of that fact, gearing up for the life they were headed toward but that he had not fully accepted yet. He did not share what he brought back with his brother, in part because most of these were such small sums, but also because he sensed that Franklin wanted him to keep his confusion to himself. But that, for a time, was the truth of how a lot of these smaller holes came to be.

He heard a dull, airy thud as the shovel made contact with a plastic box. He reached down to pull it out and was still hunched over, refilling his hole, when a pair of headlights turned on and off on the road behind him.

A voice called out,

"Hey, old man? You see this?" It was the men Melvin had sent to follow him.

Johnny straightened his back and started walking toward the car. The rear passenger side window was covered with a piece of blue tarp.

He bent down and squinted at the driver. "Which one of you two geniuses shot my nephew?"

The driver shook his head. "You see how we were just sitting there, not bothering nobody? Matter of fact, if you recall, you're the one who came to us, came knocking on my window. And what did I tell you? Told you to go on about your business, act like we not there. And yet for some reason, here comes your nephew, knocking again. Only he's telling us we got no right to be there, telling us we got to move off from in front of his grandmother's house or else there's going to be trouble."

"Like I give a fuck about his grandmother," the man in the passenger seat said.

Johnny nodded. "So you shot him?"

"No, Johnny. I did not shoot him. I told him I didn't have anything to do with his grandmother or her house. I told him, very calmly, to step away from my car. Reminded him he didn't own the street, had no business trying to tell me where I can and cannot park my car. He didn't have to like it but Clyde and me weren't going anyplace until we felt like going someplace else. So what does he do? Picks up a rock, starts banging on the window. That's when Clyde got out of the car."

"Your nephew's an asshole," Clyde said.

"Two of them tussle for a moment, Clyde knocks him to the ground. Next thing I know he's reaching into his pocket, and before I even realize, he is pulling out a weapon. Shoots himself in the foot." The driver shrugged. "Wasn't really much left for us to do after that."

"So you saying he did that to himself? Where did he get this gun from?"

The driver frowned. "It wasn't mine."

"Actually I heard some of his little friends asking the same thing," Clyde said. "Said he got it out his grandmother's bedroom drawer. Said his grandmother kept it for protection. I don't know the woman personally so what you say, Johnny? She the type to keep a gun? For protection?"

"Guess he got what he wanted though, huh?" the driver said. "Because, of course, I had to move the car after that. And what I want to know is, why? Did you send him out there? Tell him to do that?"

"No. I wouldn't do that."

"You sure?" The driver squinted. "I mean, you not trying to fuck with us are you, old man? Because Melvin did warn us about you. We know you capable of some real dumb shit or else you wouldn't be in this situation, now would you? But we also know you're not actually stupid."

He turned to the man sitting next to him. "Think about that, Clyde. He can't be stupid. No way he could have lived this long being stupid."

"No," Clyde said numbly. "He can't be stupid."

"All right, then. So if we start from there, with the idea that you're not actually stupid, then I am willing to accept that you are not the one who sent that silly fool out there like that. Because if you are not stupid, it means you must realize that our being here don't actually change anything. You're the one who took Melvin's money. You were the one dumb enough to get caught. And I understand you probably feeling frustrated by all that right now but you got no cause to take it out on us. Because it is what it is. Understand? Everything just is."

"It's called being responsible," Clyde grumbled, "for your own actions."

"Okay," Johnny said. "Except I'm not taking anything out on you. I tried to tell that boy to leave you alone."

"Yeah? Well, try harder," the driver said. "Because if something like that happens again? We're not going to come out to talk to you about it like you see us doing now. We're holding you responsible."

"Keep your family in check," Clyde said.

Johnny nodded. "That all?"

"That's all. Now go on back to your damn hole."

Johnny backed away from the car. He didn't understand what Andre thought he was doing, confronting them like that, with a gun no
less. He might have told himself he was doing it to help Johnny but
the confrontation didn't make any sense except as a means of com-
pensating for something that couldn't have had much to do with two
men sitting in a car. He wondered if he'd been trying to prove something to his friends he'd had with him, which side he was on, where
his allegiances lay, that when he walked through that neighborhood
he was where he belonged. He wondered if he'd been trying to prove
that to himself. Johnny told himself he needed to remember just how
confused the boy was and to sit him down and talk to him about that
the next time he saw him. In the meantime he needed to call Simone
and tell her to do a better job hiding her gun.

When he got back to the room Eloise was wide awake and sitting up
in bed, face outlined in the blue light of the TV.

"Where'd you go? I woke up and you weren't here."

"I thought you were asleep." He clutched the pencil box to his
chest. "I had to run another errand."

"What kind of errand you got in the middle of the night?"

"It's business."

He looked down at the box in his hand. He set it down on the bed
and opened it.

"For the shop," Johnny said. He took his jacket off and started
talking. "Midnight estate sale. You ever heard of one of those? No, I
guess not. Well, some people keep odd hours, you know, and I got to
be vigilant if I want the really good deals. I'm always on the lookout for
something that might have resale value. We stock all kinds of things
in there."

The girl reached inside and pulled out a small ring.

"Is that what you've been doing all this time?" Eloise said. "Digging up things to sell in your shop?"

"I got to have a certain amount by the time I go back." He could feel his talk, in his weariness, weaving its way back toward the truth, as if somehow guided by the steeliness of her gaze.

"Why didn't you just say so?"

She tossed the ring back and forth between her hands, like she was trying to figure out its weight. "How much you think you could sell this for?"

He hung up his jacket in the closet and shook his head. "Maybe a couple hundred." He figured that was pretty much all he could expect for the whole box.

She put down the ring.

"Next time you go out to dig I want you to take me with you. I don't want to wait in the car anymore. I want to get to St. Augustine, I want to see the shop. And I bet if I was helping you, if we were both out there digging, we could probably get your errands done twice as fast."

"Let me think about that." He lay down on his bed.

"I'm serious, Uncle Johnny."

"I am too."

He shut his eyes.

THURSDAY

6

THE CROWN

It felt like he'd shut his eyes for only a minute but when he opened them again, light was coming through the sides of the heavy curtain. A new day had begun; the TV was on and Eloise was already sitting up in bed, apparently clean but once again looked as though she was wearing the same outfit she'd had on when he met her.

"What's in that bag you brought with you? I mean, don't you have anything to put on but those same dungarees?"

"What are you talking about? These are my clean clothes."

"Oh. I'm sorry. Well, maybe you could help me out by wearing a different color?"

"How is that going to help you out?"

Johnny smiled. "Why don't we go to the mall? I'll take you shopping, let you pick out something—just, please, a different color."

She nodded her consent.

Johnny washed his face and put on a clean suit. The two of them went downstairs to a small room with plastic chairs where the motel offered their complimentary continental breakfast. Johnny got a cup of weak coffee and a muffin while Eloise filled a Styrofoam bowl with fruit loops. They sat down next to a mousy woman busy fussing with a toddler, while an exhausted-looking man sat next to her and stared blankly at the TV screen suspended above the orange juice dispenser.

The woman with the toddler nodded toward Eloise and smiled.

"How old is she?" she asked Johnny.

"Thirteen."

"Well, you are lucky to be traveling with such a sweet young lady. I can tell she is very well behaved."

He nodded. When he'd paid for the room the night before it flashed through his mind that someone might ask him what he was doing traveling alone with a thirteen-year-old girl. Now it occurred to him how anonymous he and Eloise must have looked, just as anonymous as everyone else in that room. No one thought to question their being together. The woman assumed he was Eloise's grandfather the same way Johnny assumed the haggard man slumped in the seat next to the woman was her husband.

He drank his coffee, watched Eloise spread margarine on an English muffin, and looked out the patio doors where an elderly black woman sat beneath a large umbrella, dunking a tea bag into a cup of hot water while she watched two small boys splash and holler in the pool.

After they finished eating they got back in the car and headed out to the mall. He didn't think about it until they pulled into the parking lot, but the truth was Johnny did not like going to malls. He couldn't stand the crowds, the cheap products, and vapid scrutiny those spaces specialized in. Back in St. Augustine there was one small store in a downtown mall that was the only place he could find his preferred brand of orthopedic inserts for his shoes. He found the experience of going to get them so disconcerting that the last time he'd been there he bought ten pairs to avoid having to go back again.

Now, as he walked through the bright, airy space with Eloise, listening to Muzak chirp around them, something felt different. He watched a couple of teenagers open up their registers in a kiosk in the middle of the main aisle, and a man in a shirt and tie set up the AT&T booth, and he wondered if it was because it was still so early that there weren't many other people around.

They made their way to the department store, pausing to let a strange band of elderly racewalkers in sweatpants pass. When they stepped inside they were greeted by a bright-eyed sales clerk.

"Good morning," she said.

Johnny nodded and tipped his hat. Eloise sprinted ahead of him and started rummaging through the racks of teen clothes, a serious look on her face. She picked out a couple of T-shirts and a pair of jeans that looked exactly like the ones she was wearing until she turned them over and he saw the glitter decals arrayed along the back pockets, the shine of which she seemed to find enormously pleasing. She disappeared into the dressing room for a few minutes and when she came back out, she walked to the register.

She set her clothes down on the counter, then reached into her pocket for the money her mother had given her.

Johnny patted her hand.

"I got this," he said, and reached for his wallet.

The sales clerk took his money and shook her head, as if there was something adorable about the girl trying to pay for her own clothes.

"Well, don't you have a nice grandpa? Just be sure to tell him thank you."

Eloise's head shot up at the sound of the mistake, but she didn't bother to correct it. Instead she rolled her eyes and shrugged while Johnny watched the woman smile.

Something *was* different. He squinted at the woman, studied her face, her kindly unguarded expression. Then he looked at his niece and realized what it was: Eloise. Just like at the motel, everyone around him assumed he was her grandfather. He was no longer a threat to them because he was old. But somehow, because of the girl, he was good too. He was a caregiver.

The woman folded the new clothes into a shopping bag and handed it to Eloise.

"Hold on to your money, now," the woman said. She winked at Johnny. "Always good to have a little something in your pocket."

"And up your sleeve." Johnny tipped his hat. He put his arm over his niece's shoulder and smiled as the two of them walked out of the store.

They walked toward the food court, stopping when they reached the video arcade. He bought Eloise a slice of pizza, an orange soda, and a roll of quarters, then got her settled in a booth. All the while he was still thinking about how he'd never really considered how there might be some way to use his old age to his advantage.

Imagine it, he thought. Making your way through this world without the constant sense that everybody could see you coming. That was a luxury Johnny had never had, one that could not be bought or stolen.

He glanced down at H. P. Smith's watch.

"Let me take your shopping bag out to the car so it doesn't get in our way." He pushed the roll of quarters across the table toward her. "I'll be right back. You go on and start having fun."

"Okay, Uncle Johnny. If you say so."

Johnny smiled. *Uncle Johnny.* He had to admit he liked the sound of that. Walking back through the mall, even though Eloise was no longer by his side, he could still feel it: old age, the illusion of frailty, a warm sense of anonymity flooding his entire body. Nobody stared as he walked past; no one clutched their purse. He was just somebody's kindly old uncle putting his purchases in the car.

He hurried toward the glass doors. By the time he got outside, the lot was starting to fill up and there were cars now parked as far as the edge of the highway. He found his car, unlocked his door, and took off his hat. He laid his jacket across the front seat, remembering something Franklin told him once.

"We're never going to get anywhere until you accept what we are."

"And what's that?"

"Don't you already know? You really need me to tell you? You make maps and I scale walls. Isn't it obvious? We're thieves."

He opened his trunk, stuffed the bags inside, and pulled out a tripod and a shovel. Because, of course, it turned out that Franklin was right. Johnny was a thief.

He walked back around to the front of the car, reached into the glove compartment, and pulled out a stolen theodolite. Then he walked toward the edge of the lot and didn't stop until he reached a tall rubbery tree in a small cement enclosure wedged between two cars. He set the theodolite up on the tripod. Then he hoisted his shovel and started digging.

Ten minutes later he pulled out a child's Spider-Man lunchbox and plastic thermos, price tag still attached.

He was already covering up his hole when a mall security guard in a golf cart rolled toward him, walkie-talkie in hand.

"Just what do you think you are doing, sir?"

"Surveying. Why else would I be out here, as hot as it is?"

"Surveying? Why are you doing that?"

Johnny shook his head. "I would assume somebody's thinking about paving an extension, I would assume somebody's trying to figure out how to make more room for all these cars."

"That right?"

"Stands to reason," Johnny said. "I'm just here taking some final measurements, before the crew comes out to start laying down concrete."

He turned back around, finished covering his hole, then folded up his tripod. Behind his back he could hear the man talking to his supervisor over his walkie-talkie.

"I'll ask him," the man said. "Sir? You got a card? Some kind of credentials?"

"No."

"Then I'm going to ask you to wait until I come back."

"Can't wait," Johnny said. He checked his watch. "I got appointments all over the city this morning. You all are just going to have to work this out amongst yourselves. Just get it straight before tomorrow. Sanchez and his boys not like me—they got a temper. They come out here and you don't have this all figured out, you're going to have a problem."

He hurried back to his car. He watched the man wheel away in the golf cart and then opened up the trunk.

When he got back to the arcade Eloise was still sitting where he'd left her, alone in the plastic booth.

"You were out there digging again, weren't you?" she said as he slid into the seat across from her. "What'd you get?"

"Not much." It was a relief not to have to lie anymore. He was grateful for her acceptance of all the half-truths he'd told her the night before.

Eloise frowned.

"What's the matter? You like your new pants?"

"Yes."

"Then what's wrong?"

"Nothing. Just seems like a waste of a good summer is all. Every time you disappear like that I start thinking how I could be home doing something fun right now, like watching TV. This how it was with my daddy? You just leave him alone in shopping malls while you off running some errand?" She shook her head. "If you're so worried about keeping people safe, how come you weren't around when my daddy got sick?"

"Excuse me?"

"You heard me. It's just a question. I'm just asking. You keep saying how close you were. And Aunt Simone was going on about how tight-knit the Ribkins are. But when push came to shove there weren't any Ribkins with him. There wasn't anybody trying to take care of him but my mama."

Johnny bit his lip. His eye twitched as he found himself reminded how little he knew about her or what she'd been told. "That what your mama told you?"

"It's true, isn't it?"

"It's not entirely accurate," Johnny said.

"What does that mean? Either you were there or you weren't."

If she didn't already know her father had overdosed, he wasn't sure it was his place to tell her now.

"All I can say is I tried to be. Tried for a very long time. Honestly, Eloise? By the time I even knew your daddy and your mama had left town it was already too late. Understand? Franklin was already gone."

"Well, that's what I mean. How is that possible? If you were so close?"

Johnny shook his head, thinking things he knew better than to say.

"We'd had a little . . . disagreement."

"About what?"

"I don't know. Sometimes people argue, disagree about things. Even brothers. Don't mean nothing."

"Yeah but what things? I want to know."

He shook his head. Truth was they'd been arguing about Franklin's relationship with her mother. Johnny was mad about the amount of time Franklin was spending with Meredith, about the things the two of them were doing together.

"Just tell me, Uncle Johnny."

He looked around the room and happened to glance up at the TV hanging above the concession stand.

He took a deep breath. "About six months before your daddy met your mother, a politician asked Franklin and me—"

"Hold on. A politician? What are you talking about?"

"I'm trying to explain. A politician asked us to retrieve something for him. Thing was, turned out this was not a good man. Not the kind we wanted to be doing favors for. But we didn't realize it until it was too late. Whole thing put your daddy in a kind of funk. And after that I guess, in a sense, we were arguing about what we should do about it."

"What politician?"

He nodded toward the concession stand. "That one."

She spun around in her seat and looked up at the TV. It was another campaign ad for candidate Dawson.

"That one? On the TV? My daddy knew him? For real?"

"It's not something to brag on, believe me. I mean, I'm not voting for him."

"Mama never said anything about Daddy knowing Dawson."

"It was before they met. But the point is, your daddy was still upset about all that when he got together with your mama. Got a little reckless with his health. Stopped doing the things he needed to do to take care of himself. And every time I tried to talk to him about it, it just seemed to make him mad. So maybe I thought if I just gave him some time, some space, he would get over it."

"But he was sick."

"Yeah I know." Johnny nodded. "Had what you might call a long-standing illness. But, see, he'd always been so good at managing it, made it kind of hard to see just how sick he actually was sometimes. Never seemed to stop him from doing the things he wanted to do."

"What things?"

"Climb walls." He shook his head. "You know what your daddy was doing the last time I saw him? He was climbing a twenty-story building. Remember that group I told you about at Simone's? The Justice Committee? Well, one of our former members, my friend Flash, needed something that had been locked up on the fifteenth floor. And your daddy, as sick as he was, just hiked his pants and scaled it. Went straight up the side like it was nothing. Can you imagine someone doing something like that?"

"No."

"Try. Because it was amazing. You see somebody do something like that and the last thing you think is this person needs help. And yet that was the last time I saw your daddy alive."

He stopped talking, suddenly sad that she would never have the chance to see her daddy scale a wall. Because he found, when he looked at her, that it wasn't hard to imagine what it must have been like for Eloise growing up alone in that town, the kind of whispers that probably followed Eloise and her mama everywhere they went in Lehigh Acres. Franklin and Meredith were in a pretty bad way when they moved back, and however hard Meredith had worked to keep herself together since then, they'd probably given the girl enough to live down before she was even born. And on top of that, to be burdened and blessed with some kind of strange talent that made people feel it was all right to chuck cans at your head . . .

"Let's not talk about this anymore."

"Okay."

"I mean not now. We'll have time to talk when we get to where we're going." He smiled. "Guess what? All that digging I did yesterday? I'm getting pretty close. Just got to make two, maybe three more stops and then I should have all I need. And then we're on our way, heading up to St. Augustine."

The girl said nothing.

It occurred to him that that was why she was with him, what Meredith had wanted him to teach her. That you could come from something, even be something that made you stand out or off to one side, and still find a way to be strong and happy. That was what their brief time together was really asking of him: *prove it*.

"Hey, girl, you know, I think you right. I probably could use some help out there, if you think you're up to it."

"I am."

"Then that's it. From now on, we're a team."

He slapped his palm on the table. "Time to hit the road."

On their way back through the mall he stopped by a toy store and bought Eloise a pink rubber ball.

It was raining when they got back outside. They pushed through the doors and the bright lights and Muzak were replaced by the pounding of hard slashes of water streaked across a gray sky. He threw his arm around Eloise's shoulder and the two of them went running, splashing over puddles as he led her back to the car. He sat there for a moment as the moisture fogged up his front window. He looked out at the sky and thought about what Simone had said about him being all Eloise had. It wasn't entirely true—she had her mother. But he wanted her to know she had him too now.

They drove back to the motel for their things and paid the bill. He helped the girl hoist her bag into the car and get settled in the back seat.

He started the car. The rain had stopped by then and the broad sky flashed before him like a vision of a world so cool and radiant it glowed.

....

Two hours later they arrived in Buena Vista. They drove by a large commercial boulevard, then turned left and passed through a pair of stone pillars and glided through a world of manicured hedges and rolling green lawns. Johnny parked the car in front of a large white hacienda-style house with a red tile roof, a property edged by a cement wall and a long row of sturdy pine. Johnny leaned back in his seat and watched a heavy-set woman pushing a stroller at the end of the block. Two doors down a man with stooped shoulders, face hidden beneath a large straw hat, was raking leaves. Across the street was a UPS truck, the driver busy writing on a pad he had propped on his lap.

Besides that, the block was empty.

Johnny took off his jacket and rolled up his sleeves, then picked up the ball from the back seat of the car. He got out and walked along the row of trees that separated the house from the adjoining property. He tossed the ball over the wall and slowly walked back to the car.

"Now go get your ball."

"Somebody probably saw you do that, you know," Eloise said as he climbed back into the car.

Johnny shook his head. "Only one who saw me was the UPS man and he's busy thinking about something else."

She looked out the window and saw it was true: the truck was already turning around the corner.

"See? What you don't realize is that most people got more important things on their minds than trying to figure out every suspicious thing they might see out the corner of their eyes, especially this time of the day," Johnny said. "Take that house. Kids are in summer camp while the parents are out working. Only one inside right now is the maid. That's why the best time to rob a house is eleven o'clock in the morning. That's what I've heard anyhow."

She stared at him.

"I must have read it in a magazine," Johnny said.

She shook her head. "And you just want me to go get the ball?"

He took off H. P. Smith's watch and handed it to her. "I want you to walk around the block first. Wait twenty minutes. Then knock on the door and when the maid answers, tell her your ball got tossed over the wall."

It wasn't like he was asking her to lie. It was her ball and getting tossed was, in fact, what had happened to it.

"Walk straight out the kitchen door and head toward the back wall. Turn left, go past four trees, and look down. Right next to your ball will be a rubber bag tied up with a piece of twine."

Eloise stared out the window. She'd told him she wanted to help and he knew very well that as old and harmless as he may have looked walking through a mall there were still certain doors he could not just stroll through, certain passageways other people would always try to keep locked to him. Even if all he was really looking for was an escape route.

"What if they don't believe me?" Eloise thought for a minute and then she said, "I could tell them my family lives next door and—"

"Don't do that," Johnny said quickly. He looked around at the mansions they were surrounded by and then at the girl, still in her grungy jeans, rain-frizzed curls shining around her face. "I mean, don't let the walls fool you. People who live in houses like these tend to know their neighbors. Tend to keep track of who belongs where."

"Well, what if I was a cousin of somebody, visiting from out of town?"

"Or better yet, a relative of somebody who works there. See? Then it would make sense if nobody bothered to mention you before."

She squinted; he smiled.

"Stands to reason, don't you think?"

"All right, Uncle Johnny. If you say so."

She slid the watch over her hand and let it flop around her wrist.

"The more you explain the more complicated it gets. Now go on."

He watched her walk down the block. Once she turned the corner, he started the car again and went back through the stone pillars and onto the wide boulevard. He kept driving until he reached the entrance to a botanical garden. He pulled into a crowded parking lot.

Walking to the main entrance he passed a yellow school bus parked in front of the gate and found himself forced to make his way through a group of squealing children in sun visors, T-shirts, and blue shorts, swarming like angry bees around a couple of teenaged camp counselors with pimply foreheads. Beyond them, in the shade of a small pavilion where you bought your entry ticket, a woman with a long blond ponytail tucked beneath a red baseball cap was standing behind a small folding table, handing out samples of heirloom tomatoes seasoned with a marinade prepared with the herbs grown inside.

AN AUTHENTIC TASTE OF THE REAL OLD SOUTH read a small banner taped to the wrought iron fence behind her. That was what the garden was known for: "History you can taste." Inside they maintained a wide variety of herbs and vegetables that predated the Civil War, species of fruits you could no longer find in any store. Johnny thought it was a wonderful place, a unique calling card, and respected how difficult it must have been to maintain while keeping it open to the public.

They were very particular, however, about people trying to steal seed.

He paid his entry fee, and before he was allowed to push through the turnstile, he was asked to raise his arms while one of the guards waved a metal detector across his stomach and legs. He could see several other guards waving black wands over the flailing arms and legs of all the children from the tour group in front of him. When they were finished with that the children were asked to walk inside a clear glass booth that snorted quick puffs of air at various parts of their bodies. Johnny watched the hair on their heads jump in quick spasms as they laughed and squealed. Most of this, he imagined, was just for show, but the children seemed to find the indignities of all this technology delightful. After getting what he came for, he'd bring Eloise back, show her around, let her have fun passing through it too. But he needed to get it first, because what he'd come to dig up was so precious he couldn't explain how it got there, and he didn't feel like trying to lie.

"Enjoy your visit," a man said, and handed him a brochure. Johnny lingered just inside the entrance for a moment to give the children a chance to scramble ahead of him. When he couldn't hear them anymore he walked alone under the canopy of trees, then sat down on a green metal bench and looked up at the broad blue sky. Everything was just as beautiful as he remembered from the last time, when he brought his brother to meet their father.

That visit had been Johnny's idea. It seemed important at the time but if hearing Mac explain his side of things meant anything to Franklin, Franklin had kept it to himself. Mostly he'd just listened, slurping ice from a cup of frozen lemonade, nodding every now and then as he stared straight ahead. Too much time had passed, Johnny realized, and maybe in part because there was so much to say, Franklin seemed unable to say anything at all.

Still, the visit was important because it had reminded Johnny of something: who he was not. Not his father, for example. Not the type to sit there, stuttering through a list of excuses for why he hadn't lived up to his responsibilities. Johnny had made a promise to his brother when he lured him out of Lehigh Acres, and one way or another he was going to find a way to keep it.

Now he took a deep breath and walked to a water fountain. He leaned forward, took a sip, and looked around to see if anybody was watching him. Then he walked inside a storage shed and locked the door behind him.

He reached into his pocket and pulled out a small penknife, bent down, and pried the tip into the grout of the tiles beneath the sink. He used the same knife to jimmy the tile, then reached into the small hole beneath it and pulled out a black rubber bag tied up with a piece of twine. He washed the bag in the sink, dried it off with a paper towel, and slipped it into his pocket. Then he walked back out again.

He went all the way to the far wall and stood under a large oak. He stepped up on a tangle of roots and tossed the bag over the wall.

Just as he was lowering himself to the ground, he turned around and saw a man in a polo shirt with the garden's logo embroidered across his chest.

"Excuse me, sir, but you can't do that."

"Yes I can," Johnny said.

He tipped his hat, then walked back out the way he came.

He pulled up in front of the house and, a few minutes later, Eloise ran back out with the ball. She climbed into the car, reached under her shirt, and pulled out the black rubber bag.

"Did you peek?"

"No. What is it?"

"I want to show you something first."

He stuffed the bag into his glove compartment and drove back around the block.

They went through security. The puffs of air, he noticed, did not make Eloise smile the way the other children had. When that was finished he took her to the main pavilion at the center of the garden and bought her a cob of corn and one of the tomatoes marinated in herbs.

"What are we doing?"

"Just walking around," Johnny said.

The two of them sat down on the bench.

"Listen," he said. "You remember that talk about the Rib King's people Simone was giving you? Well, this is where they came from. Right here. This is where he learned to cook."

The girl looked around at the trees. "Were they rich?"

"No. It didn't look nothing like this back then. When they settled here all this was just a swamp. Didn't anybody else want this land, so for a long time people just left them alone. I don't know what happened. Something must have changed. Maybe somebody decided this land was valuable or maybe folks in the next town over got nervous about having all them free black people living so close by. So they decided to burn them out, take the land for themselves. Then it came down to a question of being outmanned. So far as we know, your great-grandfather was the only one to make it out alive. He was nine years old at the time."

He studied her expression as she looked around the garden. There was no sign of any such violent past.

"Anyhow, before all that, your great-great grandmother, the Rib King's mother, was a cook. Worked for a rich family in the neighboring town."

He held up a cob of corn. "When I look at this, Eloise, I see her hands. See her hands holding all these fruits and vegetables and herbs she used when she was cooking. That's what makes them so beautiful to me."

He smiled. He knew that a cob of corn was no real proof of the world he was trying to describe, but he didn't know how to explain what he meant any better than that. All he knew was that his last visit had seemed to require some gesture, some form of ceremony or tribute. The Rib King had had his way of paying his respects to his ancestors' memory and Johnny had his.

They finished eating, passed back through security, and walked to the car. Johnny took the black bag out of the glove compartment and handed it to Eloise.

"Now look in the bag."

The girl reached inside and pulled out a diamond-encrusted tiara he had stolen from a nearby historical museum. His great-grandmother had worked for the woman who owned it originally, and the first time he saw it, all he could think about was how beautiful it must have looked as she held it, just before she placed it on someone else's head. He'd hidden it in the garden, one gesture intended to pay tribute to another.

"What is it? A necklace?"

"No, you wear it on your head, like a crown. Here, let me help you."

He placed it on his niece's head.

"Oh, that's real nice on you," Johnny said. "See that? That suits you just fine."

He smiled as he started the car, then slung his arm over the seat and looked behind him as he put it in reverse. Two cars down, in the opposite aisle of the parking lot, was a yellow Camaro with tinted windows.

"I saw them before, you know," Eloise said. She nodded toward the two men. "Back at my house. They were parked on the corner when I came home, just before I met you."

"Why didn't you say anything?"

"I didn't think it mattered."

He looked up at her in the rearview, still wearing the crown. He started to tell her to take it off but she looked so pretty in it. Besides, it had been sitting in that hole for decades and in its unpolished state even rhinestones had more shine. Anyone who saw it would no doubt assume it was fake.

"It doesn't."

He pulled out of the lot and got back on the interstate, heading toward his cousin Bertrand's house. There was a large hole waiting for him there, the size of which seemed to reflect the relatively stable state of his life when he put it there.

7

THE KIND YOU NEED

Things were going well for Johnny when he dug that particular hole. He'd pushed through his initial ambivalence about how he and Franklin were living, and the amounts of money they were able to gather toward them had started to reflect that. It was as if he woke up one day and realized Franklin was right. Thereafter, they were no longer amateurs.

It was in the wake of this new understanding that they moved to St. Augustine and reopened their father's dilapidated shop. The shop was the perfect storehouse and cover for moving their ever-increasing stash of stolen goods. As he set about doing renovations the irony of his return was not lost on him. Growing up, there wasn't a thing about the place that he had not resented. Mac bought it when Johnny was sixteen and at the time had talked about the move with such clarity of intent, such surefooted references to "stability" and "fresh starts" that Johnny actually believed their lives were going to turn around. It wasn't until he finally got up there and saw the smile on his father's face as he unpacked his artwork that Johnny realized his father had not conceptualized it as a place to make money but rather as some sort of gallery, a showcase for his own eccentric art. If that wasn't disheartening enough, he had to watch Mac affix little price tags to each of these works.

Mac managed to make ends meet by doing what he'd done before: painting houses. After a few years he started leasing space to a series of equally eccentric craft dealers, several of whom simply disappeared before rent was due, leaving their stock behind. In this manner the space had eventually become so cluttered that it acquired in Johnny's mind the designation, "the apothecary of junk."

Now he could see the apothecary for what it was and, in truth, always had been: a safe place to hide. Unfortunately the same could not be said for the neighborhood that surrounded it, which was, without question, going through a period of serious decline. Crime was rampant, businesses were closing, unemployment rates were higher than ever. The community's already ad hoc infrastructure was not just breaking down anymore; it seemed to be buckling under. At first it was hard to understand what was happening because all signs seemed to indicate that people were on the move as never before. Barriers had been overturned, opportunities were opening up, and those in a position to take advantage began entering spaces from which they had formerly been barred. But it turned out that the distribution of mobility was not uniform. A lot of people were being left behind, locked out, and, increasingly, locked up as well. According to rumor, by 1989 one-third of all African American males had their mobility curtailed by the criminal justice system. A new nihilism began to creep into their interactions with each other, and the new drugs they were provided to soothe it only created more confusion and heartbreak. How was this possible given all the progress that had been made?

Johnny knew the answer. It was that other map, the one he'd lost everything trying to access. Every time he walked through his neigh-

borhood and looked at the turmoil and confusion around him, all he
saw was the secondary manifestations of a larger design. The manipulations of another mapmaker, the product of conscious thought. Until
someone got their hands on that map, studied it, and actually figured
out a way to navigate through it, nothing would ever really change. So
far as Johnny could tell, the only thing that had really changed was his
acceptance that maybe he was not the one for the job.

All of which contributed to Johnny's foul mood the day Franklin
found what was left of his map of time. They'd been up in the shop's
attic clearing out old boxes to make room for new inventory when
Franklin came upon a shoe box stuffed with ripped-up pieces of paper
covered in intersecting colored lines.

"What's this?"

Johnny looked down at it and frowned. After the Committee fell
apart he brought it with him from New York, thinking that maybe he
could still work on it. The last he'd seen of it was in a garbage bin. His
father, he realized, must have fished out the pieces for him, put them in
the box, and tucked it in the attic. All without saying a word to Johnny.

"Maybe we could fix it."

Johnny shook his head. It was only half-finished. Couldn't be finished until it was realized as a series of actions he had once thought
would be undertaken by the Justice Committee. In lieu of that, a lot
of what he had was still just speculation, a series of sketches outlining
possible passageways based on what he'd been able to intuit. There
were parts he'd never seen and so there was still a lot of blank space
when it came to trying to represent what he thought of as the other
side. Because for him the other side was another map.

"I'm serious. You and me, working together . . . I bet we could
do it."

He looked down at the pieces. Even if he'd wanted to try again he knew it was too late. Its colors were too faded, certain lines had started to bleed into each other, the routes they traced further obscured by numerous erasures representing his increasingly frustrated attempts to correct false starts. But he'd made those lines so long ago he could no longer remember what those corrections were, much less what he'd been trying to fix in the first place. That map was already lost to him, in some ways, before he even met his brother—by the time he got to Simone's with that duffel bag full of money.

He handed the box back to Franklin.

"Just let it alone."

That part of his life was over. He'd given up trying to figure out how to save the world; it was an attempt that had started to seem like little more than arrogance a long time ago. He'd let that go and moved on because he felt he had to; had narrowed his focus, become something else entirely: his brother's keeper. That was how he knew himself now. And over time that became his ballast, in lieu of ideals.

If Franklin still had an edge to him, Johnny was still working on ways to smooth it out, when one day a local politician came into their shop and asked if he could speak to them in private.

Johnny was sitting behind the register, reading the morning paper, when the front door buzzer rang. He looked up and saw a middle-aged man in a dark blue suit pacing stiffly up the center aisles as he gripped the handle of a large leather briefcase. The man looked nothing like their usual customers, yet Johnny had the strangest feeling he had seen him before. He watched the man make his way to the cash register, then set his elbows on the glass counter and glance down at a pair of diamond earrings lifted from a penthouse in South Beach.

"Can I help you?"

"Are you Johnny Ribkins?"

That was when Johnny recognized him from his campaign ads.

For the past few months his favorite TV show had been repeatedly broken up by commercials featuring images of this man grinning and glad-handing his constituents as he prepared to embark on his first run for Senate.

"I was told you were a professional, someone I could trust," Dawson said, "to be discreet."

Johnny called Franklin in from the storeroom. When his brother sauntered in to join them, Dawson put up his hand.

"Maybe I didn't make myself clear, Mr. Ribkins. This is a private matter."

"This is my brother," Johnny said. "Believe me, he knows what private means."

The three of them walked down the hall. Johnny led Dawson into the back office, sat down behind his desk, and told Dawson to have a seat on a large velvet sofa he and Franklin had picked up from the lobby of an art gallery in Tampa.

Dawson told them what he wanted: "A man I used to work for has some photographs, evidence of an indiscretion on my part that occurred years ago, that he is now trying to use to dissuade me from pursuing a national campaign. I've made my own peace with it, my wife is aware of it; we've sought counseling. But having it made public is an entirely different matter. The people won't understand that that is the past. Despite all the work I've done, the myriad ways in which I've tried to make amends, those photographs will be the image that gets etched in their minds."

As the man spoke, Johnny was still marveling at how different he looked from the one he'd seen grinning on TV. Without the smooth sheen of camera makeup he looked older and paunchier. It was distracting.

"If I thought this was simply about money I would pay it, believe me," Dawson said. "But money is the one thing this man does not need. He is simply a vindictive person, a bitter old man capable of doing great harm and he knows it." He shook his head. "What hurts me the most of course is thinking of the effect this would have on those who are depending on me. Not just my family, you understand. It would put an end to all the work I've been trying to do in this community."

Johnny winced at the sound of that. It was why he'd always instinctively disliked politicians. All that cowardice polished up to look like altruism. It was why, as leader of the Justice Committee, he'd tried to keep his dealings with politicians to a minimum.

Franklin, in contrast, seemed genuinely starstruck.

"You don't have to tell us. This shop has been a fixture in this community for more than thirty years, so we understand all about the changes this neighborhood has been through. Folks are lucky to have someone like you out there, to stand up for them."

"Yes," Dawson said. "Change means opportunity but it also can be dangerous if it's mishandled. I see it as my job to ensure that all of my constituents are able to benefit, that no man, woman, or child gets left behind."

Johnny nodded. He still thought it was strange, Dawson coming to them. He imagined someone in Dawson's position had people on staff to handle this type of thing. But the man kept talking and after a while Johnny realized that there must have been something in those pictures he didn't even want the people who worked for him to see.

"You do realize how easy it is to make copies of photographs, don't you?" Johnny said.

"Of course I do. It's the gesture that is important. I want to send him a message, a reminder that he is not unassailable and should reconsider his tactics. Believe me, I'm not the only one with skeletons in the closet."

"Any idea where he might be keeping these photos?"

Dawson nodded. "He's from my hometown, near Pine Hills. There's a safe in his house. Are you are familiar with that area?"

"My cousin Bertrand lives near there, yes."

"Well, I'm pretty sure he's keeping them in the safe. I worked for him for a long time and he's a creature of habit, if nothing else. What's more, I can get you inside. Every month or so he hosts large dinner parties and hires out additional staff. I'm still in touch with both his head of security and the owner of the catering company he uses."

Then Dawson reached inside his briefcase and set $10,000 down on the desk.

"Understand—you do this and then I don't want to hear another word about it. Your discretion is part of what I'm paying for."

"Consider it handled," Franklin said.

It all seemed pretty straightforward. Yet Johnny couldn't shake the feeling that something about it was not quite right. It was too much money, for one thing—but then he looked at his brother, eyes lit up by the sight of all that cash. At the time it seemed like an impressive sum but it wouldn't take very long for Franklin to work through his share.

He watched his brother count it.

"Do you understand what this job means, Johnny? When a man like that comes looking for us? It means we got a reputation—a professional reputation."

Johnny sucked his teeth. "You're a thief, remember? You don't want a reputation."

"Stop thinking small. All rich folks are thieves. Isn't that what you said? And that means they're all most likely in need of these types of services, at some point. We do this right, we don't have nothing to worry about. We're set. Besides, this is Dawson. Only one trying to do anything for this community. Haven't you seen his ads? Not about giving people a second chance. It's about giving them a *real* one. And not everyone has you for a brother. Just think about that."

In the end, stealing those pictures left his brother curled up in a ball, unsure, he said, of who he was anymore.

....

The car rolled past a WELCOME TO OCALA sign.

"Where are we going?" Eloise's head shot up in the back seat.

"Ocoee. Actually, just outside of it." His uncle Bart had moved to Ocoee in the 1920s and Johnny's cousin Bertrand still lived there with him, in the same house in which he had been born. The last time Johnny had been there was when he and Franklin drove down to steal Dawson's pictures. They'd stayed with Bertrand and Uncle Bart for two days and he hadn't been back since.

"I got people in Ocoee," Eloise said. "I mean on my mama's side."

"Your mother's from Kansas," Johnny said. The highway split off in front of them and Johnny drove down an exit ramp.

Eloise looked at the blur of trees whizzing past the car.

"They got an Ocoee in Kansas?"

"Maybe."

They moved up a sloping hill, passed through some pleasant pastureland, and then hit a red light. On one side of the street was a Dairy Queen, and on the other, a Piggly Wiggly, where in the parking lot a black teenaged boy was helping an elderly white woman load boxes into the back of her car.

As much as he loved his cousin, it made sense that the only thing that brought him back there was something that needed doing. There was no other reason to be in Ocoee really. Even as a child he'd understood the town as something to be passed through—literally. They'd taken the signs down but Johnny had never needed to see them to understand: back then this was a place where blacks were not welcome after dark.

The light changed and they rolled down Main Street, past a strip of stores that appeared freshly painted. Whenever his father and Bart went downtown to go shopping or buy gas, they'd never taken Johnny with them. He and Bertrand stayed behind, in the safety of Bart's compound, where a group of black army veterans sat with shotguns and watched the windows whenever someone stayed too long on one of his errands. That was the world in which his cousin had been raised: a world of men who were harsh and heavily armed.

They kept going until the concrete beneath them disappeared and the car rattled and shook on the hard earth. They moved up a hill, kept going until the woods seemed to fold over them like cloud cover. Even now he breathed a sigh of relief. That was how it had always been: when Johnny was a boy, all black travelers knew if you could reach Bart's woods by dusk, you were safe. In the 1940s, when the NAACP once sent lawyers out there to investigate the strange goings on in that place, Thurgood Marshall knew he was safe. No outsider would hurt you there.

What went on inside, of course, was a different matter.

Finally they reached a wide cul-de-sac of houses, his uncle's house right at the center: a squat concrete building with a wooden camel-back. As Johnny pulled into the driveway, two young girls in short-sleeved dresses were sitting barefoot in the yard. They stared at the car and, before Johnny could tip his hat, scampered up the front steps and disappeared into the house.

"This is it?" Eloise said.

"This is it."

She stared out the window.

"A lot different from Auntie Simone's."

"Whole lot of ways to be a Ribkins, girl. I keep telling you that." Johnny smiled. "This is my cousin Bertrand's way."

Eloise looked out at the yard. "What's he like?"

"Loud," Johnny said.

He climbed out of the car as an attractive woman in tight white pants and a blue and white striped shirt came out and stood on the porch.

"That you, Johnny Ribkins?" she asked in a stunningly seductive drawl. She was tall, big boned, with smooth, dark skin and a body like an Amazon. The kind of woman who made Johnny involuntarily nod.

"I'm Jeanette, Bart's nurse. Simone called last night and said you might be passing through this way."

"How did you know it was me?"

"I saw your picture," she said, and went back inside the house.

Eloise was still peering at the yard from the safety of the back seat. He walked around and pulled open her door.

"Come meet your cousins," he said.

Just then a powerful voice rang out across the yard.

"Hide your wallets, people! Cousin Johnny's back!"

Johnny turned around and saw Bertrand stomping down the front steps. A six-foot-seven, barrel-chested man dressed in a blue chambray shirt, blue jeans, and steel-toed work boots, he threw out his arms, gripped Johnny to his chest.

"My favorite cousin!"

Johnny winced as he tried to adjust to the loudness of his cousin's voice, the reverberations of which battered against his eardrums.

"Not staying long—"

"Look, man, that's all right, no need to put on airs with me." Bertrand patted Johnny on the back. "I'm just glad to see you is all.

Whatever you need—a place to sleep, some food, a shovel—you know all you got to do is ask."

Johnny nodded. "I take it you've been talking to Simone?"

"More like she's been talking to me." He smiled at Eloise. "And who is this?"

"Eloise," the girl said.

"Well, bless your heart."

The front door opened and Jeanette came back, wheeling out Uncle Bart in his chair.

"Somebody else wants to tell you hello."

Johnny looked at his uncle sitting in his robe and slippers, head slumped over his left shoulder, his formerly bushy hair reduced to short gray tufts. Johnny immediately felt a twinge of guilt. He knew about the wheelchair but had never actually seen his uncle in it; he'd never been able to picture his uncle as anything other than the tall, upright man he had been fifteen years before, when Johnny last saw him.

"How's he doing?" Johnny asked.

"Oh, he's in and out," Bertrand said. "I mean, it was rough at first, trying to get him used to the chair. But he got that fine nurse now, that seems to calm him down."

Johnny took a step toward the porch. "Hey, Uncle Bart. Remember me?"

Instead of answering, his uncle pursed his lips together and started whistling an oddly cheery birdcall.

"Now you see that? He's happy to see you." Bertrand smiled.

Uncle Bart worked his jaw, laying his upper lip flat against his top row of teeth, and the call transformed into a series of high-pitched trilling sounds.

Bertrand sighed. "Hard to believe, isn't it, Johnny? How things change? I mean, that there was once the most feared man in the county. Now he's content to just sit there and twitter and coo."

Johnny nodded. It was something all right. This was not the Uncle Bart he'd known growing up. The man always had a talent for imitating sounds, but the ones he'd made when Johnny was a boy were not delightful at all. It seemed like his uncle could look at a man's face and come back with a voice dredged up from places deep inside, sounds so personal and secret that no one else might even understand what that voice was saying. But it was never something delightful.

The twittering grew louder. Johnny turned around and saw Eloise laughing and cheering. The more awed Eloise looked, the more frenetic the birdcalls, and the more saliva appeared on Uncle Bart's face.

"That's enough now, Papa," Bertrand said finally.

"Oh, he's all right, Bert," Jeanette said. "Just telling the girl good day."

"She's too young for you, Papa. Ha ha," Bertrand laughed. "No, but seriously, Jeanette, clean him up."

Jeanette pulled a Kleenex from her pocket and wiped the man's chin. She nodded toward Eloise. "Yours?"

"My brother's child. But she's staying with me for a while."

"Well, isn't that sweet."

She swiveled the chair around, allowing Johnny to get a look at the rear view.

"She really a nurse?" Johnny asked as he watched her wheel his uncle back inside. "What kind of credentials she got?"

"The kind she need," Bertrand said.

Things had changed. It wasn't just the bird's calls; as soon as Johnny walked through the door he could see how different the compound now was. Someone had removed the bars from the windows, replaced the heavy shutters with thin white curtains. In the front hall, where once there had been a shotgun rack, a row of pink rain jackets was hanging along the wall. Small glass candleholders lined the tiled floors, and though the ghostly scents of tobacco, liquor, and sweat that Johnny remembered still lingered, these smells had been coated over by a strangely soothing blend of disinfectant and lilacs.

"Shayna left her husband—you hear about that?" Bertrand said, as if by way of explanation. "She and the grandchildren been staying with us for about a year now."

"Sorry to hear that." When Johnny last visited, Bertrand's daughter Shayna was still in college.

"I'm not. Up to me she would have done it a long time ago."

In the living room, Johnny glanced at the photograph on the wall above the fireplace: a row of proud-looking men standing on the porch. They were the original members of The Rock of Gibraltar, the organization Bertrand had founded after he left the Committee. At one point, there had been a dozen branches of The Rock located in various cities across the South. Through the kitchen window behind them, you could see several women peering out. Though ever present, women were not allowed to be official members of the group Bertrand formed. Johnny always wondered if that decision had to do with lingering resentment over the fact that the Hammer had been the one person Johnny had allowed to join the Committee after its initial formation, making their sole recruit a woman.

Bertrand turned a corner and started walking toward the kitchen. Johnny followed along behind and, as they passed through the door, saw a small lithograph hanging on Bertrand's wall of the same advertisement for Rib King sauce that Simone kept in her photo album. It occurred to Johnny that, set among all those portraits of gun-toting men, the Rib King's smile looked different somehow. More like a jeer.

Inside the kitchen two more girls were cooking at the stove. There were so many girls in the house and they were moving so fast it was hard for Johnny to keep track of their individual features, but he thought he counted five; if he had to guess he would have put them all between the ages of two and nine.

Johnny smiled. "They cook?"

"Not really." Bertrand shook his head. "I know it looks like cooking and it must feel like cooking because they sure do seem pleased with themselves when they're finished. But I really can't say much for the taste. Take after their mother that way, bless their hearts. Shayna can't cook for shit."

"How's she doing?"

"Ask her yourself. She went on a church retreat this weekend but she'll be back tonight."

He turned to the girls standing by the stove. "Go on out there and tell your sisters to clean up the living room," Bertrand commanded.

"Okay, Grandpa."

The girls climbed down and scrambled through the kitchen door. Bertrand waited until they were safely on the other side.

"I'm not supposed to talk about that particular situation in front of the girls. Shayna says I've got to be careful, that it might affect their self-esteem. They got enough to deal with, you know, coping with the fact that their daddy is a fucking idiot and all."

"Stands to reason," Johnny said. "That why she left him?"

"No. She's not that kind of woman. I hate to say it but I'm starting to highly suspect that fool may have laid hands on my child."

"She tell you that?"

"No. She won't tell me anything. I said I suspect it. I'm not sure yet. And the proof of that is he ain't dead. All I know is he must have done something mighty foul because I know what it would take for

Shayna to actually leave her husband. I blame myself for that. When she was coming up, I knew what men were capable of, because I knew what I was capable of. Thought I was supposed to protect Shayna from all of that. Sent her to that fancy private school, never let her go out after dark . . ." He sighed. "Now I know. If I really wanted to protect her I would have been better off teaching her how to shoot."

"Speaking of which." Johnny smiled at Eloise. "Why don't you go help your cousins with that living room?"

"But I want to stay with you. Anyhow I'm helping now, remember?"

"Of course I do. But I want you to get to know your cousins too. Any work needs doing, I promise I'll let you know."

As soon as she left the room, Johnny turned to Bertrand. "Just thought I should let you know I got two men following me. I don't know what security here is like these days, but they're probably sitting out there somewhere, in a yellow Camaro. No cause for any unnecessary agitation."

"Well, shit, Johnny, what are you saying? What kind of mess are you in now?"

"Working a deadline is all. As long as I do what I got to do before I get back, I should be all right."

"And the girl?"

"Well, see now, that's the part I didn't really anticipate. Found her down in Lehigh Acres and felt like I couldn't just leave her there. I didn't know they were following me at the time. But I just got to make a few more stops, take care of this thing. Figure if it gets too hectic, I can always put her on a bus and send her back home."

Bertrand sighed.

"Johnny? Can I be straight with you? You sound like a fucking mess. I mean, you know I'm not the type to tell other folks how to live their lives. But don't you think you're getting a bit old to be running up and down the road, working a deadline, as you call it? Plus you got that little girl with you now, and like it or not, that means you got responsibilities."

Johnny was quiet. It had been so long since they'd seen each other, it was only now, sitting across from his cousin, that he remembered there was a reason for it. Bertrand wasn't just loud. He talked too much.

"It's under control," Johnny said.

"Now you know that's not what I'm talking about," Bertrand said. "This is me, remember? So let's be honest. This is hardly the first time. Tell the truth now. All that money in Simone's yard? It was what was left over from that nonsense with the Committee, wasn't it? To finance that last map?"

Johnny squinted. "That's right."

"As I recall you were working a deadline then too."

"You got something you want to say to me, Bertrand? Something left over from the Committee?"

Bertrand shrugged. "I already said what I got to say. That's the difference between you and me, Johnny. I don't believe in things being 'left over.' It's why I always just come out and say what I got on my mind. I told you straight back then and I'm telling you now. Don't matter what your message is if can't nobody hear it."

Johnny said nothing. He knew that even before the Committee fell apart Bertrand thought Johnny was wasting time trying to perfect his map. As far as Bertrand was concerned, not everything needed a diagram. Some things were just as simple as that.

"You hear me, Johnny? Nobody cares what your maps look like. Nobody cares what your intentions are, what you are planning to do. They care about what you actually accomplish, how you actually walk this world."

Johnny nodded. "I got a little something out in your yard too."

"That right?" Bertrand said. "Well, you go on ahead and take it.

You hear me? Take whatever the fuck you think you need to get yourself straight. But do get yourself straight, Cousin. Because, mark my words, even you gonna get old one day." He shook his head. "How many Ribkins you got hidden down in that swamp, anyhow?"

"She's the last one, I'm pretty sure."

The kitchen door fell open and Jeanette came back in, wheeling Johnny's uncle in his chair. The girls rushed in behind them and Eloise sat back down next to Johnny.

"So you're Franklin's girl?" Bertrand said. "Only met him once. I could tell he was a nice fellow. But I'll tell you, Johnny. Mostly I remember that visit because of the theft."

"What theft?" Eloise said.

"Oh, nothing really. Just some old cracker coot lost his whistle."

Johnny smiled. He'd almost forgotten about stealing that whistle from the old man who'd had Dawson's pictures, forgotten how his cousin had told him about the cash the old man offered to anyone who would return it. But the man passed years ago, taking the offer of the reward with him.

"A whistle? That's all?" Eloise looked confused. "Was it made of gold or something?"

"Not at all. In fact, I'd say just the opposite."

"My whistle!" Uncle Bart barked out suddenly, in exact imitation of the voice of the old man Johnny had stolen it from. He slammed his hand on the table for emphasis. "When I blow, all my Negroes know they better come running."

"As I recall, no one was ever arrested for that particular crime," Bertrand said. "Whoever did that must have been pretty smart."

He looked at Eloise. "Your Uncle Johnny here got what they call natural brilliance. Might not have done as much with it as some folks would have liked, but it's still the truth."

"Well, thanks for that, Bertrand," Johnny said.

"Now, me? I'm a whole different story. All I am and all I got in this world comes from nothing but hard work. Never even finished college. Yet today I own five Popeyes and a Jiffy Lube."

"That's great, Bertrand," Johnny said. "Must be nice."

"That's exactly what it is, Johnny. Nice. It's my retirement, it's independence. It means when my child decides she's done having babies with some idiot, she always knows she has a place to go. Because Daddy is here . . ."

He stopped talking. He cocked his head and stared at Jeanette's rear end, like he was studying it. After a moment she must have felt the heat coming off of him because she turned around and glared at him.

"My shift is just about over," she said.

"Don't tell me that."

"Really now." She looked down at her watch. "I got to go."

"Stay," Bertrand said. "Wheel him out back awhile."

"We'll keep him company," Johnny said quickly.

"You sure?"

"I don't mind."

8

THE SHIELD

Johnny and Eloise walked out into the yard while Jeanette parked Bart's chair on the porch and then followed Bertrand back inside. Truth was Johnny was glad to be out of the house. He was worried about Bart's voices getting too creepy and knew from experience it was never a good idea to let the old man go on for too long. But his uncle had gone back to the birdcalls almost as soon as they were outside.

Johnny got a shovel from the shed and held it up to Uncle Bart.

"I'm going to dig a little hole. That all right with you?"

The old man clucked his tongue.

"Miss Janice don't like folks messing in her yard, now," Bertrand's ex-wife Janice's voice rang out. "What you want to do that for?"

"Don't worry. We'll cover it back up when we're done."

"Well, just see that you do."

Johnny shook his head.

"How does he do that?" Eloise asked.

"He just does," Johnny said. He was relieved when, a minute later, one of the girls came running out of the house and reached for Eloise's hand.

"Come play with me, Cousin."

Uncle Bart clapped his hands excitedly. "Yes, we gonna have us a tea party," he said, in perfect imitation of the child's voice.

"Go on ahead." Johnny smiled. "You can help me later."

He watched Eloise run off toward the shed with her cousin. Then he turned around so he was facing the driveway and took ten wide steps to the left. He hoisted the shovel and started digging.

After a few minutes, he heard his father's voice call out: "Johnny? You still mad at me?"

Johnny spun around. "Now, Uncle Bart. Don't start that."

The old man pursed his lips together and stared straight ahead.

Johnny turned back toward the road. He knew the man couldn't help it, that the voices were a compulsion. Just as he knew that, as disorienting as they sometimes were, they emanated from something protective and fiercely loyal to family. Mac had told him many times that he would have never survived his youth were it not for his younger brother. Where Mac was always small and timid, Bart was always scary—the one who wouldn't hesitate to threaten to kill somebody for looking cross-eyed at his nervous older brother. Yet, as an adult, Mac knew enough to keep Bart at a distance and had advised his son to avoid him altogether after dark.

It was a warning Johnny had tried to pass along to his brother. He glanced back at his uncle, trying to remember what it was he'd said to Franklin the night they headed out to steal those pictures for Dawson.

Just keep going.

Uncle Bart, as he recalled, had been on a nasty tear from the moment he found out why they had come and whose house they were planning to steal from. It turned out Bart knew Dawson's former employer well. The man came from one of the most prominent families in the county, owned a large agricultural concern, and just about every black man who lived in the area was on his family's payroll one way or another—which remained true even after Bart's increasingly prominent role in the state's underground economy started offering an alternative. Then, sometime back in the 1940s, Bart's always tense dealings with local law enforcement escalated to near daily acts of violence. Bart was convinced that Dawson's former employer was behind it, that his hatred of black autonomy was so intense and virulent that he had financed not one but two armed assaults on Bart's compound back in 1948. Things got so ugly that at one point the NAACP sent lawyers down to investigate but they could find no real proof of the man's connection to the various crimes Bart accused him of. Bart swore he didn't need proof; it was just a fact.

When Johnny walked outside that night and saw Bart and Franklin sitting together in the shed, he didn't know what to think. He had no idea who his uncle was trying to imitate; it was a voice he'd never heard before. And maybe it was the intimacy of the sound of it that made it hard at first to hear the threat implied by the actual words.

Don't look back, fool. Got to get out while you still can. Hear me? Run.

"You all right?" he remembered asking Franklin after he'd finally hustled him out of there. The two of them were seated side by side in the car, speeding down the dark hill on their way to pick up Dawson's pictures.

"What were you doing alone with him? I told you to stay away from him. Didn't I tell you that?" Franklin didn't always listen to his warnings. It was frustrating.

"I just went to get a beer from the shed. He came and sat down with me. Everything was cool at first, and then . . . I don't know what happened."

He looked rattled.

"Who's voice was that?"

"Not sure . . . friend of mine, maybe. First time I got locked up. Made some real good friends in there. Of course a lot of them aren't around anymore. Weren't Ribkins I guess. Didn't have anybody coming around looking for them."

Then he was quiet.

"Franklin? Are you all right?"

"You think it's true? The things he said?"

"What who said?" That was what made Uncle Bart so dangerous. His voices blended so seamlessly with memory, it made it difficult to discern what was real. "That was Uncle Bart talking. Man was just fucking with you. You know that right? Tell me you know that."

"Forget it, Johnny," Franklin said. "It's no big deal." He'd brought a bottle of beer with him and Johnny watched him toss it out the window. "I keep forgetting all you Ribkins are fucking nuts."

"Don't talk about yourself like that," Johnny said.

The old man who had Dawson's pictures lived in Winter Park, about an hour's drive from Ocoee. He was hosting a fundraiser that evening for a local politician and arrangements had been made for Johnny and Franklin to go in as part of the catering crew. When they got there they found a high wrought iron gate surrounded by concrete walls. A black guard in a khaki uniform was standing in front of the gate and asked to see Johnny's ID. He glanced at it quickly, then handed it back.

"You two take the first left. That's the service road. A man down there will be waiting for you, get you straight with your uniforms."

"Thanks," Johnny said.

"You're late, so just make sure you get back before my shift is over," the man said. "Because you're not actually on any official list. I'm out at ten o'clock. Man coming in after me doesn't know anything about you."

Johnny nodded. They drove up a steep incline for a full minute before they even saw the house. The door to the service entrance was propped open and they stepped inside and found the prep room: a large storage area just outside the kitchen, crowded with two dozen bleary-eyed black men in white dress pants. The men stood around smoking cigarettes and talking. One of them was singing in a low baritone.

Johnny heard someone call his name.

"Johnny Ribkins? Over here."

They walked toward a portly middle-aged man with a pencil wedged behind one of his ears and a clipboard tucked under his arm.

"You the ones Dawson sent? That's all I need to know. I mean that—don't tell me any more."

He handed them two silver trays.

"You're going to need these. Ever wait tables before? Just follow along and do like everybody else. You're both going to be serving the first course and then bussing front of the house. We got four bars set up out there."

"You sure no one will notice we're not part of your normal crew?" Johnny asked.

The man turned around and pulled out two white jackets.

"Your cloaks of invisibility, gentlemen," he said. "Just do the job, act like you belong here, and won't nobody be looking at your face. That's the trick of the white coat. One of them, anyhow."

They tried on the uniforms.

"The sleeves are too short," Franklin complained.

"Doesn't matter. Once you pass through that kitchen door, the uniform is all anyone will see. As for back here, if I were you I wouldn't mention to anyone who you're working for. A few of them have been here long enough to remember Dawson. I imagine most of the others have heard."

"What does that mean?"

The man shrugged. "All I ask is that when you get back to St. Augustine you tell Dawson that this is it. Understand? Tell him we're straight, that I don't want to hear from him again. I got you two inside, I got your uniforms, and I am giving you two hours. That's paid in full, as far as he and I are concerned."

The man walked away and Johnny realized he understood. However Dawson had refashioned himself in St. Augustine, back home he was a cautionary tale.

He looked at his brother, drunk and moping in the corner, pulling at the sleeves of the jacket. Whoever Dawson was, whatever he'd done, it was too late to worry about it now. They were already inside, already doing what they'd been sent to do. And Franklin had already spent his share of the money they'd been paid to do it. Johnny just wanted to get it over with.

Then the sound of a whistle came through the intercom, bleating out the first notes of a strangely familiar tune. All at once the energy of the room shifted and everyone snapped awake. Now the men were straightening their collars, swallowing mouthwash, reaching for the silver trays. The singing stopped, cigarettes were stomped out, bottles tossed into Dumpsters as the men slipped their jackets over their shoulders.

"Five minutes now," the man with the clipboard said.

The door to the kitchen fell open to reveal a long metal table covered with salad plates. Johnny and Franklin fell in with the others, started stacking salads onto their trays because they saw the other men do it, and then stood in line by the doors to the main dining hall.

"Dinnertime, gentlemen."

Another whistle blew, the doors fell open, and the men began streaming out, passing swiftly from the harsh fluorescence of the prep room to the soft golden light of chandeliers hanging above a large crowded dining hall flanked by red velvet curtains. There were at least a hundred people in formal dress seated around four long tables set up on either side of the center aisle, and at the opposite end of the hall, a podium had been set up. As the men in white coats funneled into the room, a man in a tuxedo walked across the podium, leaned forward, and tapped on the microphone.

"Ladies and gentlemen, our speaker tonight . . ."

As soon as Johnny passed into the room with his tray something inside of him bristled. It occurred to him that back in the final days of the Justice Committee, this was exactly the kind of room that had kept him up at night. The kind of room that made him realize if they really wanted to do something to promote the cause of freedom of movement they would have to change course.

"Thank you, Mr. Chairman," another man on the podium said. "First, I want to thank you for your generous donations to the campaign . . ."

It was that other map, the way it kept insinuating itself into so many seemingly disparate encounters. He was looking for access points and eventually realized that maybe, instead of focusing so much on the movements of all the men busy shouting back and forth on podiums, what he really should have been tracking were the people who had put them there. The donors.

". . . I say 'the' campaign and not 'my' campaign because, of course, this is not just about me," the man continued. "This campaign belongs to all of us. All of us who understand what is going on, that our government has been hijacked by special interests. All of us who have decided that we've had enough, and will stand silent no longer, that the time has come to take our country back."

Johnny moved down the crowded aisle. The donors, he came to believe, were the key to accessing the hidden map. When he tracked their movements he could see the money trail following them everywhere they went. He started thinking that maybe if he followed the money he could trace it back to its source.

"We have seen our country enter a new era of lawlessness," the man said. "We know we cannot ignore this new reality. We have to stand firm, stand together. We know that covering our eyes and pretending we can't see the problem won't make it go away. Trying to hide in the pocket of special interest groups, like my opponent, is only going to make it worse," the man said. "Half the county is strung out on drugs and welfare or the drug of welfare. But that is going to end. The time has come to stand up and say no. Criminals belong in jail, not receiving handouts . . ."

That was all the money was supposed to be. It was currency, it was access, and once he had that he could finish his map of time and use it to fashion a proper door, find a way to prop it open so that anyone who wanted to could come in after him.

Now Johnny shuffled down the aisle with his silver tray of salad plates. It occurred to him that if he'd been looking for a means of access he might have started right here. Because the only thing moving through this particular corridor was the wait staff.

"Under my administration we are going to build more prisons, take the bad guys off the streets so that decent people don't have to be afraid anymore . . ."

The wait staff, the men in white coats. The never-noticed yet always-there. And even if they weren't an answer, their existence at the very least spoke to the fact that there was always more than one way of looking at the problem of access. But he was so caught up in one pattern of thinking, so obsessed with money, that by the time he realized his mistake it was already too late. That line of thought affected all the lines that came after and, he began to suspect, his perceptions of those that had preceded it. It had become so enmeshed in what the map now was that it could not simply be erased without having to start all over again.

"What's more, we are going to put them to work, let them earn their keep, as opposed to making law-abiding citizens pay for their crimes."

Something was happening. People were now tapping the sides of their glasses with their forks, cheering wildly as they rose to their feet. A woman at the table behind him pushed back her chair just as he was lowering a plate, jostling the silver platter balanced on his right arm. A ladle of salad dressing tipped over, running over the side in a dark red smear that splashed across her elbow. She winced as if she'd been physically struck.

"Excuse me. I didn't see you—"

"That's your job, isn't it?" She glared at him. "To see me? Isn't that what you're paid to do?"

Johnny managed to make his way to the other side of the room. He pushed through a heavy wooden swinging door and set his tray down on a small side table set up just outside it. When he looked up he was standing in a large hall, an enormous staircase rising to his left, the roar of the dining hall replaced by the soft click of heels and murmur of voices, as men in white jackets moved here and there, passing out hors d'oeuvres.

He kept walking down the hall. He picked up a handful of toothpicks tucked in dirty napkins that had been left on a window ledge and a wine glass smeared with pink lipstick that had been left on the arm of a leather sofa. Finally he turned a corner and found the room he was looking for: a small parlor, with a dozen men and women sitting in velvet chairs sipping cognac and smoking cigars.

"The origins of modern industry," a man's voice said. "The rest is gobbledygook . . . Back then everyone knew their place."

Johnny passed through another set of wooden doors. He turned right and walked into the bathroom and unlocked the window. Then he walked back out again.

As he shut the doors behind him, he heard a whistle bleat out the same notes he'd heard in the kitchen; he looked up and saw a man sitting in a green velvet chair with a glass case balanced on his lap. He was holding up a small wooden whistle, and something about the way the others in the room leaned toward him, their chairs turned ever so slightly in his direction, made it clear to Johnny that this must have been the host.

"That's it?" asked a woman.

"What do you mean?" the old man with the whistle said.

"I guess I was expecting something more. Something louder."

"But that's the beauty of it, don't you see?" the man said. He tucked the whistle back inside its case. "It's small and the sound it makes is rather subtle, which meant they had to listen for it. That straining to hear was part of their training. Because they knew if they didn't hear it, whatever happened as a result was their fault. After a while, they were so afraid of missing the sound, they could hear it all the time. They spent their whole day listening for something that wasn't actually there. Understand?"

"I suppose."

"You don't understand," the man sniffed. He set the glass case back down on the side table. "But that right there is why my daddy was my daddy. And your daddy wasn't."

For some reason, everybody laughed. They were still laughing as Johnny walked out of the room.

When he got back downstairs he found his brother leaning across one of the bars in the front hall. He'd taken off his jacket and was talking to a skinny woman in a long yellow dress. Johnny watched the woman reach into her pocket for a pen and write down her number on a cocktail napkin. Then she sauntered back toward the dining room.

Johnny frowned. "Put your jacket back on. We're still on the clock."

"What are they going to do? Fire me?"

Johnny shook his head. "It's up in the study. There's an outer room and a whole group of them sitting in there smoking cigars. You need to get to the smaller office in back. Go around to the side of the house— it's the seventeenth window from the right. It's unlocked."

Franklin reached around the back of the bar and helped himself to a shot of bourbon.

"You got all that? The seventeenth. Sixteenth and eighteenth will take you into the outer rooms and there's a whole lot of people in there."

"I know how to fucking count, man." Franklin swallowed his drink and set the glass down on the counter, hard.

Johnny nodded. "You remember how to open the safe?"

Johnny had learned how to open a safe during those last months of the Committee when the expense of implementing his map began to require other skills: how to pick a lock, hot-wire a car, crack a safe. These were the skills he passed along to his brother.

"Just wait for me in the car," Franklin said. He put his jacket back on.

Johnny went back to the kitchen, where he found the cook standing by himself, crouched over the prep table, eating soup. He removed the white jacket, set it down on the counter, and went outside.

He walked back out to his car. When he glanced toward the front of the house he could see guests starting to trickle out—women in long dresses being helped into coats held out by men in expensive suits. They stood shivering in front of the house as they waited for the valets to bring their cars around.

At the back of the house, Johnny counted out seventeen windows, and when he looked up and squinted, he could barely make out the vague outline of a white jacket, a strange moonlit shadow slowly levitating up the flat plane of the sidewall.

Once, Johnny had seen himself as part of a massive shift, as someone who had the power to help make a better world. Now he and his brother slipped through the shadows, trying not to draw attention to themselves, hiding behind white jackets. And mostly he was all right with that. He'd never really recovered from his failure with the Justice Committee and, in an effort to never again inflict his confusion on anyone else, had freed himself of any sense of responsibility to anything larger than himself and his brother. But sometimes, when he looked at Franklin, he couldn't help but wonder if free was really the right word for what they had become.

Twenty minutes later Franklin finally walked out, stumbling through the service door with a stolen bottle of whiskey in his left hand and a large manila envelope in his right.

"Let's get out of here." He tossed the envelope into the back seat.

Johnny started the car. They drove back down the service road. After they'd passed through the front gate and were back on the main thoroughfare, Johnny turned and looked at his brother again.

"You still upset about what Bart said?"

"No. It's this . . . What are we doing here?" Franklin shook his head. "The man should be in jail, not running for political office."

Johnny thought about the man on the podium.

"I was thinking the same thing. It's why I don't like politics. Always someone standing in front of a curtain smiling at you, trying to figure out how to say what you want to hear. But if you look behind that curtain, you're gonna find something ugly, every time."

"Well, I don't want anything to do with it," Franklin said.

"What can you do? That's how this world is. I used to think you had an obligation to try to change it but . . . I don't know. Maybe you really are doing something just to survive."

He could feel Franklin watching him in the dark.

"Why don't you look at the pictures, Johnny," Franklin said.

It occurred to Johnny that the two of them were not talking about the same man.

"Are you even going to look at them?"

Johnny frowned. "No. And judging by your expression, you shouldn't have either." He gripped the wheel. "Man paying ten thousand dollars to get back some photographs. What did you think you would find?"

"What he said—a youthful indiscretion," Franklin replied. "Well, he doesn't look particularly youthful in those photos. He looks like a grown man messing with little girls." He shook his head. "We shouldn't be involved in helping him cover up something like this. It's not who we are. What kind of people did he think we were, even asking us to do something like this?"

"Exactly what we look like. Thieves."

Franklin shook his head. "All this time, all these people we been stealing from? A part of me has been telling myself that it's all right because, let's face it, anybody got that much fine stuff hasn't really got anything to lose. Because they can always get more. But this is different. I feel like we are crossing a line somehow. I feel like now that we know, we have an obligation to tell people, to let them know what kind of man they're voting for."

"Maybe you should have thought about that before you spent the money Dawson gave you," Johnny said.

"That's not important."

"Of course it is," Johnny said. He felt weary all of a sudden. Frustrated because this was typical. Bail him out, clean him up, find him something new to climb—that was what Johnny's life felt like sometimes. And all because his brother had no sense of consequence and often seemed to lack the most basic understanding of how things worked. That there were some facts that Johnny could not get around, that Franklin could not simply climb over.

"Franklin, you're a thief. The only reason you know the truth about anything is because you stole it from somebody else. How do you plan on explaining that? And even if you could explain it, why should anybody listen to what you have to say?"

"Because it's the truth. We're not bad men, Johnny."

"No, we're not. But you know as well as I do that there's a lot of room between being a bad man and being a good one. We're just men is all."

Franklin frowned. "Why don't you just look at the pictures, Johnny."

He did look. He looked when they got back to Ocoee, when he went to have copies made, and then a second time, later, after his brother was asleep. And so far as he recalled, he didn't find anything he hadn't expected to see. He hadn't understood what his brother wanted from him, what was actually provoking all that anger. It seemed obvious to him that going public with those pictures would only draw unwanted attention to themselves; it wouldn't change anything. Because as far as he was concerned, Dawson was not the problem anyway; he was just a symptom of the problem, a secondary manifestation of a larger design. The man was filling a slot, and that meant if he went away he would just be replaced by someone else, someone no better and probably worse. Nothing would ever really change until someone figured out how to make it stop. Until then that was just how things worked.

No, something else was bothering him that night, something else that made it hard for him to sleep. After Franklin went to bed, he went out and stood on the porch, not at all surprised when his uncle came out to join him.

"How'd it go tonight?"

"Just fine."

"What's that mean?" Bart smiled. "You kill anybody, Johnny?"

Johnny squinted at his uncle. "Now, Uncle Bart. I know you and that man got some bad blood between you. But don't talk crazy. What do you think would happen to me if I tried to do something to the man in his own house? At a dinner party?"

"Why you think I never sent nobody else out there? But you? You're smart enough to get it done and too smart to get caught. Escape routes come natural to you, Johnny. I know that as well as you do."

"Maybe so. But I'm not a killer, Uncle. I just make maps. You know that."

"You just got to believe in yourself. Have a little more confidence."

Uncle Bart nodded and smiled. It was a dangerous smile and Johnny remembered thinking his uncle was getting mighty reckless in his old age. Throwing out voices, insinuating secrets, dredging up things he knew damn well were better kept hidden. If Johnny was honest, he was not really surprised when, a few months later, he got word from his cousin that Bart had been shot in the back by one of the men who worked for him. It was how he wound up in the chair.

That night, Johnny just wanted to get away before the man could start talking again. He climbed back into his car and drove down to the bottom of the hill. At first he'd just wanted to get out of reach of his uncle's voice, but then he kept going, all the way back to Winter

Park. He went back to the old man's house, managed to get past the gate. He was already standing inside the house before he fully realized why he was there. He wanted that whistle.

....

Fifteen years later Johnny was crouched in the dirt staring down at a rusted metal box. Inside it was a manila envelope, a fat wad of cash, and a whistle. Weirdly, when the old man realized he'd been robbed, that small piece of petrified wood was the only thing he cared about. By the end of the week he'd taken out a full-page ad in the local paper, announcing that he was offering a reward for the return of the stolen goods, "no questions asked." But the whistle was the only item he actually bothered to specify.

Weirder still, when Dawson found out what Johnny had done, he thanked him for it.

"I can't believe I didn't think of it myself. The gesture was downright elegant . . . I mean, talk about thinking outside of the box. How did you know about that whistle anyway?"

Johnny looked at his brother scowling in the corner and said nothing.

"Franklin? Your brother is a brilliant man. My advice? Study his ways, you could learn a lot from him."

"You think so?" Franklin said. "Well, that means a lot, coming from you . . ."

Now, Johnny took out the whistle, set it on the ground, and crushed it beneath his foot. He wouldn't even have bothered digging up that hole if it weren't for the cash and fistful of jewelry he'd grabbed along with it that night.

He pulled out the money and stuffed it in his pocket, then looked down at the envelope wedged along the bottom of the box, which contained copies of the pictures that, ultimately, had served no purpose other than to horrify Franklin. In some strange tribute to his brother's memory, he opened up the envelope, pulled out the blurry images, and forced himself to look again.

It was a series of pictures taken through a motel window that showed Dawson having sex with several different young girls, none of whom could have been over the age of sixteen. As Johnny looked at them now, he was a little taken aback by how raw the photos were, so raw he had to wonder about his own state of mind back when Dawson sent him to retrieve them. When he was fifty-six, they'd been pretty much what he'd expected; looking at them now, at the age of seventy-two, it seemed to him that no sane adult who'd ever had a daughter, sister, or mother would ever cast a vote for Dawson if they'd seen those images. He flipped through the stack quickly and then stopped when he came across a photo of a girl staring straight at the camera, almost as if she were aware it was there. He realized he had seen her before.

Meredith.

Meredith as he'd never bothered to imagine her—as a very young girl.

When she still looked like Eloise.

"Johnny? What are you up to?" his father's voice called out from the handle of his shovel. He could feel it vibrate in his palm. "How come you don't come around like you used to?"

"Uncle Bart, I thought I told you to stop that now," Johnny said.

Uncle Bart stared straight ahead. And a voice Johnny hadn't heard in years called out, as clear as a bell: "Forgive me, Johnny. You always were my favorite."

The back door pushed open and Johnny looked up and saw Eloise standing over him. Quickly, he shoved the stack of photos back inside the envelope.

"Dinner's almost ready, Uncle Johnny."

"How's it going in there? You having fun with your cousins?"

"Oh, we're having a lot of fun." She smiled. "Sure you don't need my help?"

"No. I got it. Be right in."

He waited until Eloise went back inside. His hands were shaking as he set the box on the ground and started filling the hole back up. When he was finished he patted it down with his shovel.

"Hey now, what you got there, son?" a friendly voice called from the porch.

Johnny held up the steel box, showed it to his uncle.

"What do you think?" Johnny forced himself to smile. "Money."

9

ENTER THE DRAGON

By the time Johnny walked back to the kitchen, Bertrand was already seated at the table, the corner of a paper napkin stuffed into the collar of his shirt. All five of his granddaughters were fussing over the stove and Johnny watched Eloise crouch down and peek at something in the oven. He thought about all the time he'd spent studying her features while they were riding in the car, searching out ways she might have looked like his brother when Franklin was that age. Now he understood why that resemblance had been so hard to find.

The girl favored her mother.

"Something the matter?"

"I'm just tired." He pulled back a chair and slid into a seat across from Bertrand.

"I know what you mean." Bertrand nodded, responding to Johnny's morose expression but misreading it. He thought it was the food. "You're going to find, when dealing with children, that sometimes it's best to just play along. Take a few bites, try to smile . . . Later we can slip out and I'll take you to Popeyes."

Johnny's hat was whisked from his head as one of the girls set a plate down in front of him. Small, stubby, garlic-smeared fingers poked at his neck as another girl reached around and tucked the corner of a paper napkin into the front of his shirt. Then all five of his cousin's granddaughters came and stood around the table, watching and waiting for Bertrand to take the first bite.

Bertrand raised a forkful to his mouth and swallowed hard. His eyes watered as the food went down but somehow he managed to smile.

"Delicious," he said.

The girls clapped and cheered.

"Might take a little less salt next time. But y'all are getting better, that's for sure." He set his fork down. "Luckily you all got other talents. We are a talented people, Eloise. Don't forget that."

"Well, you got that voice."

"What do you mean, 'that voice'? I talk loud, so what? I'm a big man so that's just normal. You think that's all I got?" He shook his head. "Girl, I spit fire. Why do you think everybody used to call me Captain Dynamite? Didn't Johnny tell you that? Tell her, Johnny. Tell her it's the truth."

Johnny shrugged. "It's true."

Bertrand leaned back in his chair. "All kinds of people in this family, but so far as I know, I'm the only dragon."

Johnny shook his head. Spitting fire wasn't exactly what his cousin did, though he figured that was close enough. More like a puff of smoke and a popping sound, like a firecracker or a gun going off in the distance.

"Now comes the big surprise," Eloise said. This time, when she spun around from the stove, she was holding out a pie. She smiled as she set it down on the table.

"I made this for you, Uncle Johnny."

He watched the girl cut him a piece and he felt sick inside. He didn't want any gifts from her, couldn't see how he had done anything to deserve them. She was a child he hadn't even known existed until a few days ago, then somehow found himself responsible for. And now he wasn't sure he had the right to look her in the eye.

"What's the matter, Uncle Johnny? Don't you want it?"

Johnny glanced at his cousin. He could only imagine the lecture he would get if Bertrand knew about those shameful photos Johnny had tucked in his back pocket. He shook his head.

"Maybe later. I tell you I'm not feeling well."

"Well, shoot, I'll take a piece," Bertrand said. He reached across the table, cut a large slice, and hoisted it back to his plate.

"This looks delicious. You really make this? Your mama teach you how to cook like that? Because this is outstanding."

Eloise sat down next to Johnny. She carved out her own small piece and poked at it with her fork.

"Come on, girls," Jeanette said as she ushered the little girls out of the room.

"Let's let them eat in peace."

Johnny watched his cousin devour his piece of pie, then lean forward and reach for another.

"I'm not kidding girl, this is great. The Rib King would have been proud. Man might have been known for his sauce but his pies were something else. Isn't that right, Johnny?"

Johnny said nothing.

"You know who I'm talking about, right?"

"Yes, sir. Aunt Simone told me about him."

"Yeah? Well, what did she say?"

"She told me he was a great man. Told me how he lost his family, how even after all his people's land got stolen out from under them he never forgot who he was. She said that was why he was so successful in life."

"And did she tell you about how he went back? How he spent the rest of his life tracking down the men who had burned down his town and stolen from his people and tried to make them pay for their crimes?"

Eloise looked up.

"Now you see? That right there is the difference between Simone and me. She always leaves that part out, when as far as I'm concerned, it's the most important. He went *back*. Tell her it's the truth, Johnny. Tell her right now."

"It's true," Johnny said.

"You got to make sure these children know these things. You've got to just come out and say it. He went back, that's the kind of man the Rib King was. And that smile they put on that can? Just like all the money he ever made from that sauce? It was just a cover for what he was really after." Bertrand winked. "Not enough to just know who you are, girl. You got to handle business too. If it comes down to it, and it always comes down to it, you got to be prepared to do whatever it takes to take care of your own."

Johnny looked at Eloise. He still had that envelope rolled up and sticking out of his pants pocket, underneath his jacket. He wiped his mouth and pushed back his chair.

"I'll be right back," he said.

Johnny walked outside, went around to the side of the house, and stood in the bushes. He needed to be sure of what he'd seen and pulled out the photos again. There was no mistaking it: the girl in the pictures was Meredith, though not a Meredith he'd ever known. It was Meredith before the camouflage of the wig and makeup she'd been hiding behind when Franklin introduced her to Johnny all those years ago.

Accepting that changed everything, all the strange behavior in the months before his brother finally left. He remembered the two of them sitting together in the shop one night shortly after they returned to St. Augustine, staring up at one of Dawson's campaign ads flashing before them on a TV screen.

"Do you know, Johnny," Franklin told him, "I do believe that motherfucker might actually win."

Next thing Johnny knew, there she was: Meredith from Kansas. That was what Franklin had told him; he must have meant that was where he'd tracked her down. Tracked her down, brought her to St. Augustine, and then for some reason started spending all his time with her. And only now Johnny was able to see that there had been a reason for it, that Meredith's sudden appearance in his brother's life wasn't a sign of Franklin's decline, but instead had been intended as some sort of rebuke. And, knowing his brother, maybe more than that: a threat.

He looked out at the trees. Would it have made a difference if he'd just let Franklin go public with those photographs? Because in the end they hadn't been necessary. The truth had come out another way. It didn't always happen, but that time it had: the revelation of crimes even more pertinent to Dawson's fitness to hold office than having sex with a teenaged girl. Graft, corruption, a systematic network of bribes—these were the crimes that forced Dawson to withdraw his candidacy.

Franklin should have been there to watch his campaign implode.

Johnny pulled out a lighter and set fire to the corner of the envelope, watched it burn down to his fingertips, and then let it go. He set his foot down on the smoldering flame, stomped on it until the whole thing was reduced to embers. The girl in the photos was not Eloise but that was who it looked like. And all he knew was that Eloise was the last person he ever wanted to see a picture like that.

"You get what you need?" a voice called out from the shadows of the porch.

Johnny spun around and saw Bertrand walking toward him.

"I guess so."

"Good. Because it occurred to me that when we were talking earlier, I might have sounded a little harsh. I need you to know it's only because I care about what happens to you. If I didn't care I wouldn't say anything. Just let you keep going the way you're doing until one day you wind up face down in a ditch somewhere."

"I know that, Bertrand."

"Then what's the problem?" Bertrand squinted down the road. "It's them, isn't it?"

Two doors down, parked in front of a small wooden house, was the yellow Camaro.

"Those the ones following you, right? Why you're acting so strange? What's got you so jumpy?"

"Actually that's not it at all."

"You sure? Because if you want I can take care of them for you." He set his left fist against the palm of his right hand and cracked his knuckles. "I'm still Captain Dynamite, remember? It's no trouble."

"No, Bertrand. Just let it alone, let me handle my own business my own way."

"So handle it then. Go on out there and let me see you handle it. Because it looks to me like you're running scared."

"I'm not scared, Bertrand. It's just that those two work for someone else, same person I used to work for. And that means if something happens to them he'll only send two more. They're here to watch, make sure I get back by that deadline."

"They're not here to watch you, Johnny. They're here to let you know you're being watched."

"Maybe. But the point is they are not the problem. You just think they're the problem because they are what you happen to be looking at."

"If they're what I'm looking at it's because they're the ones got the nerve to get in my face. Why do you try to make everything complicated, Johnny? If somebody sent them down here they did it for one reason only. To intimidate you. And that means this is not about you owing somebody some money. It's about power. And guess what, Johnny? It always is." He shook his head. "But maybe that's the difference between you and me. I wouldn't give somebody power over me like that."

Johnny was quiet. He didn't feel like explaining that whatever power Melvin had he'd gotten because Johnny sold him his maps.

Bertrand stared at the two men in the car.

"That's what wrong with their whole generation, you know. Got no respect, got no training. Just running wild out there and nobody willing to stand up and tell them to act right. Because all the grown men running scared. Well, how they ever gonna learn if nobody's willing to teach them?"

"Teach? That what you call yourself trying to do? You don't even know those two."

"I know enough. All that work we did just to get this far, so these kids could have better opportunities than we did, and what do they do with it? Walk around slurring their words with their pants hanging halfway down their asses? Where's the dignity in that, Johnny? What happened to the self-respect?"

"Just calm down, Bertrand."

"Don't tell me to calm down." He shook his head. "I swear, sometimes I feel like this whole world is just going to shit."

He stomped back into the house.

Johnny glanced at the Camaro. He realized he should probably hit the road again; Bertrand had never been the kind of person you wanted to let sit and think about a troublesome situation for too long because eventually he was going to go berserk. Besides, he got what he came for. He had most of the money he needed for Melvin. Except now he had something else too: the solution to a mystery that he hadn't even known existed.

He still didn't understand why Franklin hadn't just told him who Meredith was. Why he'd left Johnny out of whatever he'd been trying to do, or even why, after all the two of them had seen and done together, stealing that picture was the thing that made Franklin feel the time had come to change course. If Johnny hadn't recognized the extent of Franklin's anger it was because it had seemed to come out of nowhere. Franklin knew as well as Johnny that the world was full of crooked men and if there was one thing Johnny had taught him it was that politicians lied all the time. Making promises they couldn't keep was just part of their job. And Dawson had made promises. Talked about turning abandoned lots into community gardens, tearing down boarded up warehouses and turning them into free clinics that would offer drug rehabilitation services free of charge. He remembered hearing Dawson give a speech once on the devastation of the war on drugs and the sincerity of his promise to advocate for alternative sentencing. If one was to judge politicians by the quality of their lies then Dawson was a good one for the simple reason that he had the sense to both recognize and hold out the promise of things his constituents simply deserved. So when it turned out he was not the man he said he was, a lot of people were devastated. Including Franklin.

When he went inside, Shayna had come back and was now sitting at the kitchen table, with one of her daughters on her lap. He realized he'd forgotten how pretty she was.

"Hey, Uncle Johnny. You come here to start some trouble?"

"How was your church retreat?"

"Inspiring, as always."

He squinted. "How old are you anyhow?"

"Why?"

"Just asking. You ever know a girl named Meredith Clark coming up?"

"Oh, everybody knows everybody around here. She was older than me but I was friends with some of her cousins. She'd already run off by the time I got to high school. To Kansas, of all places, trailing after some man. She was long gone by the time your friend Flash came down here asking about her."

"Flash was down here?" He thought about that building Flash had hired Franklin to climb, the last time he'd seen Franklin alive. "Bertrand never told me."

"Well, I don't think Daddy was too happy to see him. Only took an hour for them to start arguing about something. Maybe he just figured you felt the same."

"Maybe. When was this?"

"Long time ago. Maybe a year or so after you came up here with your brother that time."

"And what did Flash want?"

"Money. What do you think?" She shook her head. "He said he'd helped Meredith and some friend of hers squeeze some money out of one of her former customers who didn't want people knowing about their relationship. She was a hooker before. You knew that, right? Anyhow, I just assumed he was talking about blackmailing Dawson."

"So you knew about that?"

"Everybody knew about that. It's just one of many reasons can't nobody stand him around here. You know that girl was only fifteen when she got mixed up with him? Would have served him right if she had told people about it but of course he just paid her off, just like he paid off all the others. Flash said he'd helped set up the deal but then she took off without paying him his cut. He was trying to find out who her people were, where she might go if she was trying to hide from somebody."

Johnny nodded. So now it was confirmed: Franklin was clearly the friend helping Meredith and they had been going after Dawson during the final months of his life. That was why Franklin had brought Meredith back from Kansas, not just plotting some sort of revenge, but apparently getting it, too, because from what Shayna said it sounded like money had actually changed hands. How much money Johnny didn't know, but if Dawson had been willing to spend $10,000 trying to get some pictures, he could only imagine how much he might have offered to keep Meredith quiet. Enough to send Flash down here looking for it. For all he knew, that was the real reason Franklin and Meredith had left town so suddenly. Maybe they were trying to lay low until the election was over; maybe it was what Dawson had paid them to do.

She nodded toward the yard. "That's Eloise's mother, isn't it? Meredith? Looks just like her. She still alive?"

He blinked. "Very much so."

"Well, I'm glad to hear it. Might not have said the same when your friend asked me. Like I said, I didn't really know Meredith. Just knew what other folks said."

"And what was that?"

"That the apple doesn't fall far from the tree. Her daddy drank himself to death before she was even born and her mama took off and left her when she was five. Wound up being raised by an aunt who didn't want her nohow." She sighed. "But, see, I didn't understand any of that stuff back then. And children can be very judgmental. Especially when they don't know what the fuck they're talking about."

He looked out into the yard and saw Eloise playing with her cousins, dismayed to find her up to her old tricks. She was standing with her eyes closed, arms held out at either side, while three of her cousins stood in front of her and took turns throwing rocks at her head. In the minute he sat there watching he saw how the rocks coming at her got faster and faster, more aggressive with each turn they took. Light tosses turning into angled throws, the rocks getting bigger and bigger—yet somehow his niece managed to catch every one. There was a smile on her face as her hands wheeled in front of her body, catching each rock, then releasing it so fast she had already caught another before the previous had time to bounce onto the porch at her feet.

When he couldn't take anymore, he got up, walked across the yard, and stood in front of her.

"Stop doing that."

"Why?"

"I told you I don't like it."

It took the other girls about fifteen seconds to realize the game was over and in the meantime he found himself being pelted with stones. A last large rock was hurled toward the porch and Johnny caught it in his right hand. He raised his arm, made a gesture like he meant to throw it back, and they scattered off, squealing and laughing as they disappeared into the yard.

"But why?" Eloise said. "It's a talent, isn't it? Why do you act like I should be ashamed of it? Nobody else is ashamed . . . I want people to see what I can do too."

"I know. But not like that. Your talent is . . . special. Needs to be showcased. Understand? Framed properly."

"Framed how? What does that mean?"

"I don't know yet," Johnny said. "But it's got nothing to do with being ashamed. I just want people to be able to see it for what it is."

He looked down at the rock in his hand.

"Come on, now. Tell your cousins goodbye. It's time for us to hit the road."

"I don't know about that. Honestly, Uncle Johnny? I've been thinking I might just stay here for a while. Give me a chance to get to know my cousins. Shayna said when it's time for me to go home she could put me on a bus just as well as you can."

"You don't even know Shayna."

"I don't know you either," Eloise said. "You're just one part of this family, Uncle Johnny. Shayna told me I'd do best to remember that."

Johnny squinted. He took a moment to study her expression, tried to see her clearly through all the other things weighing on his mind.

"It's that pie, isn't it?"

"No. Well, yes." Eloise shrugged. "I made it for you. You could have at least tasted it."

"Well, you're right of course. I'm sorry about that. But I really wasn't feeling well."

"You didn't even taste it. And it seems like you don't want me around. I know you're busy, I know you got your errands. But every time I look up you are already walking out the door."

He sighed.

"It's a debt."

"What?"

"What I got. The reason I've been in such a bad mood. The reason I've been doing all this digging and sneaking around. It's got nothing to do with you. Truth is I got to give somebody some money when I get back to St. Augustine. That's why I was down there at your mama's place. Trying to dig up money."

She blinked. "I thought it was for the shop. You lied to me?"

"I did. Little bit. Figured it was my problem, needn't concern you. Didn't even want you to see what I was doing so I made you wait in the car. But I'm starting to realize that maybe it's better to just come out and tell the truth. Because I don't want there to be any misunderstandings between us. Not going to have you thinking you got anything to do with my bad moods. Because if anything, you are the one thing that's been making me feel better about my situation, reminding me of all the things I still got to do when I get to the other side of it."

He put out his hand. "I'm asking you to give me another chance."

The two of them walked back through the house and said their goodbyes to Shayna and Uncle Bart.

"Got to hit the road. Tell Bertrand no hard feelings. Tell him I had to go."

He bent down and hugged his uncle. "See you soon."

Uncle Bart nodded his head and smiled.

"Don't forget who put you on this road," Melvin's voice called out. "Don't forget you work for me."

"No, I won't." Johnny smiled. "It's good to see you too, Uncle."

....

They wound back down the dark hill.

"Shayna said you were a con man," Eloise said. "When she came in and you weren't there she said you probably slipped out right quick to run a con on somebody. Did you?"

"No."

"Are you a con man?"

Johnny shifted in his seat. "Look, girl. I don't know if you noticed but everybody in that family talks too much. It's what you call a common trait. Right now they're upset about Shayna's divorce. She married a weak man, had all those kids by him, has got to figure out how to feed them on her own." He searched for her eyes in the rearview mirror. "Try not to do that when you get grown."

She looked out the window.

"It's interesting," Eloise said. "While you were gone I watched those girls pull apart two clocks and a transistor radio, then put them all back together again good as new. And it occurred to me that there are five of them and they have talents totally different from their mother. Yet they all seemed to have pretty much the same one. How do you think that works?"

"I don't know. Never really gave it much thought."

"Well, think about it now." She sounded annoyed. "I'm asking you to think about it."

"Okay," Johnny said. But really he had other things on his mind. He was still trying to make sense of all this new information about what Franklin had been up to before he died.

Months had passed since Johnny gave back those pictures and his brother was still not acting right. Staying out all night, not showing up for work at the shop, spending all his time with this new girl of his, Meredith. That was what had been bothering Johnny. Yet whenever he tried to get Franklin to explain what was going on they always wound up talking about Dawson.

"Remember all that stuff you used to tell me about the Justice Committee? I do. I know for a fact there was a time when you never would have considered keeping a secret for someone like Dawson."

He hadn't understood the connection between the two things, thought Franklin was just trying to change the subject no matter how many times he told him that it wasn't that.

"I'm not trying to make excuses, Johnny. It was my fault and I know that. I'm the one who spent Dawson's money before I knew what it was for. You think I don't know that was my fault? You think I don't know all you've done for me? All the shit you've put up with on my account?" He shook his head. "Sometimes I think about when we first headed out. How you came all that way to find me. I was kind of an asshole to you sometimes, wasn't I?"

"You're still an asshole, if it makes you feel any better."

"I was scared. Trying to convince myself I could handle it, that whatever this world had in store for me, I was ready for it. I think a lot of that stuff I used to say to you was really just me talking to myself."

He remembered his brother smiling at him. "I love you, Johnny Ribkins. Why, you're about the truest family I ever had. Probably saved my life, in some ways. But, see, not everybody has got somebody willing to come looking for them like that. I know that now too. And I'm not scared anymore. Whatever I've done, whatever mistakes I've made since then are my responsibility, not yours. Hear me?"

"Okay."

"You know what I hate thinking about now? What really bothers me? That after all we've been through and all you've done for me, somehow I've become just another voice in your head, telling you that you got something wrong."

These memories, and the confusion they provoked, were starting to upset Johnny. He had to remind himself that that was the past and right now he needed to focus on the present, on all the things he had to be grateful for. He had Melvin's money, his digging was done, and by this time tomorrow he and Eloise would finally be home. He knew he should be happy. But every now and then his thoughts drifted away from him, and he started thinking about Meredith's picture again. Then he'd have to take a deep breath, shut his eyes for a moment, and try to relive watching it burn.

....

It wasn't until he reached the bottom of the hill that he saw the red lights, flashing brighter and brighter the closer he got to Popeyes.

He pulled up to the curb. There was an ambulance and a small crowd of people standing in the parking lot, watching something happening on the sidewalk. Across the street was the battered hull of a yellow Camaro, Reg and Clyde standing next to it, watching.

"Stay here. I'm going to check and make sure they don't need any help."

Johnny got out of the car and pushed his way to the front of the crowd. A man was sitting on the ground with his legs splayed, two paramedics crouched in front of him trying to fit an oxygen mask over his nose.

It was Bertrand.

Johnny turned around and looked at the battered Camaro. He charged across the street.

"What did you all do?"

"Do?" Reg shook his head. "I had to help him find his pills."

"What?"

"His pills." He looked traumatized. "We went to Popeyes to get something to eat. Were just sitting in the parking lot and next thing we know there's this popping sound like a gun going off; I looked up and saw sparks flying everywhere. I tried to pull out of the lot and crashed into a tree. Your cousin was standing in the middle of the road, shouting something about how he was going to teach us a lesson in respect. Then he kind of just crumpled over."

"Crumpled over?"

Reg glared at him. "Your cousin has a heart condition. Didn't you know that? It's what the pills were for."

"A heart condition?" Johnny looked back at Bertrand being lifted onto the stretcher.

"Is he going to be all right?"

"I don't know. How am I supposed to know?" Reg turned to Clyde. "Why didn't you do something?"

"I did do something. I ducked," Clyde said. "Then I moved the car. You were so busy messing around with that fool you didn't even think to move the car, did you?"

"Messing around? Is that what you call it? I probably saved that man's life."

"All I know is somebody needed to move the car." He looked at Johnny. "You thought we hit him with it, didn't you?"

Johnny stared across the street as the paramedics loaded Bertrand onto the back of the ambulance.

Reg shook his head. "Why did he do that?"

"Old and crazy," Clyde shrugged. "Who knows? Maybe the pressure got to be too much for him and he snapped. The point is he did it to himself."

"I understand that," Reg said. "Still. It's just sad."

"It's like what I was telling you before," Clyde said. "Can't keep going on like that, not listening to reason, not paying attention to how things work. There are rules. That's just the way it is."

"Yes, I think I got that," Reg said.

"Good. Because I don't care how smart you think you are. If you can't figure out that much you always gonna be more of a danger to yourself than anyone else is."

They shut the ambulance doors.

"Keep fucking around and one day you wind up just like that fool there."

Johnny turned around and realized Reg and Clyde weren't watching the ambulance. They were looking at him.

"Now open your trunk," Clyde said.

"What?"

"You heard me. You are gonna pay for these damages. Matter of fact, you're going to buy us a new car."

"Wait a minute now. I can't do that. I didn't have anything to do with this."

"Yeah, I know. It's what you said the last time, when your nephew cracked the window. And you just an innocent bystander, just standing there with a trunk full of money."

"It's the truth."

"Maybe. I don't really care. Which is the same as saying it doesn't really matter."

"Look, now. Bertrand did this. He was wrong to do it and I'm going to tell him that. Just give him a couple days to get back on his feet. We can straighten this out."

"You straighten it out. He's your family, your responsibility. Or did you not hear what Reg tried to tell you the last time? Keep your family in check."

"But—"

"You were warned. Take some responsibility. Have some self-respect."

"But—"

"What did I just say?" Clyde shook his head. "You know what your problem is? You think everything is about you. Think this is your story just because you happen to be in it. But you're wrong; it's about *us*. Reg and me, what we are going to do, the choices we are going to make, and all we been through trying to follow you around in that car. And right now I'm telling you, you are going to open that trunk. Hear me Johnny? Don't make me hurt you. I don't want to have to hurt you. In front of that child."

Johnny looked at Eloise sitting in the back seat of the car, then back at the two of them.

"Just open the damn trunk, Johnny," Reg said.

What else could he do? He opened his trunk.

Clyde reached in, rifled through Johnny's things, and pulled out a stack of bills. He glanced over his shoulder.

"Heard your cousin talking about me and Reg, just before he fell out. Next time you see him ask him how I'm supposed to respect him if he don't respect me?"

He reached back in and pulled out another fistful of bills. "How am I supposed to respect you if you don't respect yourself?"

He shoved the money into the pockets of his jacket and shut the trunk.

Johnny watched them walk back across the street, then opened the trunk and counted what was left. Clyde had taken all the money he'd dug up since leaving Meredith, and then some. When he pulled out of her driveway he'd needed to come up with $20,000. After all that digging he'd done since then, he was now $30,000 short.

He closed the trunk.

"What was that about?" Eloise asked him as he got back in the car. He sank down in the driver's seat, leaned his head back, and shut his eyes.

"Uncle Johnny?"

"Give me a minute."

Part of the reason he'd accepted Melvin's terms was because he knew the money was there. He'd never doubted his ability to get what he needed, and even after he'd given Meredith the money to pay her mortgage, even after he realized Simone had gone ahead and taken the money she needed to pay hers, it never occurred to him that his situation would not come down to a question of his own endurance. But now he only had three days left. And even if he did have the strength to keep digging the way he had been, the truth was he was running out of holes.

"Uncle Johnny?"

On top of everything else there was a little girl sitting in the back seat. Where exactly did he think he was he taking her? And if he couldn't pay Melvin back, what did he think would happen when they got there?

"Change of plans." He swiveled around. "Listen, Eloise. Starting to look like my situation is a little more complicated than I thought. Might be you were right, maybe you should just stay here until I get things figured out."

"What? What are you talking about?"

"Might have spoken too soon."

"Too soon? What does that mean? You just asked me to give you a second chance."

"I know. And I still want that. Turns out I might not be quite ready for it yet."

"So, what, now you saying you don't want me with you no more?"

"No, girl. That's the opposite of what I'm saying." Johnny shook his head. "I don't want to disappoint you anymore."

"Then don't."

Across the street he heard the engine turn as Reg and Clyde started the Camaro. He watched as they took off down the road, clearing Johnny's line of sight of the billboard that had been hidden behind the car. It was a VOTE DAWSON sign and it had been defaced.

"Maybe you're not my daddy's brother after all."

"What?"

"You heard me. I mean you're nothing like he said you were. Not at all. If my daddy's brother made somebody a promise he kept it."

Johnny shut his eyes. "How you figure you can tell me what I would do?"

"Mama told me. It's what daddy told her. Told mama all about his brother coming to find him when nobody else bothered. Told her how one day, out of the blue, Johnny Ribkins showed up on his doorstep and just like that everything changed. Told him he had a talent, that all the people who'd been telling him all his life that there was something wrong with him were just ignorant, that what he had was a gift. And for the first time he started to feel like maybe it was true. Started to believe it, that he was gifted. Started to believe in himself, to feel like there wasn't nothing he couldn't do if he set his mind to it. What's more, he wasn't alone anymore. Because now he had a brother."

"That's what your mama told you?"

"She's been telling me all my life. Why do you think she wanted me to come with you? You were my daddy's hero. Don't you know that?"

Johnny said nothing. She was making him feel bad, reminding him that she was not simply his niece but always also his brother's child. And that meant any promises made and broken were not just between the two of them. He was also responsible for his brother's share.

"That's why he was working so hard to fix that map."

"What map?"

"Your map. The one that got all busted up. Mama said that's what he was doing when he got sick. Trying to fix it and then he was going to give it back to you like a present."

"A present, huh?" He stared at Dawson's billboard. Someone had drawn dollar signs over the eyes, blackened his teeth and replaced them with jagged fangs. Hanging over the whole thing was the word "sell-out" written in an angry red scrawl.

After a while he took a deep breath and said, "Tell me something,

Eloise. Your mama ever tell you anything about your daddy leaving some money?"

"Why?"

"Just curious."

"Well, he left a lot of things in the attic . . . boxes mostly. One time I found a real nice ring up there. But, no, I don't know anything about any money."

Johnny realized that was probably true. If Meredith had had any money she wouldn't have stayed in Lehigh Acres; if nothing else he believed her when she said she'd been stuck there. Yet only three weeks passed between the time she and Franklin took off for Lehigh and when Johnny got the phone call letting him know that his brother wasn't coming back. He had a hard time imagining how the two of them could have figured out a way to spend whatever money they'd gotten from Dawson in so little time. So what had happened to it?

"Maybe he hid it," Eloise said.

"What?"

"I told you my daddy used to hide stuff sometimes. Maybe he did like you did at that fort. Put it someplace he wanted to get back to someday. If you need money to pay off your debt, I bet we could find it. I mean, if we worked together, like a team."

He smiled. "Pretty quick, aren't you? You're a smart girl, you catch things? Not a lot get past you?"

"I guess."

He nodded. "Catching things" was what she called her talent, but what did that really mean? They'd been riding together for four days and the whole time he'd been so worried about getting Melvin his money that he hadn't even bothered to try to figure out what her talent actually was. All he'd seen so far was a facility for catching cans and rocks thrown at her head. It would make sense if there was more to it than that.

"Why don't you go ahead and show me what exactly it is you do. Your talent."

"Now?"

"Yes, now. Why not?"

They got out of the car, stood in the empty parking lot. Johnny walked backward until they were about ten feet apart. "Go ahead, now. Let me see you catch something."

She shrugged. "I can't catch something unless you throw it first."

"What should I throw?"

"Whatever you feel like. Don't matter how heavy, don't matter how hard. If you can throw it, I can catch it. I always do."

He looked around the parking lot, trying to find something to throw at his niece. He spotted a tree branch, a lighter, a handful of broken glass, an empty beer can someone had crushed underfoot. He bent down and picked up a rock.

"What are you waiting for?"

He looked back at his niece. There was another reason he had held off doing this; it was more than just having other things on his mind. The truth was there was something depressing about what she did, something that made him feel sad. Because she was right: she couldn't catch something unless someone else threw it first. It didn't really matter what she called it, there was no getting around the implication of violence. The fact that the blows never connected didn't seem to have much to do with that part.

Yet this was her talent.

"You really like doing this?"

"What do you mean?"

"I mean does it make you happy? Standing there, having folks throw stuff at you like that?"

"Is it supposed to?"

"Yes, honey. I think so."

A talent, so far as he'd always understood it, was inextricably connected to the person who had been blessed with it. Simone was the illusion of seamless beauty just as Uncle Bart was the voices he threw; Bertrand was a man who believed he could spit fire and Franklin was the fearless need to climb. It was the same with Johnny making maps. Not something he could really not do—it was who he was. No one's gift was easy, but for the person who had received it, it was a source of strength and strange comfort that was difficult to understand and even harder to explain.

When he looked at Eloise she did not look comforted. She looked resigned.

"Maybe we are going about this wrong. Why don't you tell me what you do enjoy?"

"I don't know. Normal stuff. I like playing cards. I like video games." She looked confused. "Mama says I'm good at math."

Johnny nodded. There was something he was not getting and he couldn't map out her talent until he figured out what that was. He realized he was going to need more time.

They walked back to the car.

"Listen, Eloise. I'm sorry about what I said before. I didn't mean it. Just got frustrated."

"It's all right."

"It's not though. Because you and me? We still got things to do. Can't just give up now. After all this riding you've already done in the car? Wouldn't be right. No, I got to get you to St. Augustine. Got to keep going." He started the car. "Feel like I need to show you what I've done with that man's money, explain why I'm in all this debt in the first place. And after I do that, you and me are going to figure out this talent of yours, help you find your place. Because your mama told you right. Your daddy wasn't alone and neither are you. You believe me?"

"I do."

"All right then." He got back onto the main road. "Just got to make a couple quick stops first."

10

FLASH

Once, a long time ago, a couple months after stealing Dawson's picture and just a few days after being introduced to Meredith, Johnny was lying in bed staring up at the ceiling, worrying about his brother. He didn't know where Franklin was, hadn't seen him in three days, and although such disappearances were no longer unusual they still kept him up at night. There had been several times in the past few months when he'd managed to work himself into a frenzied panic, gone running through the city's streets on a desperate search for Franklin, only to find him drunk and sitting with a group of his friends in the back booth of some downtown bar. Franklin always insisted he was just busy, that he had something going on that didn't concern Johnny; as soon as it was all worked out, the two of them would talk. In the meantime, he'd much appreciate it if Johnny would give him his space.

These encounters left Johnny feeling foolish and lonely but did not make him worry any less. He was aware by then that something had changed, that the barrier thrown up between them after he gave Dawson his pictures had become a wall. He could feel his brother getting lost behind it, disappearing behind a veil of drugs and drinks and parties, creating not only distance but disappointment too. Because the simple truth was that, deep down, Johnny had always expected more.

That was the source of the anxiety welling up inside him, making it hard to lay still. He wasn't sure how much of his brother's current behavior he was actually responsible for. So he stared at the ceiling and soothed himself by trying to come up with a reason to once again set out into the night and track his brother down.

Then the phone rang. Johnny picked up and was confronted with a voice he hadn't heard in years.

"Johnny, my brother. How you been keeping?"

It was Flash: long lost member of his ancient Committee. The one who'd canceled his membership, more or less, by skipping town. When the going got rough he'd simply run back to his family, move on to something else. Now here he was, all these years later, laughing and talking fast.

"Long time no see, right? Just in town for a few days and thought I'd look you up—"

As if he didn't remember why the group had fallen apart or who had been to blame.

"You busy? Can you meet me for a drink? We should talk."

Twenty minutes later Johnny found his old friend sitting in a bar lit by candles, dressed in a light blue suit and matching gators, a thick gold watch strapped around his wrist, smile as wide as a starry night sky. He stood up and embraced Johnny as soon as he saw him walk through the door.

"You look good, Flash."

"What can I say?" Flash grinned. "I got no complaints."

"What have you been up to?"

"This and that. Had a proper nine-to-five for a couple of years. Now I do consulting work."

"Consulting?"

"For a marketing firm. Product placement for the urban demographic. It's freelance, so I do other stuff too, as a means of supplementing my income."

Johnny nodded. He wasn't surprised to hear his old friend had landed on his feet. Flash was always sharp like that, always finding some way to work something out for himself, one way or another.

"And you, Johnny? Hear you been doing some freelance yourself. Working with someone everyone thinks is your brother."

"Who is 'everyone'?"

"Relax, Johnny. I know things because I make it my business to know. I'm what you call a conduit. And you appear to be occupying a peculiar territory where the only ones who don't know you are the ones who, in a sense, care. Understand?" He slapped Johnny's arm. "You're a legend, Johnny Ribkins. In certain circles. It's what you get for living so long. But who is this Franklin?"

"He is my brother. Half brother, technically. I didn't meet him until after you left."

"And now you two work together? He's your new crew?"

"Something like that."

"Interesting," Flash said. "Well, look here, Johnny Ribkins. I got a favor to ask you, if you think you're up to it. Not really a favor because, of course, you'd be getting paid. But it just so happens that, in my official capacity as a consultant, someone asked me if I could help somebody else with a little problem they've been having. And I was sitting there, listening to this man talk, when it occurred to me: what we need is a map."

He told Johnny what he wanted them to do. There were some documents that needed retrieving from an office safe in a high-rise, high-security building. It sounded perfect and the money was right—

which meant in part that the money made sense. Johnny had learned his lesson about accepting unaccountably large amounts of cash from his experience with Dawson. And also he remembered thinking that it was just the excuse he'd been looking for to go out and find his brother. In order to do what Flash was asking, Franklin would have to climb the highest wall he'd been asked to scale in years.

The two of them shook hands, then sat for a while, laughing and talking about old times. He eased into his friend's company, let himself be soothed by the glitter of Flash's smile. Before he knew it, it was two in the morning and the bartender flipped on the lights. He and Flash walked outside, stood on the corner. Johnny promised to talk to Franklin and they would all get together the following night to discuss details. They slapped palms and gripped fists and Johnny hugged his friend goodbye. And he realized he felt better again, better than he'd felt in a long time, although, in truth, not a thing had changed.

Fourteen years later Johnny looked through his front window and saw the Tallahassee skyline etched across the foggy horizon. He and Eloise were entering the state capital at rush hour and as they reached the downtown exits the traffic sped up and Johnny leaned forward and squinted, trying to focus on the road. Suddenly they were surrounded by gleaming high-rises, wrought iron fences, and flowers. Campaign season was in full swing and Dawson's smile was just one within what looked to be a crowded field of candidates jockeying for billboard space along the side of the road.

"Where are we?"

"Going to see Flash."

"From your group?"

"That's right. From my group." The way Johnny figured, either

Flash had gotten his hands on the money Dawson had paid Franklin and Meredith to keep quiet or he hadn't. If he hadn't, then there was a chance it was still out there somewhere and Johnny was pretty sure he could find it; there was still a chance he could settle his debt with Melvin in time. He just needed some information first.

They crossed a bridge, turned a corner, rolled past a gas station, a laundromat, and a check-cashing store. He pulled up to a curb, put the car in park, and looked up at Flash's childhood home: a small, concrete slab house with a brown tiled roof and encircled by a chain-link fence. The last time he'd been here was fourteen years before when, in a fit of rage, he strapped Franklin's share of the twenty-five hundred dollars they'd made doing that job for Flash to a water pipe running beneath it. He'd been mad about Franklin's behavior, annoyed by how much time he spent with Meredith, and was planning to tell Franklin the next time he saw him that if he wanted his money he'd have to go fetch it himself.

"So the money you're looking for is just sitting in his house?"

"No. I mean I hope not." The money under the house was bait. Johnny was hoping he could use it as a lure to get Flash talking about what he was really interested in: what Dawson had given Franklin to keep quiet about Meredith, which he was convinced had to be an exponentially larger sum.

He reached for his hat. "Be right back."

"But I told you I don't want to wait in the car," Eloise said. "I want to help. We're a team, remember?"

"I do. But sometimes being part of a team means you got to do what I tell you. Means you got to trust that I'm trying to tell you to do something for your own good. Right now I'm telling you to wait in the car."

"That doesn't sound like a team to me."

"Well, maybe I'm not explaining it right." He reached down and straightened his tie. "We can talk about it more when I get back."

As he pushed open the door he glanced at the group of teenagers standing on the front porch of a small duplex across the street, laughing as they listened to the music blasting through the open windows of a parked car.

"Lock the doors."

He climbed out, stood on the sidewalk for a moment, and waited for the click of the lock behind him. Then he walked up the steps alone.

Fourteen years before, he, Flash, and Franklin met in a bar one night and shook hands. He remembered how hopeful he'd felt, how excited he was for the two of them to meet. If anyone could sympathize with whatever it was his brother was going through he was sure it would be Flash, who had tumbled through so many of his own bouts of confusion and grief, yet always managed to right himself in time to land on his feet. He'd just assumed the two of them would get along, would feel about each other the way he felt about each of them: like they were brothers.

It was why he'd been so disappointed when it turned out they hated each other.

"Your brother is a fucking drug addict," he remembered Flash telling him later, the next time the two of them were alone.

"Now, I apologize for being blunt. But pretending you can't see a thing that's right in front of your face don't help anything, you got to realize that. And I know an addict when I see one, even if I've never touched the stuff. Not even when I was dealing."

Johnny winced. He'd been responsible for that: part of the confusion of the Justice Committee's final months was his decision that they all needed to go undercover, assume aliases. He'd had his reasons for doing it; it was a response to the amount of scrutiny they'd started to get once Bertrand left and founded his own organization, The Rock of Gibraltar. The FBI seemed to assume that the Committee was just another branch of The Rock, all the more suspicious because they shied away from the kind of noisy public demonstrations Bertrand's group was becoming known for. So the Committee started meeting in secret, while in public its members slipped into other lives. Simone started auditioning again. The Hammer got a job teaching at a local community college. Flash was to play the part of a small-time drug dealer. Their eyes on the corner, their ear to the ground. Something like that, something that made sense at the time.

"Remember that, Johnny? Me? Dealing drugs? Shit . . . Never mind. That's past, just let it stay there. Point is I can't have him fucking up this job. Not on my watch. I'm a professional. I got a reputation too."

He'd made Johnny promise to talk to Franklin. All that had come of it was Johnny finding out that the feeling was mutual.

"He's a hustler, Johnny," Franklin said the next time they saw each other. "Can't you see that? Because the only reason you couldn't is if you just don't want to. Showing up out of the blue like this, after all this time. And I know, y'all got history, been through stuff I wouldn't understand. Well, you're right, I wasn't there. And I'm telling you I wouldn't trust that motherfucker any further than I could throw him out like trash."

A sign on the buzzer by the door said WEYPOOL RESIDENCE. That was Flash's real name: Winston Weypool. Johnny pressed the bell and heard the flat, low bleat of a buzzer going off somewhere inside. A child seemed to cry out in response, but no one actually answered the door.

Johnny cocked his head. Through the window, past the bars and behind a thin white curtain, he could see the silhouettes of several people
moving through the living room, the blue light of a TV screen pulsing
on and off behind them. Johnny remembered Flash telling him once
that, growing up in that two-bedroom house with his mother and five
brothers, he'd gotten into the habit of sleeping in the bathtub just to
have a little privacy. Johnny had joked that maybe that was how Flash
developed his instinct for always coming out of whatever mess he had
to deal with looking so clean.

He pulled back the screen and knocked on the wood behind it.
The door cracked open and a girl looked up at him from behind a
chain.

"Yeah?"

"Here to see Flash. He around?"

The girl closed the door.

A moment later, it opened again and a gray-haired woman with an
unlined face was standing in front of him.

"What do you want?"

"Looking for Flash. I'm an old friend."

"Flash?" The woman laughed. "You must be real old then. Ain't no
Flash no more. I haven't heard someone call Winston that in years."

"Any idea where I might be able to find him?"

"Why? What do you want with him?" She squinted. "And more to
the point, who are you?"

Johnny got back in the car. He drove beneath the bright lights of the
city for a little while and then pulled to a stop in the parking lot of
a downtown hotel. He paid for a room on the fifth floor and he and
Eloise had a nice dinner in the restaurant in the lobby.

"Did you find what you were looking for?"

"Not yet. Flash doesn't live there anymore. We'll go out to see him tomorrow, get it all figured out. What?"

"Nothing. I mean, you are the mapmaker, I got to assume you know what you're doing. But if you don't mind my saying, it does seem to keep you zigzagging around an awful lot. I would have figured someone who made maps would travel in straighter lines."

"That's because you don't understand what a map is," Johnny said. "It's all right, most people don't. Think a map is an answer when really it's a proposition. Don't tell you nothing except where you already are. Understand?"

"No."

"Say you trying to get somewhere and don't know how, realize you need a map. I can graph your perceptions, show you where you standing in relation to something else. Also, because I'm a particularly good mapmaker, I can graph out the possibility implicit in your perceptions. That's an important part of navigation, help you figure out a way from here to there. But the reality is that every move you make is also potentially a new starting point. And because of that a lot of times when the *here* changes, the *there* changes too. It's why sometimes you wind up having to map your way out of your own map."

"I thought a map was just a picture of what's really there."

"What's really there is the map."

She shook her head. "That's confusing."

"It's not though. It just is. Think about it. Let it sit with you for a little while."

He felt something bubble up from the pit of his stomach and raised his hand to his mouth.

"You all right?"

Johnny nodded. His stomach was bothering him and at first he thought it was something he ate, then realized it was probably the prospect of seeing Flash again.

"Why don't you go on upstairs and watch TV? I'm going to go across the street and try to find some Pepto-Bismol. Be up in a minute."

"You want me to get it for you? I don't mind."

Johnny smiled. "I'm all right. But I want to head out early tomorrow. You should get some rest."

He watched her get on the elevator, then walked across the lobby, out the door, and through the parking lot, heading toward the bright lights of the Walgreens across the street.

The girl was right, his life had taken many strange swerves to get him to where he was now. If he hadn't taken Melvin's money he might have never gone back to Lehigh Acres and might not have realized Eloise was there. And if he hadn't wound up helping both Meredith and Simone to pay off their mortgages he wouldn't have been compelled to keep digging; he might have never looked at that picture of Meredith and therefore never realized who she was. And if he hadn't seen the picture again he wouldn't be in Tallahassee, holding on to the hope that Flash, of all people, might have the information he needed to finally get himself out of his current bind. Every step he'd taken had led him to the next, to exactly where he was now. Had become his path. All he could do was keep following it and have faith that there was a reason for it. Right path, wrong path—it was *his* path and maybe the best he could do was try to be true to it. Keep going, keep trying to be the best man he could be, keep working to ensure that some good could come out of it. Even if things with Flash didn't turn out the way he wanted, even if it turned out he could not find the money and pay Melvin back, he was still hoping he could find some value in all the steps it took to get him this far. Because at least when he sent Eloise back to Lehigh Acres she would not be going alone. All the money he still had in his trunk was going with her. If Melvin couldn't be satisfied with what Johnny had to give him then he wasn't getting anything at all. The only thing left unsettled in his mind was how to deal with Reg and Clyde until then.

He pushed through the door of the store and searched the aisles until he found a bottle of Pepto-Bismol. He walked to the register, where a thin man with a scraggly beard and wearing an enormous black sweatshirt was hunched over a gossip magazine. He set down the bottle and looked around the counter, a small, crowded space full of scratch-and-win cards, condoms, a jar of pickled eggs. They were selling mini Reese's peanut butter cups for five cents, loose cigarettes for a dime, and single-serving bags of Hubig's pies. He stared at the logo on the bag and remembered something. He reached for an assortment of pies.

He paid the man, then went outside, twisted the cap off the Pepto-Bismol, and took a swig. He tucked the bag of pies under his arm and walked back across the street, looking for the battered yellow Camaro.

He waited for Reg to slide the window down.

"What do you want?"

"Got you something."

Reg looked inside the bag. His upper lip curled back.

"Pie? That's what you think we want? What we make you think of?"

Johnny shrugged. "I guess you must have when I was standing in that store. Look, I just wanted to thank you for helping my cousin find his pills. Occurred to me that in all the confusion about the car, I never actually thanked you for that."

"Don't worry about it," Reg said.

"But I do worry about it, see? You didn't have to do that. It says something about you and I want you to know that, whatever else happens, whatever else is going on, I do realize that."

Reg frowned. "Just go on back inside, Johnny."

Johnny shook his head. "Things seem to keep getting real hostile out there and I'm not exactly sure why. You two are not responsible for my problems with Melvin. Just doing a job, what you were paid to do. Besides that, I don't know you. All I know is, somehow or other, we all wound up working for Melvin."

Reg blinked. "If you wanted to know who we were you could have just asked. I would have come out and told you that I made a couple dumb mistakes when I was younger; had a real hard time finding a job after that. Clyde? He's actually been to college. Got an associate's degree in business administration. Didn't know that, did you? He didn't make any mistakes but he had a real hard time finding a job too. Surprised? I mean, the man makes an impression, doesn't he? I know he does; Clyde knows it too. The thing is, he's actually very good with numbers. Yet he couldn't even pay off his student loans.

"Clyde and me, we're in the same car, we're in the same boat. Neither one of us can actually afford to get out of it. We work for Melvin because he offered us jobs. Said he had a nose for spotting talent and thought he could find a place for us in his organization. But first he wanted us to do this. Test of loyalty I guess. Why else hire someone who has nowhere else to go if they're not going to be loyal? And guess what, Johnny? We are loyal. Now I'm real sorry about what your cousin did, sorry because someone had to pay for that. But you need to understand that however your situation turns out, whatever Melvin winds up asking us to do, that is pretty much what's going to happen."

"Okay." Johnny shrugged. "Figured as much. Just so long as you admit that it's not true, the part about you having nowhere else to go. That's an illusion, see? Something other people use to control you. You give it power by buying into it, but there's always another way."

"Yeah? That right? That how shit works for you? How you've lived your life? Is that how you wound up in this situation you're in now? Because I hear you Ribkins talking to each other sometimes, going on and on about how gifted you are. Well, Clyde and me? We can't walk through walls. We don't have any superpowers. Is that really what you expect? What it takes? Just to be treated with respect?" He sighed. "Never mind. That's not your problem, is it? Not your issue . . . But thanks for the pie."

"Where'd you go?" Eloise asked when he got back to the hotel room.

Johnny set the Pepto-Bismol down next to the TV. He turned to Eloise and smiled.

"You know, you were so busy fussing at me yesterday you never even asked what I dug up from Bertrand's yard. Don't you want to see it?"

He handed her a small box.

Eloise set it down on her lap. She opened it up, poking her finger at the jumble of gold chains stuffed inside. They were all tangled together and she dumped them onto the bed and combed her fingers through the knot, separating individual pieces like strands of hair from a braid.

Johnny sat by the window. Out in the parking lot he could see Reg and Clyde sitting in the Camaro, eating pie.

"What's this?"

Eloise was holding up a small gold vial suspended from a long chain. She handed it to him and he turned it over in his hand. It was a pendant with a latch and when he pressed his thumb against it, the top popped open.

He handed it back. "It's like a little pocketbook. You wear it around your neck and take it around with you wherever you got to go. Keep your hands free."

"What did people put in it?"

Johnny shrugged. "Whatever they thought they needed most, what they wanted to keep closest to them," he said, although perfume or poison were the only things that came to mind.

He looked at Eloise.

"I bet your great-grandfather had something like this, as much time as he spent on the road. Remember how Bertrand told you about him going back? Well, it was the truth. Until he got swindled out of the patent, that's what he used most of that sauce money for, trying to find the ones who had burned his people out. He'd track them down, pay them a visit, slip them some poison. That's how he got his revenge."

"How'd he get them to take it?"

"Put it in something sweet. Like a piece of pie."

"What if they didn't like pie?"

"Everybody likes pie," Johnny said. "Anyhow, they all ate it, one way or another."

"How many people did he do that to?"

"A lot," Johnny said. "At first he just wanted to find the people who were directly responsible, make them accountable for their crimes. Problem was, he didn't actually know who they were. He was just a child when they burned down his town and the only reason he survived was because his mother had managed to hide him in the one place no one could find him. By the time he got old enough to do anything about it, all he had to go on was the name of the family his mother had worked for and the name of the town where they'd come from. I guess he just wanted to make sure he got them all." Getting revenge on the people who had destroyed his community had been the Rib King's one true obsession. Mac had told him that after their mother left him over it, the three brothers realized they couldn't make him stop and so instead each found their own way to cope with it.

"You can't see it in the ad for that sauce, and I notice Simone and Bertrand don't like to talk about that part, but the truth is your great-grandfather was a very troubled man."

Johnny bit into a Hubig's. He looked at Eloise, still staring at the pendant.

"I don't mean to upset you or anything, but it's the truth."

"I'm not upset."

Johnny nodded. "Why don't you keep that for a while?"

"For real?"

"Sure. Just remember. You don't have to do like he did. Make up your own mind about what it's for."

He smiled. "Go ahead and fill it up with something nice."

FRIDAY

WINSTON

Turned out there was only one Winston Weypool in the phone book. Johnny wrote down the address and realized it was in the city's nicest suburb, a neighborhood on the exact opposite side of downtown from where the other Weypools lived. It took them forty-five minutes to get there and then they spent another ten winding down tree-lined streets, past an endless series of mini-mansions with circular driveways and decorative front pillars. At last they reached Flash's house, a one-story ranch with a long, flat roof and an immaculate front lawn that was, in that neighborhood, conspicuous for its small size.

He pulled up to the curb. A long-legged boy dressed in a white button-down shirt and dark blue pants was standing in the driveway, shooting a basketball at a hoop nailed above the garage.

"That's what all this is now, isn't it?" Eloise said. "You trying to map your way out of your own map? That's how you wound up working for this Melvin person? Trying to get somewhere you thought you wanted to go?"

"He just happened to catch me at a bad time. He came around one night, looking for Franklin, when it just so happened I was looking for your daddy too. This was during the time when he and I were having our disagreement, so when Melvin told me he was friends with Franklin and your mama I thought he might be able to help me figure out what was going on with them."

She stared at him. "If you wanted to know what was going on why didn't you just ask mama?"

Johnny nodded. "I could have done that. Should have done that. Looking back, I wish I had. But see, Melvin was the one who came looking for me."

The boy stopped playing and squinted at the car.

"I don't understand why you can't just tell this Flash person what you're after."

"I told you before. If he knew what I was after he'd just start trying to piece things together, try to figure it out for himself. And if he did figure it out he'd just take it. There's a good chance he's already done that. I won't know until I talk to him."

"But I thought he was your friend."

"He is my friend. That's how come I know him." He shrugged. "Man has other qualities."

The boy walked toward the car. Johnny rolled down the window.

"May I help you?" the boy said, his English just as crisp and clean as the collar of his shirt.

Johnny smiled. "Winston Weypool live here? I'm an old friend."

"My father is not available at the moment."

"Is that right?"

"It is," the boy said firmly. "Something I can help you with?"

Johnny looked the boy up and down. "I don't think so."

"Who are you talking to out there?"

A man in his midsixties, wearing a tan guayabera shirt and a pair of Bermuda shorts, came out and stood on the porch. Winston had put on some weight since last they saw each other and his hairline had receded, but his legs were the same thin, tight bands of muscle they had been when he was still called Flash.

"That you, Johnny Ribkins?" Winston said. He hurried to the car.

"Just passing through. Thought I'd stop by, see what you been up to . . . I didn't know you had a son."

The boy stepped back from the car.

"He said he was a friend of yours."

"I got it, son, you go on back inside." He waited until his son passed through the front door, then leaned over the driver's window.

"Mama told me somebody came by the house, looking for Flash. You didn't leave your name." He angled his head, trying to get a better look into the back seat.

"Who's that with you?"

"Eloise. Franklin's girl. You remember Franklin?"

Winston smiled. "Another Ribkins. So what do you do?"

"I catch things."

"Like what?"

"Everything."

Winston nodded. "She's cute."

Then the front door opened again and a pretty woman with a wide face and gentle, sloping eyes came out. She had short, curly hair, was wearing a long blue denim dress, and was at least twenty years younger than Winston.

"Who is it, Winston?"

"No one, baby. Old friend."

He looked at Johnny. "That's my wife, Sara. Sara, honey, say hi."

"Hi," Sara said.

Johnny nodded. "I should have called first."

"Naw, man. Just been a while is all. But I guess I always figured you'd show up here sooner or later."

He smiled at his wife. "This here is Johnny Ribkins, baby."

"Johnny Ribkins? For real?"

"In the flesh," Winston said.

"Well, you are mighty welcome, Mr. Ribkins," she said excitedly. "I've been wanting to meet you for a long time."

Winston shook his head.

"What are you waiting for, man?" He took a step backward and hit the car door with the flat palm of his hand. "Come meet the family."

The first thing Johnny noticed when he passed through the front door was a large display case full of trophies. Mounted on the wall above it were two framed portraits of the boy from the driveway sprinting across a finish line. In one he had his arms raised above his head, yellow ribbon streaming across his chest. The other was a side view that captured the boy in a leaping midstride. Besides the display case the room contained a velvet sofa, an area rug, a floor lamp, a coffee table, a TV set, and a single wooden chair with a stack of bed linens resting on top. An upended Yamaha keyboard was leaning against a sliding glass door that led to the backyard.

"Nice place," Johnny said.

"It's small," Winston said. "Believe me, for what I'm paying, we could have got something three times as big over where we were before. But the boy's got to be educated somehow. Best high school in the city is right up the block."

"That right?"

"Fuck yeah. None of them rickety playgrounds and rundown buildings like they got back in our neighborhood. Here they got computers in every classroom, everything top of the line. Living out here? It's worth it just for the sports facilities alone." He shook his head. "I tell you, Johnny. Rich folks don't play when it comes to taking care of their own."

He turned toward Eloise.

"Now, honey, I know Junior is excited to meet you. But truth is you all are coming right at the start of chores and homework time. You're going to have to excuse him until he's finished."

"That's all right," Eloise said.

Junior went and took a seat at the kitchen table, opening up a heavy textbook.

"Running a tight ship I see," Johnny said.

"Got to, man, when you got this much going on," Winston said. "But I give him an hour every night, let him choose between Xbox and TV. It seems fair."

"Oh, it's real fair," Sara said, grinning feverishly at Johnny. "It's more than fair. You see, we understand how important discipline is, Mr. Ribkins. We still follow the Principles."

"The Principles?"

"From the Justice Committee."

Johnny glanced at Winston.

"How long you two been married, anyhow?"

"Going on sixteen years now," Sara said.

Johnny nodded. It meant that the last time he'd seen him, Flash was already married and had a son.

He hadn't mentioned it.

"Well, I got to say, Sara, you certainly don't look old enough to have been married that long."

"Well, thank you, I guess," Sara said. "You're right, of course—I was only eighteen when Winston and me got together. Just some silly girl hanging out on the corner when he picked me out. Picked me out, pulled me up . . ." She sighed and looked around her. "And just look at us now."

Johnny smiled. "Well, this certainly is a lovely home."

"Oh, it's not just the house, Mr. Ribkins," Sara said. "You'll see. We still keep it pretty old school around here."

"Old school?"

Winston shook his head. "She just means we understand we got to do whatever we can to make sure our boy has all the opportunities he deserves. Not lose sight of the big picture, keep our eyes on the prize. And our boy's got real talent."

He nodded toward his son. "You should see him run, Johnny. Wins just about every meet he competes in. Could win them all if he pushed himself a little bit more."

Junior blushed and said nothing.

"Well, he's your son," Johnny said. "So I guess it stands to reason."

"That's true. But, you know, that's the funny thing about living out here. Everything so pretty. Truth is I do believe he would be a mite faster if, every now and then, he had somebody chasing him."

Junior glanced up.

"Daddy just playing," Sara said. "We don't want nobody chasing you, now."

Junior slammed his textbook shut and stood up from the table.

Winston laughed as his son stormed out of the room. "Don't mind him. He's still a little upset with me now. You know how kids are. Sometimes they start complaining about nonsense. You should have heard the way he was needling me about that Xbox, talking about how he just had to have one, how all his friends at school had one. Like it was something I owed him." He shook his head. "Sometimes you got to remind kids who they are, all they got to be thankful for. I had to take him back home. Woke him up in the middle of the night and drove him out to the old neighborhood. I dropped him off on the corner without his money or that fucking cell phone. Told him if he wanted that Xbox so bad, all he had to do was find his way back here."

Sara frowned. "That wasn't good, now."

"Oh, he was all right," Winston said. "He didn't know it but truth is I was out there watching him the whole time. I swear, at one point I thought he might pee his pants. And I'm sorry but it is kind of funny. I mean, I grew up there, and Sara too. Yet somehow this kid come out thinking everything creeping around in the dark is some kind of scary monster."

He smiled. "I bet he don't fuck around now, when he go to Zurich."

"Zurich?"

"That's right. Switzerland. We're about to go international. They got a summer training program for kids like him, ones that got it in them to be world-class athletes."

"Never heard of it."

"Of course you haven't. It's not for us. It's for *them*—rich folks. They don't tell people like us shit all they do. You got to find out for yourself. Investigate. But that's how we doing things now. Just like these fucking rich kids," Winston nodded. "Mark my words, Johnny. You're going to see that boy in the Olympics one day. My child is a superstar."

"Winston got real big plans for everybody," Sara said. "But I don't have to tell you. You were on the Committee, you know what kind of man he is, what he's capable of doing, when he puts his mind to something."

Winston smiled. "Now, baby. That was a long time ago. Johnny doesn't need to hear about all that. Anyhow, he was there."

"I know he was." She nodded. "I've seen you, Johnny Ribkins. I know your face from the scrapbook. Winston doesn't like to brag about all the stuff he's done, but we've got the scrapbook. And that's why I'm so glad to finally meet you. While you're here you are going to have to sit down and tell me about it. What was it like? Working for Winston? Helping him do all that stuff, fighting for freedom, trying to uplift people and change the world?"

Winston blinked. "Honey? Why don't you take Eloise here out back, show her that Xbox. Give me and Johnny a minute to catch up."

Eloise looked at Johnny.

"Go on and have some fun, girl. I'm all right."

She hesitated for a moment, then stood up and followed Sara down the hall.

Johnny turned to Winston. "You're gonna have to tell me about these principles, now."

"That was for Sara. Believe it or not, she was kind of a mess when we first got together. After she got pregnant with Junior, the Principles really helped straighten her out."

Johnny thought about that for a moment. Then he said, "Well, I guess it's not like we didn't have principles. Just never saw a need to write them down."

"Probably should have," Winston said. "Might have helped a lot of other people too. But, as I recall, you had other things on your mind, at the time."

"Well, she seems real nice."

"She is. A good mother. She was back then too, underneath the nonsense. But you know how some folks make you squint if you really want to see them? Well, I did squint, and then I could see it . . . something about her that reminded me of the Hammer."

Winston smiled. "Never mind all that, Johnny. Why don't you go ahead and tell me what really brings you around?"

Johnny shrugged. "Guess I haven't changed as much as you."

"I don't know about that. What's on your mind?"

"Just a little retrieval is all. Remember that twenty-five hundred dollars you paid us to break into that office safe the last time we got together?"

"What about it?"

"My brother's share is buried under your family's house."

"What? Why?"

"I don't remember," Johnny shrugged. "I mean I put it there . . . But unless one of you Weypools dug it up, I figure it's still there."

Winston shook his head. "I don't understand. What would possess you to hide money in my mama's house?"

"I was upset with Franklin at the time. Trying to teach him a lesson. Nothing to do with you. You might recall we were going through something when I introduced you. It seemed to me he was getting a little reckless with the way he went about trying to get his hands on money, what he did with it when he had it. Him and that girlfriend of his. Meredith."

Winston nodded. "You mean trying to blackmail Dawson?"

"That's right. He told you about that?"

"Me? No. I mean I heard, but from somebody else. Lot of people knew about that, Johnny. Pretty slick, I got to say. What with the timing. You know they froze Dawson's assets when he was indicted. That fifty grand he gave your brother was probably the last check he wrote that didn't bounce for a very long time."

"Is that right?"

"I know for a fact that there were a whole lot of people on Dawson's payroll looking to get paid that didn't."

Johnny nodded. Now he had an amount: $50,000, more than enough to cover his current debt to Melvin. And he was pretty sure from Winston's expression that he hadn't been able to find it.

Winston shook his head. "I still don't understand what any of that has to do with you taking it upon yourself to dig a fucking hole under my mama's house."

Johnny shrugged. "I was mad. That's all. Figured he was bound to come around needing it eventually, and the way you two were going at each other . . . I knew that was the last place he'd want to go to get it. You help me get back inside, I'll cut you in for fifty percent."

"Fifty percent?"

"That's six hundred and twenty-five dollars. Not much but it might help to pay for that trip to Zurich."

"Interesting," Winston said. "You know, Johnny. My family and I have passed through some real hard times since we last saw each other. Times when we really could have used that money."

But then he smiled. "On the other hand, you're right. It's money, which means it would just be gone. And my son needs it now."

The two of them shook hands and agreed to meet the next morning while Sara was at work. Then they had lunch together, and when they were finished, Eloise and Junior went into the back room to play video games. Winston grabbed two beers from the refrigerator and he and Johnny sat down in the living room while Sara went to get her scrapbook.

She came back with a large red clothbound book with the words "The Making of a Man of Principle" written across the cover in blue letters. Inside, the book was divided into sections separated by color-coded tabs. The first section, entitled "Out of Darkness," was a mug shot of Winston at age nineteen, a sad memento of the arrest for armed robbery that had ended his own dreams of a career as a professional athlete.

The next section, entitled "Membership is Privilege," contained four photographs of the Justice Committee at various points in their lives together. The first was a picture of the four original members standing outside the diner in New York where they used to hold their meetings. On one side was Simone, in a leather jacket and dark green turtleneck, hair pulled back in a high, tight bun. Next to her was Bertrand, hair close shaved and wearing only a thin flight jacket, despite it being the middle of winter. Then there was Flash, wearing a beat-up varsity jacket; Johnny stood at the edge of the frame in a suit, tie flung over his shoulder. Johnny smiled as he stared down at it, struck by how young they appeared, and also by what a motley crew they looked when they first got together.

In the next photo they were standing by the side of a stretch of state highway in Mississippi, Flash at the center of the frame, pointing to a NO DUMPING sign. In the period between when the first picture was snapped and the second, some changes had taken place that the photograph only caught small gestures of. Simone had cut her hair and Bertrand had stopped shaving his. Flash had taken off his varsity jacket and was now wearing a simple button-down shirt and khaki pants. The only one who appeared unchanged was Johnny; he was still wearing a suit, still standing off to the side, turned away from the group. His mouth was slightly open as if he had been saying something to whoever was taking the picture.

The third photograph was of Bertrand in the crowded recreation room of a church in Alabama, shaking hands with an influential preacher they had worked security for on three separate occasions. Flash stood behind them, grinning and flashing peace signs, while Simone could be seen in the background, standing in a corner of the room leaning over a card table, holding out a brochure. Her hair was now the high Afro it would remain throughout her time as the Siren. Johnny remembered that day well, not simply because of the preacher's speech that had so inspired him, but because that was also the day they met the Hammer. He scanned the photo looking for some sign of her in the background but found none.

It wasn't until he turned the page and stared down at the last photograph that he saw the Justice Committee in its final incarnation, with the Hammer, their sole recruit. It was a group photo taken back in New York, a few months after she had joined. Flash had a wide smile on his face, eyebrow arched and left hand stroking his chin as he scrutinized the camera. Bertrand stood next to him, face forward, arms crossed in front of his chest and with a wide-legged stance, staring the camera down. The Hammer was smiling as she looked off to the side, as if someone else had just called her name. And there was Johnny, hands shoved in his pockets, still dressed in a suit.

Those four photographs constituted the entire section. When he flipped the page again, he came to a new tab and a new section, entitled "Strength in Unity." This part of the book was composed of a series of news clippings with seemingly unrelated headlines: "Student Protest at Columbia Broken Up by Tear Gas"; "Albany Sheriff's Office Announces Controversial New Policy on Riot Control"; "Thwarted Car Bombing Yields No Suspects." Johnny had been there when each of those stories appeared in the papers, so he knew that the link between all of these seemingly disparate events was the Committee itself. This section went on for twenty pages, each crammed with story after story of the group's exploits, yet not a single one of the articles mentioned the Justice Committee or any of its members by name.

To compensate for the erasure, someone had taken a yellow highlighter and marked specific passages in each article, passages that represented what could only be called glitches in the narrative that were directly attributable to the group's excision from historic record. In some, these were points in the account where coincidence came into play; the writer would have the reader assume that someone simply got lucky, that actions which had proved fateful to the outcome of events were therefore devoid of intentionality.

"Fortunately for the protesters, a fire three blocks south created a roadblock, preventing the perpetrators' escape . . ."

In others, the highlighting served to draw attention to the elliptical nature of the narrative itself: a missing sentence or a disjuncture in logic that the author of the article had failed to account for, yet which constituted the missing causal link between otherwise disconnected events.

"The attack is said to have occurred between three and four this morning near an abandoned mill twenty miles from the main road. Two unidentified men, hearing the boy's screams, pulled the child from the well sometime before dawn."

On several of the later pages the highlighted passages were accompanied by a small asterisk that directed the reader to commentary written in pencil in the lower right-hand margin of the book. These comments were often short and ultimately as cryptic as the articles themselves.

"Fortunately, residents of a nearby town, possibly alerted by the sound of gunfire, were able to get to the scene in time . . ."

*(The nearest town is fifty miles away)

"Investigators dispute this claim, however, noting that no shell casings were found at the scene . . ."

*(Aha!)

What Johnny noticed about all of this highlighting and scribbling and filling-in of blanks was that none of it actually helped to make the narrative presented in the articles more legible. They all seemed to be geared toward interrogation as opposed to clarification. The scrapbook was, he realized, not so much an account of the past as an annotated manual on the art of reading between lines.

"No one is certain who started the fire."

*(A dragon perhaps?)

By the time he went through all twenty pages Johnny had decided it was a very strange book, one that had the effect of making him feel even more disconnected from his own memories of the events the articles referred to. He read the comments, noted the highlighted sections, and could see the logic in what Winston had done, but found that, more often than not, he did not agree with it. Something was missing. Faith, an actual train of thought, the through line of some clearly expressed purpose. It was simply not the map Johnny would have made of their time together. But then, he did realize that these were Winston's memories, and he was free to do with them what he chose.

Other sections had titles like "Dawn of New Beginnings," "Freedom is Implied by Choice," and "Sense of Purpose Bred of Discipline." Johnny realized these titles, in and of themselves, constituted the Principles that Sara had referred to earlier. The whole time he was looking through the book he could feel the intensity of her gaze upon him, and after a while, that was why he kept reading—because he did not feel like returning her gaze.

He came to a section titled "Pushing Forward" and a photograph of Winston dressed in a suit, standing on a podium, and shaking hands with a man holding up a plaque. Johnny could tell by the cut of Winston's hair and the width of his lapel that he had finally reached the phase of his journey that had begun after the group disbanded, the part of his life that had gone on without Johnny.

That was when Winston snatched the book from Johnny's hands.

"All right, Sara. That's enough, Johnny's probably tired. We can show him more next time."

It was two in the afternoon by then and time to say goodbye; if Sara even noticed how little Johnny had contributed to the fleshing-out of memory she didn't say. She smiled and hugged him at the door and he and Winston shook hands and said they'd see each other the next morning. Then he and Eloise got back in the car.

Johnny asked Eloise what she and Junior had talked about while they were outside.

"Nothing. He was just trying to teach me basketball," Eloise said. She shook her head. "I don't think it's my thing, Uncle Johnny. Did Flash tell you where the money is?"

"Not yet. I need to talk to him again. We're going back again to-morrow. Or you are, at least. I want you to stay there while Winston and I run a little errand. While you're there I want you to be careful around those Weypools."

"Why? I thought they were family."

"No girl. That's just something we say."

"Flash isn't your cousin? Then how come you said he runs so fast?"

"He just does."

Johnny turned around in his seat and looked at her. "You think only a Ribkins could run that fast? That we are the only family that has something special? No, it's not true, and I'm sorry if you got that confused somehow. There are all kinds of people out there, got talent just like you. You need to remember that because sometimes it's hard to see it. That's why you got to be smart enough to really look."

Eloise nodded. "Well that's just it. I did look. Saw the way he was watching you when he first came out of the house. He smiled just as soon as he realized I could see him. But I caught it. I don't think he likes you, Uncle Johnny."

"Well, your daddy felt the same way."

....

"What if you weren't wrong?" Johnny remembered Franklin telling him once during a conversation they'd had shortly before he disappeared with Meredith. "Or just, what if that's not the right word for it? I mean, what if you were actually on to something? With your map?"

"No. It doesn't matter anymore. Things have changed, we're living in a different world."

"All I'm saying is we'll never know, right? Just admit that much at least."

"Maybe. What does it really matter now?"

"It matters, Johnny. To me. It's history. History matters, you should know that. As much as Ribkins like to sit around and talk about where you come from, about your ancestor, the great Rib King."

"I don't do that. That's Bertrand and Simone. Not me."

"But that's because you don't feel like you need to. You've got all those stories memorized, don't you? Already know them by heart. But me? I never knew any of that before I met you. I never knew a lot of things before I met you." He smiled. "It matters. History matters. Believe me. If you can't see it, I can. And your map, Johnny. All the work you were doing back then. What if it wasn't the cause of the confusion, wasn't the reason the Justice Committee broke up? What if it really was a way out? And the two things weren't actually related in terms of causality?"

"What is your point?"

"What if something else was going on? What if someone was actually trying to stop you from finishing? Maybe even someone working on the inside?"

"You mean Flash? No, it's not possible. We might not have agreed about everything but he would have never betrayed me like that."

He watched Franklin shake his head. "All I'm saying is we'll never know. I wasn't there. But, see, I'm here now. And I'm telling you it matters. Your map matters, history matters. One day I'm going to prove it to you."

Johnny stared straight ahead for a moment, trying to picture his brother putting that map back together without any help. Johnny should have been the one to explain it to him, that trust was its own line running through it. If Franklin didn't understand that much he didn't really see how he could have made much progress putting the pieces back together. Because without that, the whole thing fell apart.

Johnny looked at his niece. "Eloise? I don't want you worrying about me. I need you to trust me. Understand? I know what I'm doing."

As soon as he said it he wondered if it was true. All he really knew was that he *was* doing it, following his path where it led him. But what if he didn't get the information he needed? What if his path compelled him to swerve yet again?

The car whizzed past a small amusement park and Johnny skidded to a stop. The girl sat up.

"What's wrong?"

"You ever play Putt-Putt?" Johnny said.

"No."

He pulled into the parking lot.

"What are you doing?"

He nodded toward the park. "Putt-Putt."

"I don't know how to do that."

"So I'll teach you. Come on. Let's see if we can't have some fun."

They played a couple rounds of miniature golf and Johnny bought her some cotton candy. They went over to the bumper cars and he stood by a fence, watching Eloise laugh and smile as she whirled the car around the track. Took two turns on the Ferris wheel together and then Eloise tried out the Tilt-A-Whirl. Then they got a couple slices of pizza and sat together at the concession stand.

When they were finished, they walked back to the car.

It really wasn't much compensation for all he'd told her they would do, all the fun they were going to have. But he was glad he'd stopped. Because as hard as he tried to map out every move, he knew that things didn't always work out the way he planned.

SATURDAY

12

WEYPOOL

When they met up in front of Winston's house the next morning he seemed surprised Johnny had brought Eloise with him.

"The only other option was leaving her at the hotel. It's not a problem, is it?"

"No, man, it's not a problem." He stared at Eloise, sitting next to Junior on the couch. He smiled. "Of course not. I'm sure Junior appreciates the company."

They went back outside and climbed into Johnny's car. As they pulled out of the driveway Winston turned to him and said, "I want you to know I was sorry about what happened to her daddy. I didn't want to say anything in front of the girl but it's the truth. I know your brother didn't like me. But I was still sorry to hear it."

Johnny shook his head. "You met him at a strange time. He was going through something."

"I remember. The drugs," Winston said. "He OD'd right? That's all it was?"

"What do you mean, 'all'?"

"I'm just saying . . . He did that to himself."

Johnny stared at the road. "You thought maybe Dawson had done something to him, didn't you?"

"No, not Dawson . . . payroll." He shook his head. "I told you there were a lot of people mad about not getting paid. And the truth is . . . that stuff with Meredith? Everybody already knew about that. I mean the people who worked for him. They all knew Dawson was slipping, getting out of control. Deep down I bet you even he knew it. I mean, you listen to him talk on the TV now and he acts like being run out of office was the best thing that ever happened to him. I don't even think he's lying. People are like that, you know. Complicated."

They rolled past downtown.

"Of course you're still just repeating what you heard?"

"That's right," Winston said. "I know for a fact there were people trying to deal with him, but they were trying to take care of it in-house, see? Trying to control the fallout. Because there were an awful lot of people on Dawson's payroll. A lot of other people went down when he did. Dawson was a problem but he was their problem . . . And I know your brother might have thought he was doing a good thing, taking down a corrupt politician or whatever. But sometimes I did wonder if it didn't get all turned around in some folks' minds. You know how that happens sometimes. Especially when you're talking about money. Especially when you're dealing with people trying to get paid."

"Is that what you were doing? Trying to get paid?"

The car turned down an exit.

"I talked to Shayna. I know you went down there, asking about Meredith. I know what you were really looking for was money."

"Yeah? So what?"

"Did you find it?" Johnny asked.

Winston laughed. "Shit, Johnny. Is that what all this is about? Is there even any money at my mama's house?"

"Did you find it?"

"No."

"Where did you look?"

"Every place a normal person would think to." Winston shrugged. "I knew Dawson tried to pay him off so when I heard about Franklin's unfortunate demise I just figured there was a good chance he probably hadn't had time to spend it yet. That's all. That's just normal. I can't help it if I'm not stupid, Johnny."

"Shayna said you told her you were in on it together, that you had some kind of deal."

"Who? Me and Franklin? No. That's crazy. He didn't even like me. I mean, I might have said that to Shayna but it wasn't true. I was lying—I do that sometimes."

"So you're saying you don't know anything? He never talked to you about what he was doing?"

"I don't know any more than what I'm telling you right now. If that's the money you're really looking for and it's still out there I can't help you find it now. If I could I would have helped myself fourteen years ago."

They turned a corner, wound back through the Weypools' neighborhood.

"Honestly, Johnny? You want to know the truth? The only thing Franklin and I ever talked about was the Justice Committee."

"Is that right?"

"It is. He was very interested in your map. Said it was a shame that no one had ever gotten a chance to walk it. He said if somebody got it in them to come up with something that beautiful and complex you ought to at least see where it leads."

"And what did you tell him?"

"I told him the truth. I told him if he really wanted to know what the Justice Committee was about, where we were trying to get to, then he needed to talk to the Hammer. She was always the real heart of that organization as far as I was concerned."

Johnny was quiet for a minute. He knew that when Flash said "heart of the organization" he really meant his own heart. A part of him always knew that Flash had been in love with the Hammer back then, even if it was something never said out loud, at least not to him. It was a corridor he'd glimpsed from the corner of his eye while his sight line remained focused on something else. Another route he'd never bothered to trace.

"Listen, Winston. About that . . . Whatever else happens, I want you to know that I never had any hard feelings toward you about leaving the group the way you did. In fact I know I should have apologized a long time ago, not just to you but also to everybody in the Committee. Because I know that what happened was my fault."

"What are you talking about?"

"I'm talking about that last map." Johnny shook his head. "I was so busy working on it, I know I lost track of a lot of other things going on around me. Seems crazy to me now, thinking I could just pull you all along with me, especially when it was all so complicated I couldn't even explain it. All I could do was ask you to trust me. And sometimes I think about all the good we might have done if only we had just stayed together, if I had had sense enough to know when I had gone too far and just stopped . . . if that last map hadn't required quite so much trust . . ."

They pulled up to the curb in front of Winston's mother's house. Winston looked at Johnny. Then he laughed.

"Is that how you remember things? No. You're wrong. Your brother was right about that much at least. Your map was beauti-ful, Johnny. Don't you know that? It wasn't confusing at all. Might have worked too, if—well, so long as we're being honest here—the only part that bothered me was those roles you had us playing. The covers."

Johnny was surprised. He thought about the aliases he had asked them to assume after Bertrand left and formed The Rock. It seemed such a minor detail, such a small part of a much larger plan.

"You had me out there pretending to be a drug dealer. When you knew very well that was the last thing in the world I would ever be. I got to admit I got pretty upset about that. Everybody else got to be something respectable. Why did I have to be a criminal? Did you really *need* a criminal? And even if you did . . . why did it have to be me?"

Johnny sighed. "I was so busy worrying about other things at the time . . . I imagine I was trying to come up with something other people wouldn't question. Something they would simply believe."

"Why? Because I had a record?"

"Maybe. Probably. Yes."

"I was nineteen when I got arrested. A box cutter fell out of my pocket, that's the only reason they said I was armed."

"I guess I was thinking that, so long as you knew who you really were, what you were really doing, it wouldn't matter what anyone else thought."

"Well, see now? That was your mistake. That's where you fucked up, Johnny Ribkins. Because you could have made me anything at all. Why couldn't I have been a social worker, living a decent life? Why couldn't I have been out there helping the community? Why couldn't I have been married to the Hammer? Like that herb she's married to now?"

Johnny was taken aback. But somehow he sensed Winston was telling the truth.

"Well, you're right, of course. Believe me, if I had another chance I would do things differently. A whole lot of things." He shook his head. "What else can I say, Winston? I was wrong. I'm sorry."

Winston squinted. "You really mean that, don't you?"

"I do."

"Well, Johnny, I'm sorry too."

He nodded down to his lap. He was holding a small pistol and it was pointed at Johnny's stomach.

"Now tell the truth. Did you really hide money in my mama's house?"

"I did."

"Then let's go inside."

They climbed out of the car and walked down the front walk, Winston holding the gun at Johnny's back. He unlocked the door and flicked on the lights. Johnny looked around the Weypools' living room. Plaid armchair, TV set, circular area rug strewn with plastic toys, pile of clothes waiting to be folded into a laundry basket in front of the couch.

"Jonathan Ribkins, do you know where you are?"

"Weypool residence."

"That's right. You are in my family's home, the house I grew up in. What makes you think you have the right to come back here after all this time and offer me twenty-five percent of money you got stashed *in my own house*? Doesn't that sound crazy to you?"

"It does now," Johnny said. "So what, you going to shoot me over it?"

"I can't imagine it's going to come to that. You?" He held up the pistol. "No, this is just to help you focus. Because I want you to move *fast*, understand? Don't think too much. Don't talk. Don't stall. All you got to do is show me where that money is. Then you can take your apology and your questions and that girl and go right on back wherever it is the two of you came from."

"So that's how it is?"

"That's how it's been for a long time."

Johnny nodded. "You know, I don't think you've changed as much as you think you have, Winston. And that's why . . . well. You didn't think I was stupid enough to come here alone did you?" He nodded toward the window. "Busted yellow Camaro, parked across the street. Go ahead and look. If I'm not out of here in ten minutes, two men sitting inside it will be coming in after me."

Winston peeked out the window. He smiled.

"You haven't changed either have you, Johnny? Still the same old slick. Think I've never heard that before? Always someone coming in after you, because you nonviolent, right? Always somebody else folks need to be watching out for, somebody else who's got the nasty temper and you're just blocking the door. There's nobody in that car. It's empty. And that right there is the kind of thing I'm talking about, what this gun is for. The kind of bullshit you don't have time for anymore."

A voice came from the front door: "It also happens to be true."

Johnny smiled. Clyde and Reg were already inside the house.

"You two work for Johnny?"

"No. It's just we can't let you shoot him. Understand? You want to shoot him, you're going to have to wait until the end of the week. And then you're going to have to get in line." Reg shook his head. "Dang, Johnny. Why everybody want to kill you so bad?" He nodded toward Winston. "What'd you do to him?"

Johnny looked at his old friend.

"I trusted him."

....

"You're going to have to put that little popgun down now," Clyde said.

Winston shrugged and handed the gun to Clyde, who checked the chamber.

"It's empty."

Winston shrugged. "I told you it was just to help you focus. You think I'd need a gun to put you down if I wanted to? You should think about that sometime."

"What does that mean?"

Winston shook his head. "It's like that gun. After all we've been through. Truth is you don't know what I'm capable of, do you Johnny? Don't know me and never did. You just think you do."

"That's enough now. Y'all going to have to work out your problems some other time. Understand?" Clyde said. "Where is your money this time, Johnny?"

"Down in the basement."

The four of them went down to the basement, looked around the crowded floor. If it had been cleaned since the last time he'd been there Johnny could see no sign of it. Same waterlogged cardboard boxes, dusty luggage, and pieces of broken furniture. Johnny pointed to the three-legged remains of a La-Z-Boy recliner sagging in a corner, underneath a *Luke Cage: Hero for Hire* poster taped to the wall.

"Under the chair," Johnny said. "It's strapped to a sewer pipe underneath the floorboards."

Reg pushed the recliner toward the center of the room. Underneath it were the four tiles Johnny had dug up; instead of grout they were held into place with rubber cement. Johnny crouched down, pulled out a pocketknife, and jimmied the tiles, which seemed to pop out with relative ease. He handed Winston a shovel.

"Start digging."

Winston took the shovel while Johnny stood and looked at Reg and Clyde standing on either side of him. He knew it didn't really change anything between them—they were still just abiding by the terms of their contract; he had a couple more days was all. For the moment, however, it meant they could step in and be heroes. And he didn't know what they felt about that; all he could do was study their faces, make a map of what he saw there.

Reg, at least, looked relieved.

"Now that we got you here, I got to ask," Reg said. "What's really going on between you and Melvin?"

"Didn't he tell you?"

"Oh, he told us some things. We know you took some money from him. Melvin said he couldn't have somebody disrespecting him like that, that it set a bad example."

"A bad precedent," Clyde said.

"That's right. A bad precedent. But, see, Clyde and me? We figure there's got to be more to it than that." Reg shook his head. "You should hear him every time he calls. Gets so mad he starts yelling and spitting into the phone. Clyde thinks you must have messed with his mama or some shit."

"Shut up, Reg."

"I don't know that man's mama," Johnny said.

"Well, you must have done something pretty foul to get him so upset. It's not like him."

"You sure about that? How well you figure you know him?"

"Well enough. Yeah, we sure. He's a businessman, see? Keeps cool, or at least he did. Not like him to fly off the handle. Always talking about the third way."

"Third way?"

"Between a rock and a hard place. See? That's the law. And Melvin, he knows the law. Knows all the ways to maneuver around it without ever stepping outside."

"Everything got a loophole," Clyde said.

"That's right. That's exactly what he said: the loophole, the third way." Reg looked at Winston digging in the corner. "Isn't that something? You got your holes and he got his. Difference being his don't get his hands dirty. Just the opposite in fact."

Johnny nodded. "You two learn a lot from Melvin?"

"Wouldn't be working for him otherwise," Clyde said.

"And see, that's the problem. When he sent us after you, he told us to watch you. Said you were trying to slip out on him, that you thought you were smarter than everybody and that it was about time somebody proved you wrong. Said if we watched you closely we would learn something. What not to do." Reg shook his head. "Finally I had to tell him it looked to us like you were just out there busting your ass, trying to pay off your debt."

Clyde sucked his teeth. "That's enough, Reg. You talk too much. Just shut up."

"Somebody must have gotten something confused."

"Well, don't look at me," Johnny said. "I don't confuse that easy."

"That's what I'm trying to tell you," Reg said. "Neither do we."

"How old are you two anyway?" Winston called out.

"Why?"

"You're young yet. Still looking at things wrong. Maybe it's not Melvin who has the problem."

"What do you know about it?"

"Who? Melvin Marks? That's who you all work for, right? I know him."

"Bullshit."

"Tall fellow? Light skinned? Got a nasty scar under his left eye?" Winston shook his head. "I tell you I know him. Matter of fact, I'm the one who introduced him to Johnny."

Winston smiled. "You didn't know that either, did you, Johnny? At first I just assumed it was why you were here. Who do you think sent Melvin to find you all those years ago?"

Johnny squinted. "What do you mean, sent him to find me?"

Winston shrugged. "I want my original cut. Like what we talked about last night, back at the house. Fifty percent."

He turned around and went back to digging the hole.

A moment later he hit something hard with the blade of his shovel and found a latched opening in the wooden floorboards underneath. When he opened it up, he was staring down at a length of pipe that ran beneath the house. He stuck his hand inside and found a large black rubber bag duct-taped to the underside of the pipe. It was stuffed with dollar bills.

Reg nudged Clyde with his elbow. He nodded toward the bag. "Look at that."

Clyde snorted. "That's not enough, man. Not enough money to change anything."

"Well, it's something. It's a start," Reg replied.

"Really? Is that what you think? Because it's not what you said in the car." Clyde looked at Johnny. "He's mad because I took that money from you. Thinks we should give it back, let you pay off your debt and the three of us work something out when all this is over. Even tried talking to Melvin about it, and guess what? Melvin agreed with me. You were warned. I told you we were holding you responsible for keeping your family in check. But now I'm standing here looking at you, and I'm thinking maybe Reg was right. Too late to be starting anything. You only got three more days. So what's the point?" He pulled out his gun.

"What are you doing?" Reg said.

"Taking responsibility for my actions. According to you, I take that money, somehow I become responsible for whatever happens to him. When I didn't steal from Melvin. I wasn't the one stupid enough to get caught. Don't seem right but maybe it's true. All I know is I'm tired of thinking about it. I want to go home."

"All right, Clyde," Reg said, "you made your point. Put that away."

"I want to go home. I told you we should have stayed in the truck, let these two work it out amongst themselves."

"Man has three more days." Reg slipped in front of Johnny, angling his body to block Clyde's view of him. "I'm just trying to give him that."

"I want to go home. I'm tired of chasing after him. We can't even figure out where he's going half the time. Just rolling around in circles, dragging us along behind him. And for what?"

"I gave him my word, told him I'd let him know if anything changed."

"Well, go ahead and tell him. Guess what Johnny? Things have changed. You don't have enough time to raise that much money and I'm not giving back what you owe me on account of the car. And that means it doesn't matter where you go or what you do because it all ends up the same." He pointed the gun at Johnny's head. "This man here is going to die."

"Maybe. But not today." Reg reached behind him and pulled out a pistol of his own.

"That's enough now," Winston said. "Everybody just calm down. Put those guns away. Last thing anybody needs to be doing is shooting each other. In my mama's house."

"Get out of the way, Reg."

"I told the man he had a week," Reg said. "Told him I'd let him know if something changed, give him enough time to send the girl home, gave him my word. You took his money, whatever you feel about that is on you. But I'm not letting you make a liar out of me too."

Johnny looked at the two of them standing in front of him pointing guns at each other. He realized that maybe Clyde had been telling the truth the night before, when he said that it wasn't really about Johnny, that Johnny just thought this was his story because he happened to be in it. Maybe it really was about Reg and Clyde.

"Everybody is trying to make me into something I'm not," Reg said. "I'm tired of it. Understand? That stops right now."

Then there was a sound at the top of the stairs. The door to the basement fell open, unleashing a narrow shaft of light and a little girl's voice called out.

"Uncle Johnny?"

Out of instinct, Reg and Clyde lowered their arms, tucking the guns under their shirts.

Johnny groaned. "Eloise? Is that you?"

She took two steps down the stairs and he could see a pair of dirty Adidas, white socks, and brown ankles.

"What the heck are you doing here, Eloise? I told you to stay with Junior."

"I was worried about you."

"You don't have no cause to worry. Just go on back. How'd you get here anyhow? Junior with you?"

"I took the bus. He's still at home."

"Well you just go back upstairs, get right back on the bus. Wait for me to come get you."

She took a step down the stairs and then leaned over, peering over the railing at the four men.

Johnny bit his lip. "You shouldn't be here."

"Yeah, but, I was worried . . ." She squinted around the room, trying to make sense of the scene in front of her. Winston crouching in the corner over an empty hole in the floor. Reg and Clyde standing with their heads down, hands tucked under their shirts, both shaking their heads and silently muttering curses at the same time. Johnny standing behind Reg, staring back at her.

"Everything is all right, Eloise. Just go on out of here. Do what I say."

She took another step down the stairs.

"Eloise? You hear me talking to you? Because I expect you to mind me. Hear? Go on back. I'll be there in a couple hours."

She took another step down the stairs.

Everything happened so fast that by the time his mind processed what was going on around him, it was already over. Eloise put her hands out in front of her. Clyde wheeled around to face her and pulled the gun out from under his shirt, but instead of firing it, he *threw* it at her. It wheeled through the air and landed in her left hand as Johnny stood there, speechless, still working through his initial shock and terror at the sight of someone pointing a gun at his niece. Then Reg raised his shirt and Johnny saw the gun pry itself from his fingers, watched it spin through the air and land in Eloise's right.

Then there was a sound like a gong, first once, then twice. Johnny flinched and when he looked again, both Reg and Clyde were lying on the floor, Winston standing over them breathing hard, gripping the shovel.

He looked at his niece, still standing on the middle of the staircase, only now she had a gun in each of her hands.

"I told you I was fast," Eloise said.

....

"Give me those." Johnny snatched the guns from her hands. "What were you thinking? You shouldn't be trying to catch these things, you shouldn't even be touching them. What if one of them had gone off?"

"But that's exactly what I was trying to keep from happening."

He looked back at Reg and Clyde, both lying on the floor. Winston had already covered both their mouths with duct tape and was busy securing Clyde's hands behind his back. He frowned.

"What the heck, Eloise. What did you think you were doing?"

"Saving your life."

"Who asked you to do that?"

"Nobody. What would I look like waiting around for somebody to ask me to save their life?"

"I didn't need you to save me. Understand? What if something had happened to you?"

She blinked at him.

"I told you it was under control."

"Well, now Johnny, I'm going to have to disagree with you on that," Winston said. He was crouched over Clyde, securing his hands behind his back. "*This* fool was going to shoot *that* fool and then he was going to shoot *you*." He wound an extension cord around Clyde's wrists. "That's just a fact. Tell the girl 'thank you' and move on."

Johnny narrowed his eyes. "You going to explain yourself now? Tell me how you know Melvin?"

"I'll show you. Back at the house. Just so long as we have a deal." He looked down at Reg and Clyde. "First you are going to help me clean up though. I can't have my mama coming home to find her house like this. She'd have a stroke."

They refilled the hole, replaced the tiles, and positioned the chair back over it. Then Winston pulled Reg and Clyde onto their feet and led them upstairs. While Johnny and Eloise waited in the car, he got them settled in the back seat of the Camaro.

The three of them drove back to Winston's house. Junior was in the driveway and Johnny told Eloise to stay outside while he talked to Winston.

When they got to the living room, Winston pulled out the scrapbook.

"Remember when I saw you in St. Augustine? I told you I was doing consulting work. Product placement for the urban demographic," Winston said. "Well, Dawson was the product."

He sat down on the couch and started flipping pages. He stopped when he came to the "Pushing Forward" section and handed the book to Johnny.

Johnny looked down at the picture. Winston had snatched the book from his hand so fast the day before he'd only had time to glance at it. Now he realized the other man on the podium with Winston, the one holding the plaque, was Dawson.

"So you did work for Dawson," Johnny said. "You lied to me."

"Didn't lie. I said I knew people on the man's payroll were upset. I didn't say how I knew. And I didn't have anything to do with your brother trying to blackmail him."

"But now you saying Melvin did?"

"Look at the picture." He set his finger on the page and made a line from Dawson's face to a tall man in a dark green suit, standing in the background on the opposite edge of the picture's frame.

It was Melvin.

"Right there, man. Dawson's legal counsel. One of them anyhow. But he's the one who hired me. The only one I ever actually talked to. Called me in from out of town, said Dawson was starting a national campaign and needed a new image consultant. I was working for a malt liquor company at the time, so yes, I did think it was strange. But he offered me a lot of money." He shook his head. "Do you know that I managed to convince myself that if he was asking for me it must have meant that somehow I had acquired a professional reputation? For a quick minute I actually thought I was headed for the big time. Seems kind of stupid now. When I got there, it didn't take long to realize all he really wanted was for me to tell him about you."

"Me? Why?"

"Why do you think? Dawson knew you were the brains of that particular operation. You were the one who made the maps, right? Point your finger in a certain direction and your brother just go? Wasn't that pretty much how it worked? And here come Franklin, making all these wild accusations, showing up at his office, shouting curses at rallies. No one could figure out what he was really after, coming at the man like that, if he was just crazy. Made it kind of hard to know how to deal with him. Because if it was money he wanted, then the way he was acting didn't really seem to make a whole lot of sense. They knew he was your brother, just like they knew we'd worked together in the Justice Committee. So they hired me, asked me about it."

"And what did you say?"

Winston shrugged. "In my capacity as a consultant, I informed them that, yes, you probably were the one behind it and that, yes, there probably was cause for concern. Then I took my money and went home."

"I didn't have a thing to do with it," Johnny said.

"No? Well, honestly, it did seem a bit peculiar to me, all that shouting and cursing and pointing fingers in public. Didn't really seem like your style. I told them that too."

"And the job you hired us to do? Breaking into that office?"

"It was a test. A very expensive test it seemed to me. But they were paying for it. Some things had started going missing from the safes in

their offices. From what Melvin told me, Dawson was getting real paranoid by then, just throwing money at the problem. He was trying to figure out if Franklin was actually capable of pulling off a theft like that."

Johnny nodded. He remembered when Dawson's campaign im-
ploded: a reporter had obtained documents outlining a whole system
of corruption. Proof so detailed and irrefutable that it was impossible
for Dawson to lie. Johnny had never given much thought to how those
documents had been obtained but it would have been easy for Franklin
to access such information, if he'd decided that was what he wanted to
use his talent for. Walls meant nothing to him, making it very difficult
for people to hide.

"I got to say, Johnny. He surprised me that night. I really didn't
think your brother could climb that wall, as fucked up as he looked at
the time." Winston sighed. "Your brother really was a very talented man."

Johnny frowned. "What happened to you, Winston? Have you
completely forgotten everything we did with the Justice Committee?
What we used to stand for? You used to be about something."

"Still am. I'm about getting my son to the Olympics. It's why I
need my money."

"You need it bad enough you would threaten to shoot me over it?
Over some money?"

"Oh, now, come on. We both know you are too smart to get yourself shot over some nonsense like this, even if there were bullets in that
gun. I was just trying to make a point. That I will do whatever I got
to, to take care of my own. I don't see how you can be mad about that.
You are a Ribkins, after all."

Winston smiled. "Don't you remember all those stories Bertrand
used to tell us about your granddaddy? And every last one of them was
about doing what you had to do to take care of your own. I remember
one time Bertrand telling us about some man who took the Rib King

in after the shit hit the fan, how he was hiding in that man's basement when that posse came looking for him. I don't know if Bertrand was already trying to recruit for The Rock or what, but he just kept going on about how that man saved your granddaddy's life. Wound up getting his whole house shot up before they burned it to the ground. And Bertrand kept talking about how brave that man was, how important it was to remember his sacrifice, to honor his memory, how none of you Ribkins would even be here if it weren't for him. Because somehow, while all the shooting was going on, the Rib King managed to slip out the back.

"That granddaddy of yours sounds pretty wild, Johnny. You think he would have done the same, were the situation reversed? No, he would not."

"That was not Bertrand's point and you know it," Johnny said.

"I do know. It's the *opposite* of the point he was trying to make. That's why I was so confused by it, why it took me so long to understand what that story was actually trying to tell me. But after my son was born it occurred to me that every dynasty got started by somebody putting their foot down, being willing to do what they had to do to survive."

He shook his head. "That man who blocked the door for your granddaddy was a blessed fool. And the world needs fools, now, don't get me wrong. But we got to have some not-fools too. I can say that, see? I got the right because I have been both. But somebody has got to slip out the back."

"Dad? You all right?"

Winston looked and saw Junior coming in through the front door.

"Go on back outside, son," Winston said. "Just keep playing."

"You sure? Sure you don't need any help?"

"I don't need anything. Daddy got this. Everything is fine."

He waited until his son left the room.

"I want my fifty percent."

Johnny gave Winston his $625, then went out to his car. He sat by himself for a moment, trying to make sense of what he'd been told. He realized that he'd had no idea what his brother was doing during those last few months of his life, that in his anger he'd somehow managed to lose sight of who his brother was. Because now it all made sense. Dawson's mistake had been trying to implicate Franklin in his crimes, but Johnny's mistake had been thinking Franklin would let such an implication stand. Of course he'd gone back, had done something to make that right. That was just who his brother was.

Johnny should have known. And if he hadn't known, he should have listened, because he realized now that his brother had tried to tell him. All those times Johnny asked Franklin about Meredith, the talk they'd had at Flash's insistence, just before they scaled that last wall. Johnny had been so busy worrying about losing his grip on his brother that somehow he hadn't heard. But he could hear it now.

"Trust me. Meredith is not the problem. And even if she were . . . well. I'm a grown man. Nobody has the right to tell me what to do, how to feel. Not even you. And that doesn't mean I don't love you, but it does mean that sometimes you are going to have to trust me to do what's right. Not right for you maybe. But right for me."

Then Franklin was gone. They scaled that wall, got their money, and Johnny bought a bottle of whiskey to celebrate—then sat and stared at it for the next two days while he waited for his brother to come home. He was hurt, felt abandoned, but couldn't see until now that maybe his brother wasn't turning his back on him, was instead trying to pay tribute to his example. And sometimes the only way to follow someone's example is not to follow at all.

Sometimes you have to go out and set your own.

"What do you think you're doing?"

The door to the front porch slammed shut as Winston ran out into the driveway. Junior and Eloise were standing in the yard, playing "catch."

"We were just playing. She can catch things, she—"

"I didn't ask about her, I asked about *you*," Winston said. He looked furious. "You are a Weypool. I expect you to act like one, at all times. Understand? Don't you ever let me see you do something like that again."

"Yes, sir." Junior glanced down at the rock in his hand and tossed it on the ground. "I'm sorry."

"A Weypool man does not hit women," Winston said. "The fact that you can't is no excuse to try."

He dragged his son back into the house and Eloise hurried to the car.

"Did you get it figured out?" she asked as she climbed into the back seat.

"I did," Johnny said.

"What are we waiting for then? Let's go."

Johnny started the car. He put the gear in reverse, then turned around and squinted at his niece. "What was that anyhow? Back in the basement? With the guns?"

"I caught them. Just like I always do. It's why I keep telling you that you don't have to worry about me."

"But you did not catch them. You snatched them."

"Same thing."

But of course it wasn't. It wasn't the same thing at all.

13

AN INITIAL PREMISE

Three hours after pulling out of Winston's driveway Johnny was sitting in the parking lot of a mini-mall that contained a Jamba Juice, a TCBY, and a Sally Beauty Supply. Eloise was sleeping in the back seat and instead of waking her up he just sat there for a few minutes, staring out at the cars whizzing by on the street in front of him. After a while she sat up and wiped her eyes.

"Where are we?"

"Gainesville," Johnny said. "Used to be a park."

She watched two teens come out of the Jamba Juice, then looked around the busy street.

"And this park . . . It's where my daddy put the money you been looking for?"

"Yes." He'd mapped it out, retraced his brother's steps. Somewhere under the concrete floor of the parking lot was a bag of money his brother had put there fourteen years before.

"Are you sure?"

"It's the only place that makes sense."

"Why?"

Johnny sighed. He started the car again, drove around the block. A minute later he pulled to a stop in front of a small brick house tucked behind a wooden gate. There was a dusty brown Honda Civic parked in the driveway, with a bumper sticker that read MY GRANDSON MADE THE HONOR ROLL.

"What's this?"

"That's the Hammer's house."

"The Hammer? From your group?"

"That's right."

Through one of the windows he could see a woman standing in the kitchen talking on the phone.

"So you think my daddy wanted to leave the money near the Hammer's house?"

"I think your daddy dug a hole at that mini-mall back when it was still a park, figuring he'd come back for it later."

"Why?"

"It's like you said with the fort. Made himself a promise and wanted to make sure he kept it." He nodded toward the house. "I think he wanted you to meet her."

"Me? But I wasn't even born yet."

Johnny nodded. He'd mapped it out. Remembering who his brother actually was had made it easier to figure out how his mind worked. Meredith must have been around two months pregnant when they'd left town. He wasn't running away from anything. He was taking a break. Just like Johnny had been telling him to do for months.

Something must have gone wrong.

The curtain pulled back in the window. Johnny watched the Hammer raise her hand and wave. From the distance between the curb and the window, it looked like she was holding up a sledgehammer.

Johnny smiled. The hand was just like he remembered. Where the left arm funneled down to a slender wrist and long slim fingers, the right expanded outward into a widening band of muscle. He would never forget the first time he saw it. The Justice Committee had been working security for a popular preacher who'd recently had some threats against his life. Once the sermon was over and things were winding down, Johnny was standing behind a card table where several of the political group working in the area had set out sign-up sheets for volunteers. When he looked up he saw a shy girl of no more than twenty standing over the table. She was wearing a gray dress with a high collar and was holding a brochure in her left hand. Her right hand was hidden behind her back.

After a while, she looked up at him and smiled.

I'd like to get involved . . .

⸺⸺⸺⸺⸺⸺⸺

"I don't understand. Why did my daddy want me to meet her?"

Johnny looked at his niece. It went without saying that this was the end of the line for him. He'd run out of holes; when he got back to St. Augustine he was going to have to deal with Melvin another way. Yet he felt calm. All he could think was that if he couldn't keep his own promises to Eloise, then maybe he could help someone else keep theirs.

"Let's go find out," he said, and pushed open his door.

They were heading up the front walk when she came out to greet them, wearing a sleeveless white tunic over a pair of blue jeans and hiking boots. There was a shock of gray hair around her temples and her eyes crinkled when she smiled but besides that she still looked the same as she had when he met her all those years before.

"Johnny Ribkins, is that really you?"

"Hope we're not coming at a bad time."

"Nonsense. It's never a bad time to see an old friend. Just busy is all."

She held out her hands. "Come and hug me."

Johnny hugged his old friend and smiled.

She looked at Eloise. "And who's this?"

"My niece. Eloise."

"Niece? Well, very nice to meet you, Eloise. Wonderful, actually . . ."

"How's the research going?"

"Oh, splendid. Things have been moving much quicker since I started working from home. Not that I had much choice in the matter. The university was threatening to shut down my high school program. Liability issues, I was told. But that was not going to happen. I got young men and women coming from schools all over the county to help me do this research. Some of the most brilliant minds of their generation working right here, in my yard."

"Is that right?"

"Without a doubt. Mark my word, Johnny. *All* of my children are superstars."

She held onto Eloise's hand as she led them inside the house, which was messy but comfortable, walls decorated with framed children's artwork. When they reached the living room she removed a small pile of newspapers from a side table and Johnny saw a picture of her and her wife underneath it.

"So what brings you to town?"

"Nothing really. Just taking a little road trip with my niece here and thought we'd stop by. Couldn't pass up a chance for Eloise to meet you."

"Road trip? Where are you heading?"

"Oh, we've been a lot of places. Just got back from Tallahassee. Went to see Flash."

"Flash?" she laughed. "Okay. And how was that?"

"About like you'd expect, I imagine. Guess he hasn't changed much."

"Still moving fast? Makes it hard to get a handle on that man."

"Well, I got to say this last visit made me wonder if maybe the reason he so hard to get a grip on is not because he moves so fast. Maybe it's just that there's nothing actually there."

"I don't believe that. Come on now," she said. She poured him a glass of iced tea. "Neither do you."

"I don't know," Johnny said. "I sat and listened to him give me a long lecture while I was there. Some story Bertrand had told him about my granddaddy. And I remembered the story, I think I might even remember Bertrand telling it. But the details were all wrong. Somehow he had managed to get everything turned around, was using it as a justification for greed, for only looking out for yourself."

"Yeah, well . . . that sounds like Flash. Sorry. I really don't know what to say about that man anymore except . . . sorry." She smiled at Eloise. "What did you think of Flash?"

"I don't know."

"Fair enough. You just met him, right? Me? I've known him forty years and I don't know either. But it just goes to show . . . you can't really dictate a moral, Johnny. Just got to tell your story, put it out there, and hope somebody has sense enough to figure out for themselves what you were trying to say."

She smiled. "I tell them too sometimes, you know. Those stories about your grandfather that Simone and Captain Dynamite used to tell. To my students, you'd be surprised how much it means to them, hearing about the Rib King, all his adventures, what he went through. Especially the early ones, from when he was a child."

She looked at Eloise. "Your uncle ever tell you about how the Rib King's mother hid him in a cellar when those people came to burn down their town? Told him someone would come find him when it was safe but he had to promise to stay hidden and not make a sound until he heard someone call him by his name. So he did as he was told and stayed where he was, while all around him fires burned and raged all over town. After a while he got scared no one would come. But just when he was about to give up hope he heard someone calling his name. He looked up and saw a woman in a long white dress standing by the cellar door. She took him by the hand and led him out of town. He woke up the next morning by the bank of a river, all alone. The woman who had led him there was gone and he never saw her again, and so, for the rest of his life, he was never sure if she'd ever actually been there or was just something he dreamed up. When, of course, either way, she was real."

"A hand to hold on to," Johnny nodded.

"That's right. Hope, the power of dreams. Such a beautiful story." She smiled. "So what else? What else have you been up to since we last saw each other?"

"Oh, this and that," Johnny said. He shook his head, trying to think of what to say. "Actually I feel like I'm going through a kind of transition right now . . ." He looked at his niece. "I got to say that lately I find myself thinking a lot about things I might still be able to do to help folks coming up after I'm gone."

"You mean like volunteering with a youth center?"

"What? Well, yes. Something like that."

"I think that's wonderful, Johnny, so many children out there could really benefit from your wisdom and experience."

"Yeah, well." He smiled at Eloise. "I can't really think of anything better I got to do right now than try to invest it in the youth, in the future."

The Hammer nodded. "Is that why you came by? You need money?"

"What?"

"For the youth center?"

Johnny was confused.

The Hammer leaned forward, patted him on the knee. "It's all right. Happy to help." She stood up and disappeared down the hall.

When she came back she was carrying a large package; she set it down on the coffee table in front of him.

"It sounds like you might need this now. For the youth center."

"I hope I did the right thing, digging it up like that. But when I realized they were going to pave over the park, it just seemed foolish to leave it there. So I went and got it myself. I've been holding it for you ever since."

Johnny stared down at the package.

"How did you find it?"

"Franklin told me he was putting it there. When he came to visit me."

"So you did meet Franklin?"

"Oh, yeah. Him and his fiancée. Meredith." She looked at Eloise. "Is that your mama, sweetie?"

"Yes, ma'am."

"Well, please give her my regards when you get back home. She was very nice. They both were."

"When was this?"

"A long time ago, Johnny. They were on their way to Lehigh Acres. He'd just proposed to your mama, Eloise, and wanted her to see where he was from. And they decided to stop and say hello. He said I was the only member of the Justice Committee he hadn't met yet."

"Did he tell you what they were planning? He and Meredith?"

"Planning? Well, like I said, he told me they were planning on getting married. But mostly we just talked about the Justice Committee. He had a lot of questions. Wanted to know where we met, where we went, what we did. We must have talked for five hours. Or really, I talked. He listened. He asked about your maps. And he asked why we disbanded."

"And what did you tell him?"

"Well, the truth, of course." The Hammer shrugged. "Told him how you'd decided we needed to change course. That the time had come for us to stop playing defense, to start confronting real sources of power, and that in order to do this we would unfortunately be needing other resources. Money.

"I told him about how you spent almost a year working on that last map. I told him about how just when we were ready to put it into action, Flash managed to get himself scooped up in that raid. Told him how you wound up using most of the money we'd raised for your map in order to pay for Flash's defense. You paid his bail and he just took off, left you stuck with that bond note. I told him about how, in the midst of all that turmoil, J.D. was killed and how you blamed yourself for that, even though, of course, you didn't have a thing to do with it. I told him how you went back to St. Augustine, saying you needed some time to think. Before you left you told us to stick to our covers, that when the time was right for us to get back together, you'd let us know."

She reached for his hand. "It's been thirty years, Johnny Ribkins. But that's what I've been doing ever since."

Johnny nodded. "I should have returned your phone calls."

"Yes, you should have. But it's all right. I knew you were grieving. First for Flash, then the Committee, then your brother . . ." She shook her head. "He loved you so much. Told me about all you'd tried to do for him and how much it meant to him. But then he said something happened that made him realize it was time for him to grow up and not be so dependent on you. He said he was trying to be his own man because he wanted to give you a little more space to be yours. Because you still had work to do." She nodded toward the package. "That's what this was for, just in case you needed it."

He looked at the package. "You didn't even open it."

"It wasn't mine," she said. "Besides, I already knew what was in it. Anyhow, I liked keeping it for you. I guess I figured one day you'd have to come back for it. And then I'd get to talk to you again. Are you going to open it?"

When he didn't answer she turned to Eloise. "Honey? Why don't we give your uncle a moment to himself. You like to paint? How about I get you set up with an easel in the kitchen?"

They disappeared through the door and Johnny opened the package. Inside it was a note Franklin had written on the back of a piece of business stationery: "For you, brother, to do with as you see fit. Hope it helps." Johnny smiled at his brother's handwriting, then removed the note from the box. Underneath it was the money Dawson had given him, laid out in neat stacks. Johnny took it out of the box and counted it slowly: $50,000.

Johnny shook his head. His brother had saved him, not for the first time, he realized, but yet again. He stared at his brother's note for a few minutes, then he looked back in the box. Underneath the money was a small stack of documents Franklin must have taken from Dawson's offices at the time. Among them was an itemized list of donations followed by a long memo outlining a legal justification of expenditures. The memo had been signed by Dawson's legal counsel at the time, Melvin Marks.

"Thank you, brother," Johnny said. Then he stood up and walked back to the kitchen where he found Eloise sitting alone.

"You all right?"

"Very much so," he said, and took a seat across from her.

"Where'd the Hammer go?"

Eloise nodded toward the window. Johnny looked out and saw the Hammer standing across the street leaning over the driver's door of a battered yellow Camaro.

"They pulled up a couple minutes ago. She wanted to talk to them, check to make sure everything was cool."

"She wasn't worried, was she?"

"No, I think she meant it literally. Thought they might be thirsty." Eloise smiled. "So you got what you're looking for?"

"I did. Your daddy came through for me in the end. Isn't that something? After all that digging, all that running around. And you want to know what? He always did."

"Did he? I'm sorry I never knew him. That's what I'd like to understand, you know. What he was really like."

He looked around him, trying to figure out how to describe Franklin. He thought about the last wall he'd seen his brother climb, the job Flash had sent them to do. Maybe it was only a test but the truth was it had been perfect for them, almost like a dream. Or should have been. Whatever warning Johnny had given his brother about showing up sober had gone in one ear and out the other because Johnny had taken one look at him and realized he was wasted. And there on the spot he'd made the decision that, for the first time in years, he was going to climb that wall with him.

He told himself he was doing it to look after his brother but the truth was Franklin didn't need his help. As soon as they hit that wall something clicked in his brother's mind, instinct and reflex taking over the same way they always did. And that night, whether or not he'd recognized it at the time, Johnny saw his brother as he truly was.

I've got you.

Johnny was the one who wound up holding them back, making things take hours longer than they should have, or would have, if he'd just let Franklin go it alone. They were already halfway up the wall by the time Johnny accepted that he was the one holding them back, the one who needed help.

You got this, man. We can do this together. Come on.

At one point, he felt himself slip.

Grab my hand.

Something sank in his gut and he was still processing the shock of it when he realized Franklin had him by the arm—

I've got you, brother. Just hold on.

That was the truest likeness of his brother that Johnny would ever have: Franklin somehow managing to hoist both himself and Johnny up the side of a wall. Not just what Franklin looked like but what he'd felt like too, even right there at the end of it, just before he disappeared. The feeling had stayed with him, even when he couldn't make sense of it anymore. His brother's hand was wrapped around his, pulling him up and over. For as long as they'd known each other, every time Franklin said, "I've got you, Johnny," Johnny had known he was telling the truth.

That was who his brother was. Wild yet somehow holding on. Pulling him up over a wall. That was what Johnny wanted to share with his niece. That, in truth, was what he wanted to share with the whole world.

"Your daddy wasn't perfect but he was a great man. And he was complicated, which makes him kind of hard to explain. All I know is that I learned a whole lot from him. Am still learning, if you can believe that. And I don't really know if I'm even capable of doing justice to his memory. But I can try. As soon as we get back to St. Augustine that's what I'm going to do."

The Hammer pushed back through the door, frowning.

"They said you tied them up and locked them in the car, Johnny."

"Flash did that. One of them was threatening to shoot me at the time."

"And why is that?"

"Complicated."

The Hammer sighed.

"Well they seem like nice boys to me," she said, and joined them at the table.

Johnny looked at Eloise. "Now about this talent of yours. I still want to help you figure out what to do with it. But you got to give me a place to start. I mean an honest place."

"What do you mean, 'honest'?"

"I mean what happened back there, at the Weypools'. Because you've been lying to me too. You know very well that catching and snatching aren't the same thing."

"Well, of course I do. It's just—what you call 'snatching' is what I've been doing the whole time. That's the real reason nobody can hit me, Uncle Johnny. It would be like hitting myself."

"Because all this time you been snatching things out of people's hands?"

"Yes. I mean, they can throw it if they want to. Doesn't really make a difference to me."

"Well, of course it makes a difference. One is playing defense and the other is playing offense."

Eloise shrugged. "I know. That's why I do it. I don't want to be offensive, Uncle Johnny."

"What now?"

"I'm trying not to be offensive. It's hard enough being strange. So I always wait for other folks to throw something at me. It's just being polite."

He shook his head. "You mean to tell me that's what has been going on? All this time? You've been letting people think you need their *permission* for you to exercise your God-given talent? Because you don't want to offend them?"

She thought about that for a moment. Then she said, "I guess so. Took me a while to figure it out. Sometimes when I was little, like back in the first grade, I would just do it whenever I wanted to. Snatch a pencil, snatch a piece of chalk, snatch somebody's hat off their head. I thought it was funny but it scared people. And after a while no one wanted to talk to me except for my friend Bobby. Like if I was walking down the hall? Sometimes other kids would cross over to the other side so they didn't have to get next to me. That's how offensive they thought I was. So I stopped snatching things. But then sometimes people would throw things at me just to see what I would do. And I realized that when I caught it, it didn't seem to bother them so much. Then they would just laugh at me like they thought it was funny. So I only did it if they threw something first. And after a while it was like they forgot I didn't need them to throw something at me, didn't really need their permission. That really I could just snatch something out of their hands whenever I felt like it." She smiled. "Also I imagine it makes people feel good, thinking they've got such good aim."

"That's a terrible story," Johnny said.

The Hammer had to agree. "I'm sorry, Eloise, but your uncle's right. That story just makes me sad."

Eloise shrugged. "Mostly I feel like I'm lucky I don't have to be offensive if I don't want to be. Like I have a safe place to hide."

"Hide? Is that what you're aiming for in life? A place to hide?" Johnny said.

"You can't live trying to appease other people like that," the Hammer said. "What you've got is a gift, understand? It's a gift and you have to respect it."

"Easy for you to say."

"It's not though," the Hammer said. "It's not easy at all. But it's the truth."

Johnny reached into his pocket and held out his keys.

"Show me."

So that's what she did. She snatched the keys right from his palm. They shot across the room and he watched her fingers curl over them in a fist.

Johnny nodded. "And it always come to your hand like that?"

She threw the keys in the air and then held out her hand beneath them. This time, just before they landed back on her palm, she raised her hand in the air as if motioning for them to stop. Which they did somehow, hovering midair, just a few inches in front of her face.

"Well, now, see that? That's something altogether different. And I didn't have any idea you could do something like that."

"How is anybody going to recognize you, Eloise, if you're scared to show people who you really are?" the Hammer said.

"Your mother ever seen you do that?"

"No. Just Bobby."

"Why not?"

The girl folded her hand into a fist and the keys dropped to the floor at her feet.

"I told you. It scares people. And being scared makes them mean. They already think I'm strange."

"What is so wrong with being strange?" said the woman with the right hand that looked like a sledgehammer. "It's ridiculous, Johnny. Could you please tell this child there is nothing wrong with being strange."

"There's nothing wrong with being strange, Eloise," said the man who lived his life according to maps so complicated nobody else could figure out where he was going.

"Everything beautiful in this world is strange," the Hammer said. "If you think about that for a little bit you're going to find I'm telling the truth. You can't live your life worried about people being scared of you just for being who you are. Because what you are is beautiful. It's not your job to try and compensate other people's lack of vision. You've got enough to do just trying to be true to your own."

Johnny bent down and picked up the keys. He handed them back to Eloise.

"Do it again."

With a swirl of her hand she scooped the keys up. This time she twirled her hand in front of her face and the keys started to spin around. He watched the metal swirl in the air in front of her, catching the light from the window behind her.

It was beautiful.

"Damn," Johnny said. They spun so fast it looked like tiny balls of light spiraling out from the spinning metal spokes, catching the sunlight, bouncing off the walls, filling the room with a glittery, sparking haze.

He smiled and looked around the room, glad the Hammer was there to see it with him. Somehow, more than anything, he wanted to show it to people. He glanced out the window, looking around at the street outside until he saw the yellow Camaro with tinted windows parked on the corner across the street. He stood up.

"Where you going, Uncle?"

"I'll be right back."

He ran across the street, tapped his knuckles against the driver's window, and waited for it to roll down.

"Get away from here."

"I want to show you something."

"No."

"I mean it. I just want you to see it."

"I'm warning you, Johnny. Step away from the car. Now."

Johnny frowned. "All that stuff back in Tallahassee? It wasn't my fault."

"Shut up, Johnny."

"Come on now. I didn't mean for that to happen. It was a misunderstanding. The girl saw you with the guns and then Winston did what he did and . . . Me? I wouldn't have tied you up like that but you all were looking pretty mad at that point and it just seemed better to give you all a little chance to calm down, you know, reflect, before—"

"I'm not playing, Johnny. This is not a game. Understand?"

"I do. That's why I want you to come inside."

Johnny glanced back at the house and then turned around and squinted at the man in the driver's seat.

"Just for a minute? I'm telling you, it's beautiful . . ." Johnny sighed. "Well, I can't force you. I know that. You two are grown men. You make your own decisions. And I understand I haven't given you much reason to trust me. Just so long as you know that if you should change your mind . . . I want you to know you're welcome, hear me? Welcome to come inside."

Then he looked back over his shoulder, saw the girl watching him through the window. He backed away from the car and hurried toward the Hammer's house. Something beautiful was waiting for him inside, and who knew how long it would last.

14

MELVIN

One night, a long time ago, Johnny was sitting alone in the living room of his house in St. Augustine, watching the lights from the cars passing on the street outside spray streaks of red and white across his ceiling. There was an envelope with twenty-five hundred dollars in it sitting on the coffee table and a bottle of whiskey balanced between his knees. The money was Franklin's share of what his friend Flash had paid them to steal documents from an office in a high-rise, high-security building two days before, the last time he'd seen his brother. Franklin hadn't even bothered to come claim it. Johnny bought the whiskey that same night thinking he and Franklin would drink it together to celebrate a job well done; instead he was drinking alone.

By the time he got through half the bottle he'd pretty much decided to drive out to Tallahassee, dig a little hole, and bury Franklin's share somewhere near Flash's house. It was a petty, small-minded thing to do, but he thought the gesture would make him feel better. He'd already put his shoes on and was looking for his car keys when he heard a knock on his door. Johnny set the bottle down and stuffed the money in his side table drawer; when he pulled the door open a tall, light-skinned man in a rumpled green suit was staring back at him with red rheumy eyes.

"Looking for Franklin. He around?" his future employer wheezed. A man around Franklin's age with a wide, flat nose, chapped lips, and a long, narrow keloid scar running down his left cheek. All Johnny could think was that this was some sorry spillover from a party he hadn't been invited to, a refugee come calling from wherever it was Franklin went when he disappeared, sometimes for weeks at a time.

"It's four o'clock in the morning."

"Is it?" The man sounded surprised. "Look, man. I wouldn't be bothering you if it wasn't important, and anyhow your light was on. Just tell him you got Melvin here. He's gonna want to talk to me."

Every time the man opened his mouth Johnny was assaulted by the heavy scent of Lysol and vomit, a feat of halitosis that, Johnny knew from experience, could be accomplished only by someone on an undignified bender of at least three days. Yet this, apparently, was the kind of person whose company and laughter his brother now preferred.

"Get the fuck off my porch."

"Come on, man. Don't be like that. I just need a minute."

Johnny glanced down at the man's foot wedged in his doorway. For a moment, he considered pulling back the door, slamming it on the man's knee, and simply shoving him back out the other side. The only thing that kept him from doing it was a quick calculation of how much longer it would take the man to get off his property if he was compelled to crawl.

The man must have sensed this because the foot slid backward.

He smiled. "Hold up, now. Wait a minute. You're Franklin's brother, aren't you? Shit, man. I wasn't sure he was telling the truth. But it is you, isn't it? Johnny Ribkins."

Johnny remembered the strange reverberations of his own name coming out of the man's mouth as it suddenly occurred to him what he might have looked like to someone standing on the other side of that door. For the first time Johnny wondered if that sour breath he'd been smelling was, in fact, his own.

"I remember you. Had that group back in the day," Melvin said. "Went around guarding those civil rights people and shit. Kicking ass, taking names, and fuck if you didn't look good doing it too."

Johnny squinted at the man's scar.

"What was it you all called yourselves? The Justice Committee. Y'all were like my heroes coming up."

Melvin's gaze kept drifting past Johnny's shoulder and into the living room. Eyes scanning the stacks of newspapers and pizza boxes piled on the floor, the overflowing ashtray on the arm of a threadbare sofa, the open bottle of whiskey on the coffee table next to a pair of dirty athletic socks.

He shook his head. "I always did wonder what happened to you."

Briefly, it flashed through his mind that maybe Melvin was messing with him.

"Where's your hat, Johnny? You still wear that hat?"

Either that or he was a fool.

"Man, get out of here," Johnny said. "I don't have time for this. And I certainly don't need you to tell me who I am."

"No, I guess you don't," Melvin said. "Forgive me, Johnny Ribkins. I didn't mean to bother you. And I certainly didn't mean any disrespect. If you could just tell Franklin I stopped by . . ." He licked his lips and stared at the bottle of whiskey on the table. "If you could just tell him I've got his money."

That's about all Melvin Marks was to Johnny that first night: A thirsty, desperate look wedged in his doorway. The mention of money and the associated relief that maybe Franklin was up to something so simple as another con. The numb sense of betrayal as Johnny imagined Franklin sitting drunk in some crowded bar, laughing as he told stories about Johnny's past. The sudden need to track his brother down.

Johnny could have done a lot of things that night. What he did was pull back the door and ask Melvin if he wanted a drink.

....

"The sad thing is I thought I was just being smart," he remembered Melvin telling him that night. The two of them wound up talking for a long time; Melvin told him he was a lawyer who'd worked for a large financial institution until recently, when he was caught embezzling funds. "Trying to get ahead. Just playing the game. You know, not a game, but *the* game." He helped himself to the bottle on the table between them. "And it is a game, you know that, right? I mean, 'embezzlement' sounds pretty bad, when you put it like that. But you think I'm the worst? I was just trying to fit in. People I worked for, people I worked with . . . Everybody else was out there doing the exact same things. But that is the part I didn't get: I'm expendable. The low man on the totem pole, a cog in the wheel. Nobody cares what happens to me, Johnny. And I'm starting to realize they never did."

Johnny nodded. That much he hadn't even questioned. It was the way of the world. There were always bigger crooks hiding in the shadows, the biggest ones you never saw at all. They kept to themselves and counted their money and somehow managed to keep most folks busy fighting it out among themselves, over crumbs. In the final days of the Committee it had been an obsession of his; now it was why he didn't feel particularly guilty about his chosen line of work.

"Word came down about an impending investigation and my supervisor started getting very paranoid about communications. Told me what the story was they were giving to investigators and wanted me to make sure I had the documentation to back it up. I had to present him with signed copies of all financial transactions approved by my department. And of course, loyal employee that I am, I was thinking about protecting the firm. Thought we were a team so I did what he said. Realized too late that they weren't actually trying to hide a paper trail so much as making sure it led back to me. And I helped them do it." Melvin shook his head and swallowed his whiskey. "They fired me, but it's not over yet. I figure I got a couple days left before those indictments come down. Then it's all over." He stared around the room with a look of panic in his eyes. "I'm going to jail, Johnny."

The story was pitiful, but of course Johnny was less interested in where Melvin was going than in how it related to where his brother was now. At one point he asked Melvin straight out to tell him how they'd met.

"Just around . . . you know, a friend of a friend. I don't really remember. I run into him a lot at this bar where I go after work and after a while we just started talking. Him and his girl. What's her name? Skinny, bright red hair . . ."

"Meredith." Johnny frowned. "It's a wig."

Melvin smiled. "Not friends? What?"

"It's not my business who Franklin chooses to crawl into bed with. But he's done better, that's for sure."

Those comments, so far as he recalled, had been his one lapse into anything approaching the personal. Mostly he just let the man talk.

"I told your brother what was happening to me and he just laughed. Said he wanted to help me, that he could take care of it. All I had to do was come up with the money to pay him. Said he could fix it all with nothing more than a lighter and a ballpoint pen."

He looked at Johnny. "I'm not stupid, Johnny. Your brother . . . he's crazy, yes?"

Johnny shrugged. Of course Franklin was. But that didn't mean what he said wasn't true.

"That's what I figured," Melvin said. "Drunk or crazy or both. But here's the thing—I find myself in a situation where I don't really have much left to lose. And he swore up and down he was telling the truth. Would fix it, for a certain fee."

Melvin reached into his jacket pocket. He pulled out a folded manila envelope and set it down on the table between them.

"There's a thousand dollars in there, Johnny. Charged it to the company account. Do you know that is the one instance of an out-and-out theft they'll have on me? Because I was so careful. Might have slipped up with a couple of incriminating emails, a couple of memos . . . but nothing on the books. When, believe me, this is the least of my crimes. I've been a real shit, Johnny. Still am."

"Let me see the money."

Melvin slid the envelope across the table. Johnny pulled out a crumpled wad of bills held together with a rubber band. He picked it up and counted. He set it back down between them.

"I can help you."

"How?"

Johnny finished the last of the bottle. He reached inside the envelope and picked up the lighter and lit his cigar. He took out the pen and drew the man a map.

That was the extent of their first encounter. Johnny felt sorry for him, took the money, gave Melvin his map, and that was it. Next time he came to see Johnny, Melvin had lost his license to practice law but he hadn't gone to jail. Even now, as Johnny recalled the exchange, there was nothing about it that seemed particularly sinister.

He couldn't even say that Melvin lied to him because he'd come right out and told Johnny he was a liar and a thief. He just left some things out.

················

Now Melvin had an office on the seventh floor of a glass-walled highrise. It wasn't where Johnny asked to meet him. He called Melvin soon after he and Eloise got back to St. Augustine, told him he was ready to settle accounts, but would prefer if they could meet at his daddy's shop. He was standing in front of it two hours later when Melvin pulled up in his car.

"Feel better?" Melvin smiled.

"What do you mean?"

"Out in public. With all these people around you, all these potential witnesses? You weren't scared to come to my office, were you?"

"No."

"That mean you got my money?"

"I do."

Melvin nodded. "Good. Because you know, Johnny, I realize that the last time we saw each other I was upset. Harsh words were spoken, very harsh words. And ever since you left my office, ever since I found out that the first thing you thought to do after talking to me was pack up and leave town without telling me where you were going, I've been concerned that maybe, in the heat of anger, I had not expressed myself as well as I might have otherwise."

"You were pretty clear."

"I hope so. Because all that stuff I told you? About what I was going to do to you if you didn't pay me back on time? I meant every fucking word. Gave you a week to get your affairs in order, which is more than you deserved. And if you hadn't made your way back here in time, and if you didn't have my money, I would have hunted you down like the lying, thieving dog you are. And do you know why?

"Because of the organization. I'm trying to run a business here, trying to accomplish something, and I can't do that if the people who work for me think they can get away with acting out of turn. There has to be an order and that order has to be respected and that means this is not about you and me. It's about the organization. And what is an organization, Johnny, if not a dynamic system? It is a mechanism, if you will. One that can function properly only so long as every component is doing what it is supposed to do. That is why every component, first and foremost, has got to know its place. It's also why there is no such thing as an insignificant part, because every part is, in truth, something larger than itself. Understand?"

"I do."

Melvin nodded. "Of course you do, Johnny. You're smart. I always liked that about you. So let's see if we can't rectify this unfortunate situation, fix what's broke without bloodshed. Let you get back to your life as a broke-down old man."

Johnny nodded, reached into the pocket of his jacket, and pulled out an envelope.

"What's this?"

"A threat."

Melvin opened the envelope and frowned.

"Where did you get this?"

"Brother left it for me. Sitting in a box under the money I was going to use to pay you back. Those are some of the documents you were looking for the night we met, aren't they? Why you asked for that first map. All this time I thought the reason you never went to jail was because you used my map to get them back, then I come to find out Franklin had them this whole time. What did you do with that map, anyhow?"

"I took all the ones I could find. Kept waiting for the other shoe to drop but it never did."

"Well, now we know why. Because, I must say, it does seem pretty irrefutable."

Melvin shut the envelope and tried to hand it back.

"Naw, you keep it."

"I don't want it. This old news, Johnny. Statute of limitations for most of that stuff run out a long time ago."

"Most. Not all. But it's not about you anyway, is it? It's about the organization. Having all of this made public would be bad for business. Draw a lot of unwanted attention to your current business practices; might motivate someone to start looking for patterns of abuse. I don't imagine I'd have too much trouble getting somebody to take an interest in all this 'old news' right now, what with the elections going on. Don't know if you've heard but Dawson has been making quite a comeback. And of course a lot of that stuff implicates him as well. Be a kind of poetic justice in that, don't you think? Let him be the collateral damage for a change." He shook his head. "You should have told me you used to work for Dawson, Melvin."

"You never asked," Melvin said, looking through the file again.

"Well, I'm asking now."

Melvin set down the file. He looked at Johnny and smiled. "First time I saw your brother he interrupted a strategy session. I don't even know how he got in the building looking the way he did—but I had him escorted out. Then we started noticing some things were going missing from campaign offices. I didn't know how he did it until I tracked down your friend and he explained about your brother's talents. By then he was making all kinds of threatening and dangerous accusations, and—you know what? What the weird thing about that was? They were all true.

"You hear me, Johnny? Everything he said was the truth. I mean it was chilling, trying to figure out how someone like that, someone so clearly unhinged, could access so much information. Well, we just figured someone had put him up to it. And, of course, all roads led back to you."

"I didn't have nothing to do with it."

"I know. Figured that out the night we met. It wasn't you at all. It was a crack addict and a prostitute, having the nerve to threaten a man like Dawson. I mean, it was the craziest thing I'd ever seen. How do you even cope with something like that?"

"You offer them a bribe."

"Yeah. That's right. Dawson offered your brother a lot of money and he still wasn't satisfied. I mean he took it. It was money, what do you think? Everybody takes it, that's how it works. He just didn't stop. I brought the money to him like Dawson asked and he told me to go back and tell Dawson it didn't change anything, that he was still coming for him. 'Go back and tell Dawson: you can't steal what's already stolen.'" Melvin frowned. "Like I had nothing to do with it, like it was just between the two of them. When it was my paycheck he was fucking up, my life." He shook his head. "Your brother had me confused for a bagman, Johnny."

"Probably what you looked like then," Johnny said.

"Maybe. I told Dawson it wasn't going to work. But he was panicking by then, see? Told me to give him some time to figure out how to deal with it and then he'd let me know what he wanted me to do. So I went home and waited for his call. But see, by noon the next day, your brother was gone. And after that, Dawson must have decided in the wisdom of desperation that he was going to have to settle for a scapegoat. Me."

"Pitiful."

"I know. I really don't know what would have happened if you hadn't saved me. And you did save me, Johnny. I do realize that. Not from your brother. From him . . . Dawson."

"Did you have something to do with what happened to my brother?"

"No, Johnny. I did not. But I'll be honest with you because I've got no reason to lie. I thought about it. Probably would have. But those wheels just kept turning on their own. Your brother was running wild back then, you know that as well as I do. He left town, slipped out on me, and it took a quick minute to track him down. That's the real reason I came to your house that night. But then I realized you didn't know where he was either. I'd heard a lot of people talking about your maps, figured it was an opportunity to see how you worked. By the time I found out Franklin and Meredith had gone back to his hometown I'd already missed my chance. That's why, when you took off like that, at first I just assumed you were trying to run out on me too. Reg and Clyde were the ones who explained you were actually trying to get my money."

"I suppose I should thank them for that."

"From what I hear you already did."

Melvin closed the file. "You sure this is what you want to do, Johnny? Threaten me?"

"Test me and see," Johnny said. He shook his head. "I still don't understand why you never came out and told me this, Melvin. Why I had to figure all this out on my own."

"Why?" Melvin reached down and straightened his tie. "Because your brother was wrong about me. I'm no one's bagman, Johnny. I'm a businessman. And the fact is, you are a real moneymaker, Johnny Ribkins. Dawson was right about that much at least. If it weren't for that one simple fact, I would have kicked your ass to the curb a long time ago."

Johnny nodded. "It's what I'm counting on."

Melvin smiled. "So that's it, huh? Blackmail? Why you wanted to meet in public? Just in case I decided to hurt you?"

"I thought you'd want to see it."

"See what?"

"Where all your money went." He nodded toward the shop. "Weren't you even curious about what I did with it?"

He'd done a lot of renovations over the past few years. Converted the upstairs into an art gallery, a proper showcase for his daddy's work. Then he'd purchased the lot on the corner and converted it into a community garden. When the laundromat across the street went bankrupt, he took some of Melvin's money to buy that too. He had to tear the whole thing down and start rebuilding from scratch. It still wasn't finished, but now he could point to a sign hanging over the door: FRANKLIN RIBKINS REHABILITATION CENTER.

"Don't you recognize it? I thought you might."

Melvin looked up and down the block.

Dawson's campaign promises.

"You mean to tell me you did all this with $100,000?"

"Oh, I took more from you than that. Been taking a little bit here and there pretty much the whole time I've known you."

He started to walk away and then stopped. "By the way, Melvin. What does your organization, your mechanism, do? What is it you are trying to accomplish? I mean, you got a lot of parts working for you now, like you said. Seems to me you could do a lot of things with those parts if you decided you wanted to, if you just stopped for a moment, used your imagination, reconfigured a couple of things. Like if you decided maybe it was time to change course. It's never too late for that you know. To turn things around."

He walked inside the shop.

"Everything all right?" Eloise said as he pushed through the door.

"Better than," Johnny nodded. He took off his hat.

"I knew you could do it, Uncle Johnny."

"You mean *we*, right? We could do it. Because I might not have without your help. Might have just given up."

She was standing in the corner, looking at one of her grandfather's paintings on the wall.

"Pretty." Eloise nodded. "All these colors . . ."

Johnny squinted. All he saw was blue and brown.

"You can't see them, can you?"

"No," Johnny said. "Wish I could."

"Well, don't feel bad. Sometimes I can see time. That helps."

"What does that mean? Like, tell the future?"

"No. But sometimes I can see how stuff gets put together. From beginning to end and all the points in between."

"Is that right?" Johnny said. "You never mentioned that before."

"You never asked," Eloise said. She pointed at the picture.

"You see that little swirl of yellow? Whoever did this made that line first. Then they added the red and then mixed in the blue. It's an awful lot of paint jumbled up together. But still . . ."

Johnny stared at the picture. He remembered sometimes watching his father paint when he was younger, being confused by the amount of time his father spent blending colors together, trying to get at some particular shade. Johnny knew it had something to do with how his father saw the world, something about the contrast created by all those vibrant flashes of color folding in on one another. But when it was finished all Johnny saw was a whole lot of effort submerged within two monochrome bands.

"I'm sorry you never met my daddy. He would have really liked you." Johnny smiled. "Now that that's all taken care of, we're going to have a good time. I got a whole lot of things I want to show you while you're here."

Eloise frowned. "But it's Saturday."

"That's all right."

"No, I mean, Mama's coming back tomorrow."

"That quick?"

"The festival was only for a week. I thought you knew that."

"Well, that don't mean nothing. You don't have to hurry back the minute she gets home. You'll stay for another couple weeks, she won't mind. Then I'll drive you back."

"I can't though. I have to get ready for school."

"School?"

"Summer's almost over, Uncle Johnny. I have to get back home." Eloise smiled. "Next time."

"Next time?"

"Well, I'd like to come back and visit you. I mean, if that's all right . . ."

"Of course it's all right. I mean, yeah, I'd like you to come back . . . I'm still thinking about this time, though. You see?" He smiled. "Let's talk about this later. We'll go out, have some fun. See how you feel then."

Johnny put his hat back on. They got back in the car and he gave her a quick tour of the city. They had lunch in a pizza parlor and then he took her to the pier downtown and bought her a snow cone. They walked through the aquarium and then they went to Adventure Landing and played a round of minigolf. He could tell how much fun she was having. Still, when he asked her about it again, she insisted she had to get home.

"If it's school you're worrying about—and that's good by the way, school's important, got to prioritize your education—the thing is, we got schools right here. I don't see why you couldn't just stay with me for a little while, go to school here. And—"

"I can't do that, Uncle Johnny. Mama wouldn't let me."

"She might. We could ask. Because I'm talking about good schools, Eloise. Put an emphasis on math and science and the arts, the stuff you like to do."

Eloise frowned. "I can't, Uncle Johnny. Mama wouldn't let me stay away from her that long. And even if she did, I can't leave her alone like that. And Bobby too. I promised him I was coming back."

"Yeah, but your talent . . . I got so much more to teach you."

She looked up from the empty bowl in front of her and smiled. "Next time, Uncle Johnny. I'll come back."

Johnny nodded. Next time. She'd come visit again and he'd make sure he was ready for it, would plan it all out in advance.

SUNDAY

15

UNCLE JOHNNY

The next day they got in the car and rode back to Lehigh Acres. The closer they got to the house, the worse he felt. He kept thinking about all he'd wanted to show her, to teach her. They'd barely had time to even talk about her talent much less figure out how to use it.

"I'm telling you it's all right, Uncle Johnny," Eloise said. "I mean, if you worried about me learning something, I feel like I learned a lot. Got to visit family, learned about the Ribkins' history. Got to visit a lot of new places. Got to meet the Hammer. And I showed you my talent. And I don't know why, but really, Uncle Johnny, just showing it to you and the Hammer like that made me feel a whole lot better."

"Yeah?"

"Yeah, for real. I feel like I can handle it now. People are going to have to accept me for who I am from now on."

"Yeah? Well, that's something."

They pulled up in front of his brother's house.

"You sure you want to do this? I mean, you sure you don't want me to ask if you could stay for a few more days, because—"

But Eloise was already pushing open her door. She climbed out of the car and ran up the front steps. A moment later her mother came out of the house and Eloise practically leapt into her arms.

"You should call Bobby and let him know you're here," Meredith was saying as Johnny climbed out.

Eloise nodded and ran inside.

Meredith looked at Johnny and smiled. "How was it? She behave herself out there?"

"She was fine."

"Well, I'm glad to hear it."

Johnny nodded.

"What?" Meredith said.

"Franklin," Johnny said. "He just showed up in Kansas City one day, didn't he? Out of the blue. Got you to come back to Florida with him. He tell you why he went there looking for you?"

Meredith frowned. She glanced over her shoulder, but the girl had already disappeared inside the house. "Yes," she said.

"And when you got back to St. Augustine, did you tell him to do all that?"

"No."

"What did you tell him?"

"I told him it was crazy. I told him to let it go."

"Why didn't he?"

"I don't know. He didn't do what I said. He was his own man, made his own decisions." She crossed her arms in front of her chest. "It was a long time ago."

"But it was your idea to come down here, wasn't it? You were trying to save his life, weren't you? Take him out of harm's way?"

"I don't remember." She glanced over her shoulder. "I was kind of fucked up back then. But you already know that, don't you? Had my reasons for being that way, just like everybody else. But, you get older and after a while you do start to realize it doesn't really matter. It's the past and you got to put it behind you, try not to fuck up your own kids too much."

"Why didn't you come to me? You loved him? I loved him too. I could have helped."

Meredith pursed her lips and squinted at him. "Here is what I do remember, Johnny Ribkins. Franklin came to find me when wasn't anybody else bothering to look. He cared, for whatever reason. And as messed up as I might have been, that meant a lot to me. A whole lot. I can't account for everything that happened back then, everything that I did. But I did try. All I can do is hope that counts for something because that's pretty much all there is to it, Johnny Ribkins. What happened with Franklin was an accident. That's all. It happened. Then he was gone and somebody had to take care of Eloise. And there wasn't anybody else around to do it but me."

She shook her head. "Why are you asking me about all that stuff now? It's the past, ancient history. What do you want from me?"

Johnny sighed. "I want you to know you are a fine mother, Meredith Clark. You've taken real good care of my niece and it shows. I feel like I really got to know her on this trip and she is a lovely child. And I know it wasn't easy doing that on your own. You should be proud."

She blinked at him, then raised a hand to wipe her eyes. "I am."

"Well, the thing is, you're not alone anymore. I'm here now. And you and me? We're family. So I want you to let me help you with the girl. I seem to have come into a bit of money recently. Been thinking about starting a trust fund; should be just about enough to pay for her college."

"Really?"

"Really. And all I want in return is for you to promise that, until then, if she ever needs anything, if you ever start feeling like she's more than you can handle, you'll let me know. Can you do that?"

"You serious?"

"I am." Johnny shrugged. "That's what families do for each other. The best they can."

Meredith nodded. "You really are a good man, aren't you, Johnny? I can see why Franklin admired you so much. Why don't you come inside, stay for dinner?"

"That sounds nice." He nodded toward the house. "Mind if I have a look up in the attic first?"

Meredith didn't mind. He went inside the house and climbed the stairs to the attic. It was just like Eloise had told him: a room crammed with sloppily stacked boxes full of things Franklin had stored there over the years.

He looked until he found a small shoebox stuffed with pieces of colored paper. His map. Some of the pieces were taped together; without anybody to help him, Franklin had tried to reassemble it as best he could but of course it wasn't the same. Franklin had found new ways to fit things together, yet the lines were somehow still intact. Money was still part of it, and so was trust, but they'd been reconfigured, put in different relation to each other as Franklin started to construct his own pathways. It wasn't finished yet. But maybe, if Johnny studied it, he could figure out what his brother had been trying to do. Maybe his brother had come up with another way, something Johnny hadn't thought of before.

"You find what you needed?"

He looked up and saw Eloise standing in the doorway.

"I think so."

She nodded. He could see in her face then a sudden awareness that he was leaving soon.

"You know, Uncle Johnny, I didn't realize it until now, but honestly? I think I actually liked riding around with you in that car. I'm going to miss it. I'm going to miss you."

"I'm going to miss you too. You'll have to come visit me again soon."

"Can I?"

"Of course. Anytime you want." He smiled. "Come and help me with this box."

Eloise helped him carry the box down to his car. Once it was safe in his trunk he let her have a peek inside.

The girl shook her head. "It's just ripped up pieces of paper. How did my daddy know to keep that?"

"I don't know. But he must have realized it was valuable because he didn't throw it out."

"But *how* did he know? How do you know the difference between an antique and something that's just old?"

Johnny shrugged. "Somebody just got to want it, is all. That's all it really comes down to."

He looked at his niece.

"Now, about your talent. Before we have dinner tonight I want you to show it to your mother."

"Why?"

"Because hiding is a real bad habit. Hiding from other people, hiding from yourself . . . The older you get, the harder it is to break, so we got to nip it in the bud right now. I want you to promise to remember that what you got is a gift. And I know it's hard. But you got to understand that you were given it for a reason and that means you'll have to learn to respect it. You'll have to be strong too because, it's true, not everybody is going to understand it. But, believe me, there is someone out there who needs to see it, who's depending on you to be brave."

"How do you know?"

"Because there always is. Speaking of which, I got something for you."

He reached into his pocket and pulled out a folded up piece of paper.

"What's this?"

"It's a map."

When she unfolded it, it was a list of names and phone numbers. First Johnny's, then Simone's, then Bertrand's, then the Hammer's. The last was Flash's; Johnny had written it in pen, then crossed it out, then wrote it again in pencil.

The Justice Committee.

"Memorize that now, honey. Because you got people. I don't want you to ever forget that. You need anything, you and your mama ever run into some kind of problem, all you got to do is call one of those numbers."

"All right," she said.

He looked at her. "I said *anything*. Don't be thinking it's too small or it can wait. You call and someone will be there."

"I know."

"Call the first number first. If no one answers, go ahead and try the next, then the next, straight on down the line."

"Okay."

"If no one answers those, go back and try me again."

"I got it."

He squinted.

"You sure? Because I want you to promise me you're going to

keep calling. I might have to run an errand or something. I don't know. But the point is, even if it doesn't seem like it at that particular moment, truth is I'll be waiting for your call. Sometimes you have to be a little patient is all."

He kissed her on the cheek. "Just give me a chance to get to the phone."

ACKNOWLEDGMENTS

I am grateful for having known the luminous literary scholar Barbara Christian (1943–2000), who taught me that everything beautiful is also strange. Toni Morrison inspired me to write and also showed me how. The MFA program in Creative Writing of the University of Wisconsin–Madison offered me a space to grow under the guidance of Jesse Lee Kercheval. Ayesha Pande believed in me as we worked through many drafts of this novel together. The Rona Jaffe Foundation provided me with the resources that allowed me the time and peace of mind I needed to complete this book.

Along the way I also received crucial support from the Sustainable Arts Foundation, Hedgebrook, the Virginia Center for the Creative Arts, and the Hambidge Center. Mary Gaitskill, Mat Johnson, Stewart O'Nan, and Dawn Raffel provided early encouragement. Judith Mitchell, Ron Kuka, Rowan Hisayako Buchanan, Kevin Debs, Steven Flores, Liv Stratman, and Steven Wright helped me think through early incarnations of the Ribkins family. I am grateful to Allison Warner and Shoshona Vogel for being wonderful old friends and Zach Lazar, Sarah Lazar, and Jami Attenberg for being lovely new ones.

Thanks to everyone who worked with me at Melville House:

Dennis Johnson, Valerie Merians, Taylor Sperry, Marina Drukman, and Vanessa Christensen.

As always I thank my family: Jacqueline Hubbard, Charles Williams, Jacquelyn Woods Williams, Sandra Williams, James Williams, Peter Williams, Grigsby Hubbard, Haven Hubbard, and Sage Morgan-Hubbard.

I especially thank my husband, Christopher Dunn, for his enduring love, support, and patience as we raise our beloved children Isa, Joaquin, and Zé.

READING GROUP GUIDE

1. In this novel, many characters are changed by the passage of time. Is this inevitable? Are these changes positive or negative?

2. Is it significant that Johnny is seventy-two years old? Can he still effect social change as an old man? (Keep in mind that he's an antique salesman, and that antiques, in his own words, are things "that get more valuable with time" [p. 28].)

3. Discuss the role money plays in this novel. Is it something that corrupts? Or is it something that, while corrupting, also effects positive change?

4. What causes Meredith to change her mind about Johnny? Why does she send Eloise with him? Can we believe her claim that she's looking out for Eloise?

5. Compare Eloise's use of her "gifts" with Johnny's. How is it similar? Different? Is Johnny more honorable for having used his gifts for social uplift? Why does he judge Eloise's use of her gift so harshly?

6. Does the Ribkins family have a moral obligation to use their gifts for good? Why or why not? Do we—as people, readers,

thinkers, etc.—have a responsibility to use our own talents for good?

7. Conversely, do we have a social responsibility to help others even if we don't have "gifts?"

8. Does Johnny "dig up" anything besides money? How might those other "things" change our perception of him as a character? (e.g. memories, former ambitions . . .)

9. Can we reconcile Johnny's negative attitude toward money and his active pursuit of it?

10. Is Johnny morally wrong in his pursuit of money? How is he different from the other money-obsessed characters in this book—particularly those he criticizes?

11. Are the Ribkins as close-knit a family as Simone suggests? If so, why do they seem so suspicious of each other?

12. How are members of the Ribkins family similar to one another? How are they different?

13. Why doesn't Simone keep pictures of the Justice Committee in her photo album? Is she trying to erase the past? Can the past be erased?

14. Why don't Johnny and his family members hide their "gifts"? Might there be reasons for their being so open about what are ostensibly supernatural powers? (Conversely: what might be a reason for them to hide their superpowers?)